S.O.S. Del

By

LJ Vickery

S.O.S. Book One

S.O.S. Dell

Published by Weir River Press—USA—
Hingham, Massachusetts
Original Copyright 2017 by LJ Vickery
Cover Art by Taria A. Reed

Vickery, LJ./SOS Dell
ISBN-10 0989433315
ISBN-13 978-0-9894333-1-0

PUBLISHER'S NOTE:
This book is a work of fiction. Names, characters, places and incidents either are
the product of the author's imagination or are used fictitiously, and any resemblance
to actual persons, living or dead, business establishments, events, or locales is
entirely coincidental.

Dedication

This one is just for you, Sherrie!

Prologue

Brina escaped the party and entered the lounge, thinking only to catch a quick breather before disappearing upstairs to her hotel room. Maybe a small drink to help blot out the ugly evening would ease her into sleep. She wove through the crowd and elbowed her way to a spot at the bar.

"A shot of tequila, please," she called out to the bartender as she caught his eye. One ought to do it. She wasn't much of a drinker.

"Kind of sad. Drinking shots alone."

Brina blinked. The man sitting on the stool next to her flourished a cheeky, bright smile which stood in stark and breathtaking contrast to his smooth, mahogany skin. His deep brown eyes studied her with intelligent interest. *Huh.* The guy wanted small talk? Fine. She'd give it to him. Brina thrust her chin at the glass in front of him. "Shots are lonely, but whisky is okay?"

"Scotch," he corrected, raising his glass in a salute to take a sip. She watched the muscles in his throat work as the amber liquid slid down. *Damn.* The small droplet that remained on his full, bottom lip begged her attention. What would he do if she impulsively leaned forward and swiped it off with her tongue?

Brina gave herself a slight shake. Where had that thought come from? To hide her sudden confusion, she signaled to the bartender and held up two fingers. *There.* Now she wouldn't be doing shots alone, and since her gorgeous bar-mate had been the one to point out the error of her ways, he wouldn't dare refuse.

Two small glasses appeared on the counter, and Brina tilted her head toward them. "Drink up," she challenged.

His white teeth flashed again, and this time showcased dimples. *Wow.* As if broad shoulders and an obviously taut physique didn't already snag a woman directly in her mid-section, he had to have those dimples? Brina attempted to ignore the allure and tossed back her shot. She immediately signaled for two more.

A chuckle came from his direction. "So what exactly are we doing?" Mr. Melting-chocolate-brown-gaze raised one clever eyebrow and downed his first round.

"I don't know what you're doing." Brina made up her mind on the spot. "But I've had a horrible, awful, very bad month, and I'm going to celebrate by getting drunk." It hadn't been her original plan, but it hit her that even if she didn't mean drunk, drunk, she really did need to cut loose after playing the part of good, dutiful doormat to her new boss, week after week. And if by numbing her inhibitions with alcohol, she dared make a move on the sexy hunk next to her—who gave off testosterone like a cool mist humidifier—then so much the better. Line up the shots. The bartender received her signal and came back with round two.

"Okay. I'm in." Her new companion responded gamely by picking up the second shot and decimating it in one gulp.

"Salud," Brina agreed, and hers slid down, too.

"So are we exchanging names?" There climbed that snarky eyebrow again. Brina observed it, fascinated. It exactly matched his close-cropped hair in color and texture. Ebony, curly. She wondered if it was as soft to touch as it looked, but how weird would that be? Reaching out to caress someone's eyebrow. Even if the damned thing did seem to have a life of its own. And, *yup*. There it went again. Continuing its journey upward, as if waiting. *Oh, yeah*. He'd asked about names.

"No." She managed to speak around her semi-paralyzed tongue. "I think this should be completely anonymous." Not quite true. Bri had already recognized her bar mate as someone who had been in the US AIM offices where she worked. Someone who had done business with her boss. His name, she recalled, was Delancourt Songen. Oddly, it made her feel less like he was a shadowy hook-up, but she wouldn't let on that she knew him.

Her head had already begun to spin, and if she said—or did—something completely stupid, he would walk away knowing her name and where she worked. That would not do.

"Fine. Here's to anonymous," he agreed easily.

A third set of glasses appeared. Tall and sexy got to his feet while chugging the contents of his. "Excuse me for a moment, will you?" He gave a half-apologetic shrug.

"What?" Brina nearly panicked, so immediate was her need to keep him near. "You're leaving already?" A sharp stab of disappointment hit her mid-chest.

He winked. "Absolutely not. I wouldn't think of it," his honeyed voice assured.

Damn. He might as well have used his hand to rub away that verbal near-ouchie, the way his silky tones warmed, and soothed her.

"But if I'm going to keep up with you, I need to partake of the little boy's room."

Brina breathed out a happy sigh. "I'll wait," she told him, inordinately relieved.

She studied his ass as he walked away. *Oh. Mighty fine.* She knew it would be. Slim hips giving way to some bulging glutes that filled out his pants to perfection. Not too big. Not too small. An ass to get a hold of. She really liked that. Which meant she'd plateaued; reached the exact proper amount to drink. The fine balance between false courage and sloppy drunk was a complex science, but one that had clearly been met. A quick conversation with the bartender was in order.

Several minutes later—after her server assured her that all shots she received from this point on would be water while her companion's remained one hundred proof—her unsuspecting date returned.

Now Brina felt confident she could stay in control. And at the same time, she could seriously let her hair down.

****

Del groaned and crooked an elbow over his eyes. Sunlight streamed across his face as he lay in bed, his cranium set on detonate. Why hadn't he closed the drapes? *Oh yeah. Company.* He cracked one lid and peered at the empty space next to him. *Or not.*

His eye slammed closed.

It hurt too much to see, let alone think, but he remained pretty damned sure the lithe blonde from the bar last night had accompanied him upstairs to his hotel room.

He inhaled tentatively. Yup. The slightest hint of lemon clung to the sheets. The same scent that had tickled his nose every time she'd lifted the heavy mass of curls off her neck while they'd talked.

Before they'd done an unprecedented number of tequila shots. Before Del lost all awareness. Two things which did not bode well.

He rolled his tongue around in a mouth as dry as sawdust and swallowed thickly. What exactly had occurred?

He recalled some of it. Their meeting, of course, and how he'd experienced an instant attraction.

Between shots they'd exchanged brief, truncated histories; cities in common, college anecdotes. Nothing deep, but certainly a more interesting and fascinating conversation than he'd held with any other female in a good number of years. And all this while sizzling glances zinged back and forth between them.

After that, Del grew hazy about how the evening had progressed. But even so, he recalled the woman sending him a siren call that left no doubt as to her intentions. He didn't know whether the alcohol had given her courage, or if this was something she did on a Saturday night, but he found himself loosening up and doubling down on her tequila shots because everything she said sounded like a good idea.

Until his brain hit a wall.

He vaguely remembered taking her hand, and leading her across the lounge to the elevators. But then… *Huh.* Had he imagined the sinful, smoking hot kiss they'd shared once the doors slid closed? He could almost feel the palm of his hand inching up her silky smooth thigh while she dug her nails into his scalp. The situation smacked of all his fantasies, but how much of it had been real?

As he pondered, his stomach clenched. Then did a somersault. *Holy fuck.* It lurched.

Del's eyes popped open, and unable to fight his nausea in the suddenly spinning room, he lunged from the bed and barely made it to the bathroom where he disgustingly rid himself of the vestiges of a totally shadow-laden night.

Eventually he pulled himself upright from the porcelain, and managed a glass of water with a couple of aspirin before making his way back to the bed where he sat gingerly and looked around.

The depression in the pillow next to his told him a head had, indeed, rested there; the covers kicked back as if for a surreptitious get-away. He looked at the bedside table, took a deep breath and bent to peruse the floor. Finally Del lifted the sheets. *Nope.* No evidence of a condom wrapper. For sure then, there had been no sex. He'd obviously passed out. Failed to score. Racked up a goose egg. *Too bad.* It might have been magnificent, even if he wouldn't have remembered it today.

He silently thanked his bed companion for taking off before he embarrassed himself turning out the contents of his stomach this morning, but another part of him hoped she was okay. He seemed to recall she'd been less than steady on *her* feet earlier at the bar. He quirked his lip, smiling. He also recounted her being smart-mouthed and intelligent, and he briefly wondered if she could be found in the hotel.

He dropped his head into his hands waiting for the aspirin to take effect, groaned, and came to a realization. He'd had enough of this. *Oh.* Maybe not the pretty lady who'd picked him up, but certainly late nights spent overindulging in food and alcohol. He'd been playing the rich, debauched playboy game for months now, and it wasn't him. He'd been brought up with better values. It was time to take control of his life and get back to what he knew. He already had a worthwhile endeavor in his mind—and had even gotten it underway—albeit in its beginning stages. And thanks to the wealthy contacts he'd been courting and boozing it up with, his new enterprise should pick up speed.

Del scolded himself. Forget about tequila shots and blondes. If he'd learned anything, the two were nothing but trouble.

Chapter One
Three months later

Del listened patiently, fingers steepled in front of him as Reynold spoke across the vast, highly polished, wooden desk. Sure. He wanted to be anywhere but in the chair that sat a few inches lower than the CEO's in an office high atop Boston's Hancock Tower. But there lay the nature of his new business. He needed to show deference to those who hired him, even if one of them grated on his nerves. His eyes wandered out the window to the Charles River, rife with small, billowing white sails and rowing teams enjoying the hot, autumn sun. He'd much rather be down there.

This guy who'd hired him exemplified everything Del hated in a human being, arrogant, demanding, so sure of himself after a silver-spoon upbringing that included the right schools and beneficial connections due to trust fund status. It therefore became of great interest to Del that, right now, Reynold sounded anything but confident.

"So you see why I've called?" The president of US Amalgamated Industries Management—or US AIM, an aptly named acronym for a government funded arms exporter—tapped nervously on his desk. "She's only been here a few months, and to tell you the truth, I don't know enough about her to figure out where she might have gone."

Del sighed rubbing the bridge of his nose. "Okay. So explain again why you haven't contacted her family?"

Reynold looked decidedly uncomfortable. "Because I'm in some fairly delicate business negotiations with her father. Which is one of the reasons she was entrusted to me."

A strange turn of phrase, Del pondered, making a mental note. "Go on," he encouraged.

"We—her father and I—thought an alliance between our companies could be cemented by bringing Brina into the fold at US AIM, and that perhaps an even more, uh, personal relationship might develop."

Del got the picture, and he didn't pussyfoot around. "So you're saying this guy offered his daughter up to you in exchange for some sweet future dealings."

Reynold drew back as if slapped. "You might say that. But the relationship would, I assure you, result in nuptials," he admitted through tight lips.

Ah, hell. Del hated this stuff. This jerk-off wanted to hire him to find some coddled female who'd been hand-groomed to be a CEO's wife and used as leverage by men in power. It stunk to high heaven and Del would normally have nothing to do with it except he had ties to the unappealing individual across the desk.

Eighteen months ago, fresh out of a special operations unit stationed in South America, Del had sold a brand new personal tracking system to Reynold's company. And had made millions.

Del's mind spun back to his deployment in South America where his turn of fortune all began.

He'd been on patrol in the jungle one night, wearing his infrared night vision goggles, when he spotted a large group of caterpillars on the side of a tree. *Interesting.* He'd wondered if the glow he witnessed came from the heat of their amassed bodies.

Before he could process that phenomenon, he'd spied a sloth-like predator moving slowly down the tree toward the grouping. The animal had scooped up a handful of the writhing bodies, and stuffed them into his rounded snout.

Nothing unusual there. But what Del witnessed next, had changed his life.

Within seconds, the sloth began to glow with a greater light, much sharper and brighter than what the goggles had registered coming down the tree. Whatever properties the worms secreted, had, upon ingestion, been transferred to the hungry mammal. It had to be something in the crawly creatures' chemical make-up. Del's imagination had immediately taken flight.

Guys in his unit, operatives in the jungle, were tagged with magnetic chips in case they got lost or abducted. But enemies—with a simple scan—could often find those chips, dis-embed and destroy them, rendering them useless as a beacon which put a team-member's life in danger.

If the substance in these bugs proved edible, and did to humans the same thing it did to sloths, what would stop a soldier from ingesting the compound, therefore remaining exponentially more visible to his searching buddies through infrared? Questions had begged to be answered.

Night after night Del kept watch on the caterpillars, found their nests and eventually ascertained from their vast numbers that they bred prolifically. From there, he'd followed those animals that *ate* the bugs, and found that they gained the same glowing side effect. It didn't take long to learn the ingested compound lasted approximately forty-eight hours in a body before being flushed naturally out of the system. A very useful amount of time.

He'd experimented with different types of detection other than his infrared, and eventually hit the jackpot. When hit with ultra-violet light, the worms lit up and glowed every color of the rainbow. Intense research ensued, which clued Del into the way that some insects—bees in particular—could see the ultraviolet spectrum. With that in mind, he quickly rigged his night goggles to become photomultipliers as well as infrared. Now he could see the rainbow colors at night.

It took less than two weeks for Del to get up the courage to eat one of the crawly critters himself, but when he did, he found himself lighting up in the same way as the sloth. With no ill effects.

He followed up by bringing the bugs—and his modified goggles—to camp where he shared his discovery with his commanding officer, an honest mentor who enthusiastically encouraged Del to run with the idea.

Now, nearly two years later and out of the service, Del sat pretty with a big-bucks contract from Reynold's company for rights to the chemical compound and a much improved, sleeker version of the new goggles for military use. But even better than that, Del owned his own protective clothing line which he'd developed alongside the original chemical compound. The specially treated clothing disguised the multicolored light from enemy eyes, and neutralized the glowing compound that leached out of the body as sweat. His protective jungle-wear absorbed and deactivated all perspiration.

So yeah. He was one of the rich guys now, but it felt pretty empty. One could only spend so much cash. And with his success, he'd found out what rich people already knew. That money generated more money. And suddenly he'd been thrust into a position where his company could afford a manager for everything. Which meant *his* input was no longer needed on a daily, or even a weekly basis. Men and women with chemistry diplomas and fashion degrees had taken over every aspect of his operations and now ran it far better than he ever could. So he became a one man, partying, marketing machine.

After months of fund-raisers and cocktail soirees to pimp his new products, and with too much mindless time on his hands, an idea had finally gelled for a business he could really get his teeth into. *Protective services.* Private investigation. Call it whatever the hell he wanted, but Del became excited all over again. Here was something he could be good at, and now he had piles of money in which to pursue the possibilities. It basically mimicked the very same work that his team had accomplished, day after grueling day, back in the jungles. Search and rescue. The difference now? He'd be working in an urban jungle.

Del had reached out to a few of his ex-teammates, and *boom.* It amazed him how quickly things came together. Within days he'd recruited three guys. Three *great* guys whom he'd missed having in his life.

His buddy Sarge, hands down the best computer genius Del had ever come across, became his first score. And one who would be damned helpful. Give Sarge a snippet of classified information and within a few hours, he'd hand you back an entire dossier. Not only that, but he sported an understated sense of humor, and always kept Del off balance with his quirky comments.

Prez was a different story altogether. Slightly scary if you didn't know him, the man loved his munitions. He could assemble and disassemble a firearm in under a minute, and knew exactly how much of what explosive to use for any given situation. A damned crazy SOB, but a valuable weapons and demolition expert. Scoring Prez for his new venture had made Del pretty damned happy.

Then there was Wiley. Wiley was simply Del's best friend. The soldier who'd had his back since boot-camp, all the way through their special-ops training and into the field. If Wiley had turned him down, Del would have made things work, but by having his good buddy with him he'd made certain everything had suddenly become right with the world.

With his new team in place, Del tenaciously and brazenly made use of his new, rich and influential acquaintances. Finally, rubbing those holier-than-thou shoulders had paid off. Flaunting his new business as a must-have, the upper echelon had helped him spread the word, far and wide, touting his you-lose-it, we-find-it operation. He called his company Songen and Associates. Simple and clean. And who knew that business would come to him, instantly.

Amongst his new clients, Reynold; who'd called this morning with the urgent plea being pitched now.

Time to get to work.

Del flipped open his lap-top and fired off questions. "What is the missing female's full name?"

"Brina Capadella." Reynold sat back for the first time during the interview, seeming more sure of himself since Del looked to be taking the job.

"And her capacity in your company?" Del questioned, sending everything directly from his computer to Sarge as he typed.

"She acted as assistant to my executive secretary."

Del nodded. "We'll want to talk to your secretary. She may have information you don't."

"We've covered that," Reynold frowned. "She doesn't know anything. I don't see the need to question her again."

"Do you want my help, or not?" Del held his temper. Barely. He knew Reynold, and knew the asshole was used to being in charge, but if he got too condescending, Del would walk.

"Fine." The CEO capitulated with a heavy sigh, and not too much hesitation. "I'll make her available."

Del nodded. *Good.* "So when and where did you see Ms. Capadella last? And why have you decided she's missing?"

This, the man gave to him without reservation. "She worked late here at the office yesterday. The video feed shows she left a little after 7PM."

"I'll need a copy of that footage, and any additional video you have from outside of the building."

"My security staff will be at your disposal," Reynold agreed.

"And now tell me why this makes her a missing person?" Del reiterated.

Reynold sniffed. "She was required to meet me at a function last evening at the Metropolitan Museum at 9 PM. She never showed up."

"Which could mean a headache or a broken down vehicle." Del wanted to add that maybe the lady had simply figured out Reynold was a prick, and ditched him. But he bit his tongue.

"I ruled that out," the man came back, haughtily. "At ten o-clock, when she didn't show, I sent one of my drivers to the hotel where we put her up. To her room. She wasn't there, and it looked like her belongings had been hastily packed. I'm worried someone pressured her into leaving in a hurry."

Fat chance. It was probably just as Del suspected. The lady had clearly changed her mind about working for—or sleeping with—this idiot, and fled. Some jobs almost came with answers pasted on billboards. "I'll want the name of your man and access to the hotel room." Del made a note to check the background of the driver, just to be thorough, then sat back and gave Reynold a penetrating stare. "I understand your reluctance to contact her father, but what makes you think she didn't run home to him?"

The CEO narrowed his eyes, clearly not used to being questioned, but once again he yielded. "I called the gentleman at his office in New York first thing this morning on the pretext of another matter to see if she'd done just that. Not only did he ask how Brina fared, but he wanted to be patched through to her here in the office because he hadn't been able to get her by cell phone when he called her last night." Reynold looked suddenly less than comfortable. "I made an excuse that her phone had fallen into the lobby's fountain yesterday, and that she was currently working outside of the building, accompanying one of the junior partners to see a client." His teeth slammed together. "I also told him I'd have her get in touch later today."

Del's eyebrows raised. "You expect me to find her that fast?"

"You promoted yourself as an expert, and believe me, I will pay you well."

Del scoffed. "It's not about the money. You clearly realize that."

"Fair enough. So, what then?" Reynold ground out. "What can I give you to make this worth your while?"

"Besides my regular fee?" Del paused. "A stellar reference with your colleagues." At this juncture, the more business the better. He wanted to expand. An additional number of his old team had contacted him in the hopes of being employed. "But that doesn't mean I can locate your girl in the next ten hours."

"Just do your best," Reynold grumbled. "I'll find some excuse to put her father off longer if I have to. I'm concerned that something terrible might have happened to her."

"Done," Del concurred. He didn't believe Blithe for a moment. This woman hadn't been taken against her will. She'd simply cut and run. So Del's job would be easy. After all, how hard could it be to find one air-headed debutante? A few quick searches of her credit card records and he should have her. *Shit.* She probably couldn't go two hours without buying shoes.

There were only a few more things Del needed.

"I'll require her cell phone number, her home address in New York—even if it belongs to her father," Del warned. "And the make and model of her car." He'd have Sarge search motor vehicle records to get a license number, and they'd notify a few of their ex-teammates who'd gone into law enforcement to keep an eye out for anything unusual. An accident or an abandoned vehicle.

"Do you have anything else you want to give me?" Del asked, typing notes as fast as his brain could come up with possible scenarios. As jobs went, this one looked like it would be a slam dunk. He closed his laptop.

"I have a photo." Reynold opened his top drawer.

Duh. Del should have asked for that immediately, but he didn't beat himself up overmuch. Being in charge of operations instead of being boots on the ground meant he'd be riding a learning curve for a while at the way things were done, especially outside of the jungle.

Reynold slid a glossy across the wooden surface and even before the photo turned, Del's heart skipped a beat.

Oh, hell, no.

It couldn't be. A lot of women wore their blonde hair long and curly. Del managed to control the tremor that took hold of his hand and reached for the picture.

He spun it around.

Fuck. It was her. The woman from three months ago in the bar.

And she looked even more beautiful than he remembered.

Chapter Two

Brina entered the small cabin and took her first deep breath since she'd made her escape, but still, her brain refused to shut off. What had she missed? If she'd left a trail of any kind, Reynold or her father would find her with the amount of resources they both commanded. And until she sorted things through and came up with a plan, they were the two men she most needed to avoid.

She placed her bags on the floor to the right, while her laptop landed on a small desk against the wall. The entire cabin looked to be no more than twelve by twenty feet, with a loveseat and coffee table crammed in next to the desk, and a kitchenette against the far wall. She propelled herself forward, dropping into one of two hard-backed chairs at a small, Formica table and glanced across the room. A door from the living room—if you could call it that—stood open, revealing the foot of what looked to be a double bed, crammed into a similarly knotty pine paneled, yet tinier space. A door adjacent, next to a diminutive wedge of kitchen counter, certainly led to the bathroom.

The whole place, although Spartan, appeared neat and clean, even if the appliances had seen better days. Bri silently thanked her friend—a college soccer teammate—for providing the out-of-the-way retreat. It had been sorely needed.

Daddy. Brina lowered her head to her hands and finally allowed herself to think about her father. The tears flowed. What a complete betrayal. Apparently the man she believed she knew—the man who'd coddled and cared for her before her mother died fifteen years ago, the father she always hoped would magically reappear from his remoteness—was a complete sham. Perhaps even a monster. How could she not have known?

Maybe it had been his immediate and continued absence after Mom passed, putting his only sister, Celia, in charge of her. Or perhaps it was the time spent away from him at private boarding schools, summer camps and finally college that distanced her from what he'd become. Because really, what had she seen of him in fifteen years other than quick visits at graduation or playoff games? Even during the few vacations they'd taken together, they'd flown in on separate jets, after which business accounted for most of his time while she went sight-seeing or lounged at the pool with Aunt Celia. Other than a hurried dinner or two over the years, did she really know who he was? *Apparently not.* And she needed to find out the extent of his betrayal.

One e-mail.

Brina shuddered to think what would have happened if she hadn't stumbled across it. Not that the missive had fostered her initial resolve to leave US AIM. She'd already decided to walk out on Reynold. She didn't like him one bit. Coming into his company thinking she'd be groomed as part of his management team as a favor to her absent father had been handleable. But when it became clear Reynold would use her as a glorified secretary, a stopgap before they became a couple—*a married couple whether she liked it or not*—the idea of staying with US AIM had become abhorrent.

As much as it shouldn't matter if quitting had any impact on her father, Bri had determined she would do her leave-taking the correct—if chicken—way. She'd stayed late at work, just last night, and drafted two letters; one of resignation, and the other letting Reynold know she harbored no special feelings for him. That although their casual dating had been fun—*not*—it was time for her to move on. She remembered hoping her father wouldn't be too disappointed in her decision. *Disappointed?* That would make her laugh, now, if it were any kind of laughing matter.

Brina had waited until everyone but the janitorial staff had left before tiptoeing into Reynold's dimly lit, empty office. Leaving her envelopes on his desk while he waited for her—safely far away at the Met—had been cowardly, but she hadn't wanted to confront his smug face one more time, or listen to the reasons he would enumerate to make her stay.

It had all seemed simple. Prop up the envelopes, and say bye-bye. Until her hand had inadvertently bumped the computer's mouse, and brilliant light from the screen blanketed the room.

Damn. Her first reaction was that the cleaning crew might have noticed. Brina had held her breath and watched the door for a count of twenty. No one came. She'd been lucky.

But when she'd focused on the offending screen to turn it off, her name on the monitor had popped out. *What?* An e-mail Reynold had forgotten to close, about her? Bri had hesitated for one minute, knowing she shouldn't be reading anything off his personal computer, but dammit, this mentioned her name. Her eyes had quickly scrolled the contents.

A fairly long missive from her father had ensued, most of it had seemed innocuous enough about shipments and delivery dates. But as her eyes had skipped down to where she'd seen her name, Brina's lungs constricted in her chest, and had set in motion her fourteen hour escape from Boston.

...you'll only get to keep her as long as the dealings between us remain under wraps and go smoothly. Brina isn't stupid. If she gets any inkling of what our business involves, and you screw up, she's as good as dead, and you along with her. Do you understand? If not, let me be clear. If you sign Brina's death warrant, yours will be executed right along with it.

Unable to process the last few sentences, Bri had concentrated on the first. Get to keep her? Business dealings? So her father had sold her out to Reynold like a...commodity, in order to assure that knowledge of certain transactions stayed between the two? Transactions that had to be immoral or illegal if her father didn't want her to know about them. Considering what US AIM did for business, Bri immediately speculated that illegal arms dealing could be the only answer.

She'd swallowed hard, facing the ultimate betrayal. The next part of the missive, the implication of how Reynold would be signing both their death warrants if she found out about their dealings. Did that truly mean if she discovered the truth of what her father did—not simple imports and exports as she'd been led to believe—he'd have her...killed? The possibility had shaken Brina to her core, and rapidly propelled her back fifteen years. Her mother, the head of the family business at that time, had died under suspicious circumstances, but no cause had ever been determined. Surely her father hadn't had a hand in that? Could the man she thought she knew be capable of such despicable acts? His email had certainly pointed to that reality. *Shit.*

Brina had stood in shock for what seemed like minutes before finally gulping in a deep breath. Her instincts had taken over and she'd quickly exited the e-mail on the computer so Reynold wouldn't suspect she'd seen it.

Then she'd run.

Or more accurately walked.

With shaky determination she'd strode the half mile to her hotel, detouring one block down and dashing into the local supermarket to make as big a withdrawal as the in-store bank would allow. It would be plenty to feed and house her for several weeks. Not enough to buy a plane ticket, but she'd known perfectly well not to use her credit cards. Anyone interested would be able to track her purchases. So flying had been out, as well as bus tickets and paying for her car's gasoline with plastic. She'd definitely need more money, and help. But who could she call?

Brina had looked down at the cell phone sticking out of her purse and nearly groaned. Another possible way to find her. She didn't know much about the device's GPS capabilities, but considering her father purchased it for her—and he believed he owned her enough to pawn her off to a business associate—chances are it had tracking. With a heavy sigh she'd removed it from her bag and tossed it into the nearest trash receptacle. Her aunt would be worried that the phone no longer connected them, but it couldn't be helped. Brina had then picked up her pace and reached her hotel, where the ATM machine in the lobby had caught her eye. Bingo. An additional score. It had let her withdraw the highest limit, so she had a little more cash.

An elevator ride up—where frantic packing had ensued—before a ride down to the garage to retrieve her car. With shaking hands, she'd exited the complex and pulled out into traffic. She'd known she'd have several hours of drive time before anybody came looking for her, and by then, she'd hoped to come up with a plan.

20

The first person who'd come to mind as she'd navigated traffic, of course, was her Aunt Celia, the woman who'd been her surrogate mother until Bri had been sent off to school. But she was Daddy's sister, and still lived at the house he owned where Bri had grown up. Who knew whether or not she was involved in shady business with him? Bri didn't think so, but without knowing, she'd crossed Cee off her list.

Her second inclination had been to contact her old college roommate, someone with whom she still visited regularly. But Brina had quickly nixed that idea as well. Daddy knew her roommate, and also, unfortunately, the entire list of women whom she'd called friends growing up in New York. He'd find her in a minute if she went to any of them for help.

Without conscious engagement of her brain, she'd driven over the Zakim Bridge, headed north, away from Boston and away from New York City, realizing she needed a plan. And quickly. She'd glanced at the map on her navigation device.

North lay New Hampshire, Vermont, and Maine.

A memory had sparked. *Maine.* That was it. She'd instantly recalled a college soccer teammate who had scored a job at the University in Maine. Although they had not been best, hanging-out-all-the-time, buddies, they'd gone clubbing after games, enjoyed each other's company and gotten into some mischief together. When they'd first met, Brina had helped Maygan thwart the unwanted attention of a persistent stalker, and subsequently helped her through a very trying time late in their freshmen year, so cementing their bond. But best of all? Brina's father had no clue as to this ex-teammate's identity.

There'd been no time to doubt her actions. Only the need to act. She'd pointed the nose of her car toward Maine, and driven on through the dark, late-summer night.

The campus had been easy enough to find, and the soccer field equally so. Five hours after her initial freak-out, Brina had found herself parked next to the green where she'd hunkered down to nap until sunrise. If she remembered anything about the hard-driven Maygan, her friend would have her team on the grass at the crack of dawn for a pre school workout.

Waiting had been the hardest thing. Once the group of women had shown up, Brina had to sit and bide her time until the practice concluded. That hour had given Bri some smiles. Maygan had put her ladies through a rigorous, kick-ass training which had them huffing and puffing. Only when the last student left the field had Brina made herself known…and quickly spilled the story that had festered inside of her all night.

"Oh my God, Bri," Maygan hadn't even pretended not to be appalled. "You totally did the right thing. And of course I'll help you."

Brina had launched herself at Maygan and embraced her with a trembling hug. "Thank you so much," she sobbed. "I didn't know where to go, or who to trust."

Mayg had patted her back. "I get it. And excuse me for saying so, but your boss and your father sound like the worst kind of asses." She'd grumbled on under her breath. "And don't you worry. I have the perfect place in mind for you to hide."

Brina had followed Mayg back to her home, a turn of the century farm-house with an enormous barn in the back. They'd ditched Brina's car in the larger structure, right next to a couple of vintage Indian bikes that looked like they still saw use. Then Mayg had insisted, over a cup of decaf coffee that Brina take her ten year old-reliable on the last leg of her trip, assuring Bri that she could get a ride back to work with a colleague who lived down the street. Brina hadn't known what to say, but Mayg had given Bri directions to her destination, and had brushed it off with a "just typical Maine hospitality". Brina had thanked her over and over again, assuring Maygan she'd reimburse her for every penny's worth of inconvenience.

Now, hours later, Brina sat in a small cabin taking a good look at her new, but hopefully temporary home. The place was a vacation/hunting spot that had belonged to Mayg's grandfather who had recently passed on and left it to Maygan.

So Bri had an unrecognizable car, a roof over her head, and enough money to head down the road to the local market and buy food for the duration of her stay. However long that proved to be.

Her stomach flopped and rebelled for the first time in hours, and Brina let a semi-hysterical laugh bubble up. She'd wondered where that ill feeling had gone. She hadn't had a twinge since early yesterday morning in Boston, but it figured she wouldn't be so lucky as to have it go away.

Odd. She'd nearly forgotten her original dilemma, and the main reason she'd decided to leave Reynold in the lurch—other than him being an ass. She put a hand down and rubbed her tummy.

Indigestion? An ulcer? The two things to which Brina originally attributed her nausea had certainly proven incorrect. And she should have known better.

After one semi-inebriated, glorious night of unforgettable passion with a nearly total stranger, she was one-hundred percent, certifiably, old-fashioned, knocked up.

Chapter Three

"Fuck. How is it that one inexperienced female can disappear so completely?" Del ran a hand over his short-cropped hair in frustration. Sarge had come to yet another dead end in his computer search, and it bothered the shit out of him. Since the asshole, Reynold, had revealed the picture of Brina, Del hadn't been able to get her out of his mind. It was as if he knew he had unfinished business with her, apart from locating her for Blithe.

"Dunno, boss," Sarge shrugged and continued to tap in rapid staccato on his keyboard.

Late afternoon sun streamed into the vast board-room where they took up two chairs at the oversized conference table. Del pondered the open space. Hopefully some day when he called a meeting, the room would be filled. All factors indicated that it would be so. And probably much sooner even than he hoped.

Sarge's voice drew him back to the problem at hand.

"After her original two bank withdrawals, and the camera footage of her leaving the garage, we've got nothing." Sarge put in a few more keystrokes. "I can pull up a number of traffic-cams between here and New York City, but it will take a long time to sift through the hours of target footage."

The door crashed open and Prez burst into the room. For anyone else, Del might have figured that some

24

important, key piece of evidence had been found, but not with Prez. This was simply his normal mode of entry. The blond, Scandinavian giant flopped down in an empty chair, his coloring in sharp contrast to Del and Sarge's swarthy complexions.

"Well?" Del dared to hope.

"Nothing. The secretary said that although Ms. Capadella worked efficiently, and got along with everyone, she never became real chummy with any of the staff in the few months she was there. The woman did speculate that in the past couple of weeks, our girl acted even more closed off than normal, not even joining in typical lunchtime gatherings."

"Huh. Did she say whether Brina seemed happy enough with her position at US AIM?" Del knew, from what he remembered, that Brina's credentials certainly warranted more than a position on Reynold's secretarial staff. But she'd accepted the position, so who was he to judge? However, he'd detected one slightly disturbing piece of evidence during his surveillance search that led him to believe Brina had actually left US AIM under duress. He'd spill it as soon as Wiley showed up.

"Yeah. Although who knows for sure. Nobody got close enough to have a clue as to where she originally came from, or what she did in her off hours."

Two things he would remedy for his team in the next few minutes, because Wiley's footsteps echoed outside in the hallway.

"Guys." The whip-chord strong male nodded, grabbed a chair, and turned it backwards to effect a straddle. "By the looks on your faces you haven't found anything, and I hate to tell you, but I hit a dead end, too."

Del ran a hand over his face. "Nothing at the hotel?" he questioned.

"Nope." Wiley shook his head. "Reynold's driver who went to check on her came back clean. And I got a look at hotel security footage. He got into her room with the help of the concierge, and they both came out five minutes later, empty-handed."

"And her room?" Del probed.

"No clues there. Reynold was right. It looked like she'd packed and left in a hurry. A few small, personal items had been left behind, but nothing of interest. And going back to the previous night's footage, sure enough, she left alone."

"Well, I may have found something," Del interjected. "But I don't know what it means in the big picture." He had everyone's attention. "Our client, Reynold, isn't giving us everything he has."

Del had previously filled his guys in on the initial conversation he'd had with Reynold. The one where Reynold intimated that Brina belonged to him. They'd called bull-crap on that, just as Del had, but agreed that it didn't seem out of character for the arrogant CEO.

"When I got a hold of the camera footage from the hallway outside of Reynold's private office," Del primed. "It clearly shows Brina sneaking in last night with what appears to be two envelopes in her hand. When she leaves, there's nothing in her possession, and her face looks spooked."

"So she looked fucked up after leaving some letters or documents for Reynold that he didn't hand over to you, or even mention." Wiley sat straighter, and his friends perked up at this tidbit. Del knew why. On the surface, this case had looked cut and dried. A woman becomes fed up with a misogynistic boss and walks out. But now, with the withholding of evidence by their client, as well as visual distress from their target, something fishier seemed to be afoot.

Del knew it was time to let his team in on the information he'd been keeping from them. He braced for a ration of crap, but hell, what were friends for.

"There's one more thing." It must have been the tone of his voice, because the room quieted, and even Sarge's fingers stilled. Del needed to get this over with. Quickly. "I, uh, happen to have previously met the young lady we're searching for."

Ah, shit. Not good. A bunch of raised eyebrows, scowls, and arms crossing over broad chests were aimed in his direction.

Del plunged on, eyes focused on the intricate grain of the conference table. "It was at one of those ridiculous cocktail parties I attended a few months ago. You know, the ones that I hate so much?" He glanced up from under lowered lids to see that not one of his guys had moved an inch, and sighing he continued. "I sat at the bar, having a scotch when she came over and started slamming back shots of tequila."

That got a small amount of shuffling from his pals, and maybe a strangled guffaw.

"I mentioned to her that doing shots alone might be a bad sign, and the next thing I knew, she'd ordered some for me. So I joined her."

"You joined her." Wiley repeated with an incredulous smirk. "As in got happy and then joined her, joined her?" His astonished curiosity was mirrored on the other two guy's faces.

"Umm. Of that I'm not sure," Del coughed into his hand to semi-disguise his words.

"Excuse me?" Prez sat upright so fast his chair scooted out from under him and hit the floor. "Damn." He dragged the thing back onto its four legs and plunked back down. "What do you mean you're not sure?"

"Yeah," Sarge agreed. "We can't be hearing you right, Del." Sarge showed at least some patience. "Are you saying that you initiated a hook-up with our assignment, but you're not sure whether you actually slept with her?"

Del manned-up and gave a succinct nod of his chin. "That's exactly what I'm saying. Hear me out." He held up a hand when they all started talking at once. "I vaguely remember riding in the elevator with her, up to my room." He'd skip the physical details of his hand on her thigh that still, months later, tormented his brain. "And when I woke up in the morning, there was definite proof that she'd been in my bed. But…"

"But?" Wiley begged for a butt-kicking with the grin that split his face.

"But I don't remember doing the deed." Del admitted. He held up a finger to pre-empt whatever snark-ish comments headed his way. "And no evidence of, uh, coupling remained. No used condom anywhere, and no girl to question."

"Wow." Prez looked to be eating this up. "She left your shameful ass in bed." He shook his head, in mock sorrow. "That's either proof you couldn't perform or she's one very cold customer."

"My money's on Del being a disappointment," Sarge snickered. "He never could hold his alcohol worth a damn."

Lucky for the geek that he went back to typing, or Del might have been inclined to throw him off his chair. Not that the other two guys let up.

"I think she snuck out because she didn't want to see his ugly puss in the light of day," Wiley added.

Prez snorted. "Not to mention his pitiful…"

"All right. Enough," Del barked. "If the three of you have finished impugning my good name, we should move on. The only reason I told you this is for when we find her. So you'll know why she recognizes me."

"Or not," Prez added under his breath, unable to hold back another snort.

Really? Did Del need to hear any more of this? Fuck it. Prez was about to get the sharp edge of his growing anger. It was bad enough that he still harbored fantasies about the woman several months after their encounter. Now he was going to get shit about it?

"Wait, boss." Sarge looked up from his keyboard and interrupted before Del went ballistic and Prez got the dressing down he deserved. "Before your black-out hours, you hung out with this woman at the bar, right?"

Del took a deep breath, and other than sending Prez an "I'll fuck with you later" glare, he responded to Sarge. "Yeah. That's right. At the time I didn't know she was Reynold's arm candy, and even if I did, I'm not sure it would have stopped me. You can see from her picture," he tapped an index finger on the color glossy in the folder next to Sarge's computer, "she's something to look at."

That was a complete understatement, Del nearly groaned. Brina wasn't just pretty. She was gorgeous. If he concentrated hard enough, he could still smell her lemon scent and feel her lush, blonde hair brushing across his chest. "Not to mention I remember her having a sharp intelligence and a vicious sense of humor."

Sarge radiated impatience. "Yeah, yeah. I get it. You were attracted to her on every level. But Del. What did you talk about? You must have been at the bar for a while before you made your move. Did the two of you trade stories?"

The excitement in his voice must have been catching because Del now had three pairs of eyeballs glued to him.

"Well, yeah. We talked about our jobs and where we went to school…"

"That." Sarge interrupted pointedly. "Where did she go to school?"

"UPenn." Del didn't even hesitate. He remembered being impressed that she'd gone Ivy League. For a guy who'd attended a community college and then entered the military, a name like Penn tended to stick.

Sarge's fingers flew again. Del knew immediately that his geek was hacking into the college's system for anything and everything Brina. He felt like an idiot, not having thought of that before, but he'd been too caught up in the logistics of her get-away, and his own unresolved feelings toward her. *Note to self: Investigating personal leads can be as important as following the physical, even if the personal stuff involves you.* Yup. There sure was a learning curve to this process. A shitload different than the search and rescue they'd done out-of-country.

"I'm in," Sarge let them know after several minutes. "Brina Louise Capadella," he eventually spouted. "Graduated Phi Beta Kappa and followed up with an MBA at Wharton." He raised his brows and his typing accelerated. "Here are her more personal records." Sarge let out a long whistle. "GPA of 3.9. You sure do know how to pick them, Del. Wait. She had the same roommate for four years." Sarge grabbed a pen and wrote down a name, handing it to Prez. "Check her out. She lives in New York City."

"Nope. A waste of time." Del forestalled his man from getting up. "That's too easy, if this girl is smart. And I know she is. Not just because of her academics and the fact that—so far—she's completely covered her trail, but because she caught my interest and kept it. That's a first for me in a very long time." Del hated to admit it, but due to some very unfortunate circumstances with his first love, he always chose airheads to share his bed. It was just safer that way.

Why he had let his barriers down for Brina remained a conundrum.

What he did know was that if she were truly trying to lose herself, she would never contact anyone high profile in her life. No. She'd pick a friend who remained off the grid." Del grew thoughtful. "Sarge, check on club memberships and school, sports."

"Soccer." Del suddenly shouted, jumping to his feet and pumping a fist. "That's it. I remember trading stories about soccer since I played in high school. She had a partner in crime on her team." He couldn't help the excitement as the memory rolled over him. "This girl—a pretty good friend—had a stalker at the school who wouldn't quit. They pulled a bunch of stunts and made his life a living hell until he cried uncle. *Damn.* What was that girl's name?"

Del knew Brina had mentioned it, but it had been months ago and he'd been under the influence. If he heard it again, would he recognize it?

"Pulling up the team roster now, boss." Sarge sported a big-ass grin. They were getting close and they knew it. "Here. Take a look."

The big man spun his laptop toward Del and pointed to a picture, under which were the player's names. And sure enough, there was Brina. God, she looked adorable. Even having been drunk for a good portion of their short acquaintance, he'd recognize her anywhere. It was hard to draw his eyes away, but he forced them to drop to the names below. *Score.* The girl listed alphabetically after Brina set bells clanging in his head.

"That's her," he crowed. "Maygan. That's the name Brina said." He thrust a triumphant finger at the screen. "Full name Maygan DePalto."

"Don't touch." Sarge quickly swung the computer away from fingerprints, and initiated a new search.

Del thumped a nervous hand on the conference table in front of him. What happened if this turned out to be a dead-end? His gut said no, but...well, if it was, they'd find a different path. He'd send Prez off to New York City to interview the roommate while he and Wiley painstakingly waded through the lists of all the other girls on her team and any other clubs she belonged to. Nobody said it had to be easy, but damn, Maygan certainly felt like the right one.

"How about this, boss?" Sarge was beaming again. "There's a Maygan DePalto coaching women's soccer up at UMaine. If you were our girl, would that seem like a perfect destination?"

"It certainly would." Del beamed back.

Sarge's news had them high-fiving.

"Can you get me a contact number for her?" They were so close, Del could smell that lemon scent already.

"Cell phone info coming right up." Sarge hit the keys again. The incessant tap, tap, tap, once annoying, was currently a balm to Del's impatience.

"Right here." Sarge pointed to the number. "What are you going to do?"

"I'm going to be Brina's concerned lover," Del chuckled. "My girl up and disappeared, and I'm looking all over for her. And how else, other than pillow talk, would I have known about Maygan being her friend? Brilliant, right?"

"Sure," Wiley agreed. "But if Brina really doesn't want to be found, I'm thinking her buddy isn't going to rat her out just because some dude on the phone says he's her boyfriend."

"I'm with you on that, Wiles," Del mused. "But all it will take is a moment's hesitation for me to know if the woman is lying."

"And then what?" Prez questioned.

"And then we head to Maine." Del took out his cell phone and punched in Ms. DePalto's number.

Please pick up. Please pick up. He couldn't leave a voice mail, and Del hated to think he might have to wait to try the call again, later.

"Hello?" A female voice on the other end of the line caused Del to execute a fist pump.

"Hi. Is this Maygan?" Del used his most charming voice, the one that rarely failed him in a pick-up situation. Not that he used it a lot, but enough so that the guys teased it was his "girl voice".

"It is. Who's this?" She didn't sound suspicious yet. That boded well. He now had a bead on her natural voice, with neutral intonation.

"My name is Delancourt Songen. You've probably heard of me." Be bold. Make her think she should be acquainted with the name.

"No. Sorry. I don't know you."

"Really? I'm surprised. I mean I know we've never met, but we have a mutual friend." He gave a light laugh. "Actually my girlfriend. And we were going to come visit. That's why I'm calling. You wouldn't happen to know where Brina is, would you? She weirdly checked out of her hotel where I was supposed to meet her today, and I'm a little worried."

Dead silence echoed across the phone line as seconds ticked away. When Maygan finally spoke, Del knew they had their lead.

"No. I haven't seen Brina in over a year. I haven't spoken to her, either. Listen. I've got to go. It was nice talking to you. Bye" Click.

Del couldn't suppress his enormous whoop of success. "Hell, yeah! Who's up for a road trip?"

Chapter Four

Brina read the box again. There were no caveats mentioning hair-coloring and pregnancy, and she truly had no clue whether the chemicals would be dangerous to her unborn fetus. She chewed on her bottom lip. *Damn it.* She dropped her would-be redheaded disguise into the wastebasket with a glare. She wasn't willing—in her ignorance—to take a chance, and opening her computer to look for information on the internet was not an option. Searching with any outside signal could alert someone to her location. And the burner phone she'd picked up at the local market had only basic capabilities, and was used only to contact Maygan. She'd already called and given her friend the number.

Brina was surprised to find the object of her thoughts buzzing away in her pocket. She plucked it out and punched the green indicator. "Hi Mayg." She walked from the small bathroom into the main living space and dropped down onto the sofa. "What's up? Miss me already?"

"Bri, I'm not sure who just called me, but I'm a little worried."

"Someone called?" Brina sat up straight, instantly on alert.

"Yeah. And he asked for you by name. He told me that you're his girlfriend. He wanted to know if I'd seen you today because he discovered you'd checked out of your hotel without telling him. And get this, he said he had my number because the two of you had been planning a visit to me. Together."

"Oh God, Mayg. I'm not dating anybody and no one should have your number. What the hell? They found me so quickly," she moaned. "I'm so sorry for putting you in the middle of this."

"Don't worry about it, Bri. I told the guy I haven't spoken to you in more than a year. I think he bought it, but I didn't give him time to probe. I said goodbye and hung up," she stated proudly. "Oh, and he gave a name if it helps, or if it's even real," Maygan scoffed.

"What name did he give?" Brina attempted to remain calm. She could only imagine that it had to be Reynold himself, or someone her father had sent. Either possibility sent shivers up her spine.

"Del," Mayg replied. "Delancourt Songen. And he laid the charm on pretty thick."

All the starch leached out of Bri's backbone and she sank back onto the cushions. "Del," she breathed, barely able to get words out beyond her suddenly numb lips.

"What?" Maygan demanded. "What, Del? Shit, Bri. Do you actually know this guy?"

Brina couldn't quell the hysterical laugh that bubbled up in her throat. It escaped with a sharpness that had to sound crazy to her friend. But Maygan, bless her, only waited patiently for her to pull it together.

Did she *know* him? A hiccup followed her irrational laugh. *Hell, yes.* She was carrying a part of him deep inside her womb, but damned if she'd tell Mayg that.

"Yeah. I do." Bri finally gave up, opting for partial honesty. "I, um, picked him up at a bar a few months ago and we had a one night stand." God, that sounded way more awful than it had seemed at the time. But how could she explain to her friend that there had been an instant attraction. An undeniable chemistry? Hell, she didn't understand it herself, and she'd gone over it in her mind a thousand times since it had happened.

"A one night stand? You?" Maygan questioned incredulously, and Brina knew why. In all the time they'd spent together as under-grads, Bri had been focused on sports and academics. Despite the myriad of guys who had hounded her, she'd never succumbed to any overtures. Indeed, it wasn't until she was a grad student that she'd finally dated and had exactly two, short, unfulfilling relationships.

"Yeah," she prevaricated, still unwilling to put an intimate name to what she'd experienced with Del. "It was a knee-jerk reaction to my ass of a boss, Reynold. I wanted to see if my newfound coldness was because of him, or if I'd lost my libido."

"And?" This time Maygan's question had some cheek to it.

"Uh, let's just say that Del put a checkmark in all the right boxes, eliminating my fears." Bri's cheeks warmed, remembering. Which brought her back to wondering about another phenomenon she'd pondered for days afterward. If he performed that well drunk, what would the man be capable of when sober? *Damn*, she couldn't let her mind go there. A fascinating man who was damned near close to superman in bed? The memory had plagued her, and only with brute, mental-force had she compelled herself not to track him down. A one night stand was supposed to be just that, and Del wouldn't have relished her breaking those rules.

"You don't suppose that maybe he's tracked you down because you were good in the sack and he wants a repeat?"

Maygan sounded hopeful, and Bri wished it too, but it was best she burst that bubble for both of them.

"I doubt it, Mayg," she sighed. "Del knows Reynold. It's been some months, but our Mr. Songen was around the office prior to our liaison. From the paperwork that got sent across my desk, he sold something of military importance to US AIM. Which means he's probably working with Reynold to get me back." She seemed to recall Del saying he'd done search and rescue in the armed services, and that he'd like to incorporate those skills into a new career. Was she his first paying gig?

It was a toss up as to who was after her. It could be Reynold, fearful for his own life and wanting her back to assure his safety. But it could be her father. If he knew she'd found out he was involved in something sinister, he'd make good on those threats he sent to Reynold. Bri put a hand to her stomach, trying to calm herself and think things through.

"Mayg," she began, speculating out loud. "If Reynold values his own skin, he wouldn't have dared tell Dad that I disappeared." As soon as the words were out of her mouth, Bri could feel the veracity of them. Reynold, figuring out what she'd seen, would want to find her first and silence her in a way that would let him off the hook with her father. Some obscure accident taking Bri's life would do it. He'd play the sorrowful boyfriend, and Dad would never know the difference. Fake bereavement, funeral, and then back to arms dealing between the pair. Two huge slime-balls, Bri speculated. Possibly three? She hated putting Del into that category. Her hand travelled to her abdomen again and she rubbed it, striving for comfort.

"Whether Del is in on things with Reynold is the big question, but I think right now all we have to worry about is him, not Dad. Reynold can probably put him off for a few days, but my father will eventually become suspicious if I'm

37

unreachable." Her father called once a week like clockwork to make sure—in a gruff thirty second call—that she stayed to his agenda, and it had been eight days. "At that point I'll have him hunting me down, as well." That was if she wasn't dead first.

No matter what, her situation seemed pretty bleak. If Del had managed to get this close to her after all of her precautions, she'd have no chance against her father's men. She'd seen the scary individuals with whom he was surrounded. Bri would have to try and run again, this time leaving no possible trail.

"Bri, you stay put for now." Maygan must have read her mind. "Nobody knows about my cabin, and even if this guy Del comes to me, I'm not going to tell him anything."

Brina bit down on the inside of her cheek. Her mind told her to flee, but her body rebelled. Her energy was sapped. She'd dragged her ass, tired every minute of every day since she'd become pregnant. Leaving the relative safety of the cabin seemed like an insurmountable task, but she didn't want to endanger Mayg, either.

"I can't let you get in the middle of my problems, Maygan. We're not talking about an innocent game of hide and seek here. I have a feeling these guys play for keeps. If I'm their ultimate target, I'm afraid to think what they'll do to you in order to get to me."

With the loud huff she got in return for her speech, Bri could almost see the tough, stubborn side of her friend coming out; the one who had refused to turn in her college stalker to authorities, but had instead enlisted Brina's help to discourage the jerk.

"I'm no pushover, Bri. And I've got grand-dad's old shotgun by the door at home. Someone I don't know comes up my walkway, they'll find it right in their face."

Brina sighed and lifted the hair off her nape, feeling suddenly sweaty and nauseous. She couldn't summon the energy to argue. "Okay, Mayg. But let me know the minute anybody shows up."

"I will," she assured. "Now get some rest. You sound awful."

It was good advice. Brina hung up on her friend and couldn't even muster the energy to go make herself the cup of chamomile tea she'd coveted ever since she'd purchased it at the little general store. She'd also bought dried ginger slices and papaya. Why wouldn't the morning sickness go away now that she'd reached the beginning of her second trimester? And wasn't heartburn supposed to wait until she was beached-whale-huge before it struck? Life was unfair on so many levels.

Bri took stock of her situation before she gave in and slept for the next twenty-four hours. There was plenty to be proud of. She had managed to get herself off the beaten path, enlisted the help of a friend who'd provided the roof over her head, and she'd purchased food that would last her for several weeks, even if it was canned or dried. Not the most nutritious for someone in her condition, but what choice did she have?

It wasn't winter, so she didn't need logs for the fireplace or heat in the cabin, and if she could keep boredom at bay, she might just have a chance to survive this. Eventually, perhaps she could reveal herself to her father and concoct a plausible story for him that didn't include weapons dealing, but focused on her unplanned pregnancy. Maybe she could convince him that she'd been ashamed to stay with Reynold while knocked up with someone else's child. He might buy into it. And maybe his ego would keep him from killing the vessel that contained his grand-child. It was a long shot for a man who had always professed to love her but had never shown her any but the most perfunctory attention after her mother died. But what else could she come up with?

Another thing she could attempt, to fill the unlimited hours alone in the cabin without HD entertainment, would be to keep a journal for her unborn child. Writing had always been a strong suit for her, and now that she had plenty of time on her hands, perhaps she could weave a tale worth telling.

She'd start the story by unfolding her unorthodox beginnings with Del—keeping any hint of her alcoholic haze out of it. There were so many things she could put into writing about him. And how was that even possible? She'd only known him for a few hours, but he'd made such an impact on her. *No, not just physically.* She laughed at the irony. Besides the potency of his testosterone, there was something about the man that had touched her deeply, and in truth, until she'd found herself pregnant, she'd been sure that she'd look him up once she was free of US AIM. Those plans had been derailed when she'd peed on one little stick and seen a plus sign. If, subsequent to that, she'd imagined letting him in on their impending parenthood, in a gentle kind of way, that had gone to hell now, too. Hadn't it.

It was settled. She would write down the entire clusterfuck that was her current life, and forward it to Maygan—who would find out she was pregnant, anyway, if Bri stuck around. That way if she ended up dead, the authorities would have plenty of ammo to find and prosecute her murderers. Leaving a trail might help to bring down her father's empire, not to mention that of Reynold Blithe. She could deal with that as a legacy.

On the other hand, if she and her baby managed to survive, what a bedtime story this would be for her little one. It had espionage, intrigue and sex. *Okay.* Well, the sex part would have to wait until her child was older. Say, thirty-seven? But the rest would make for a wide-eyed telling.

Bri tore open a granola protein bar, and forced it down, washing the slightly too sweet taste away with a splash of water. She took one last look at the hair dye box where it lay in the trash, and decided against it. It wasn't worth the risk.

Dragging herself into the small bedroom, she quickly divested herself of clothes, tossing them into a heap on the floor. She pulled back the covers and slipped into bed. Nothing had felt so heavenly in a long time. She considered the possibility that she'd left the evil behind, spinning the fantasy that Del was too nice of a guy to be involved in the funny business she'd uncovered. Maybe he *was* looking for her because he needed more than just their one night stand.

Brina snorted. *Sure.* That was why he'd waited three months to start sniffing around instead of coming to look for her the morning after. Or even a few mornings after. Damned if she hadn't held out hope for a full week that he'd take the decision out of her hands. For Bri, what had begun as a fast hook-up, then turned into one of the most fulfilling and erotic nights she'd ever experienced, had instead become a life-changer. Her hand fluttered lightly over her still flat abdomen. She let herself think about Del—something she'd tried not to do overly much since she'd found out about her pregnancy.

He was a Boston native, born and bred. And although he'd been places and tried hard to erase the accent, she had detected it as soon as he'd become looser with drink. A few dropped "r's", and "i-n-g's" that became "i-n's". It was cute, coming from between such attractive lips as he spouted a vast amount of knowledge.

He'd invented something, but he wouldn't say what, and he'd been in the Army, a special operations division that did search and rescue all over the world. Bri could tell by the warmth in his voice, that these were fond memories.

She'd asked about his parents, but he hadn't given her anything. He'd simply ignored the question and put it back on her. Bri had openly told him about the early death of her mother, the aunt who'd taken over as a maternal figure, and her somewhat estranged relationship with her father. He'd covered her hand with his own when she'd told him this, and squeezed as if he understood. He'd already given her goosebumps with his rich laugh, but his touch electrified her. Nothing had discouraged her from her first, rash decision to seduce him. On the contrary, she'd grown more and more enthralled with him as the evening progressed.

Of course, there had come a point where alcohol fogged his brilliant repartee. But that had been her fault. He'd assumed that she was keeping up with him, and that if she was still coherent, how could he be any less?

She remembered him being surprised when she needed no assistance to walk to the elevator when he was anything but steady on his feet. Yet, here again, he'd surprised her. He'd taken her elbow in his strong, capable hand, and made to guide her. He couldn't have known the crooked path they'd taken, or the giggle that hovered upon her lips. She'd let him have his moment.

And in the bedroom he'd been just as attentive. He'd gently removed her clothing, worshipping every part of her body, albeit in a prone position on the bed so he wouldn't fall over. He'd made sure she'd been satisfied with his talented tongue and fingers at least twice before he'd finally given in to her pleading and stripped down.

Her first look at his nakedness had stolen her breath. His smooth brown skin stretched tautly over huge, sculpted muscles, and his erect cock stood a very healthy number of inches, stretched up and bobbing above his bellybutton. His skin had been warm on hers as he'd begun on her again with his talented digits, but she put a stop to that, needing to feel his weeping cock inside of her. When he succumbed to her pleading, and fed his length into her aching pussy, tenderly, she'd almost wept with the feeling of completeness that swept over her. It was something she'd never experienced before. It hadn't worried her at the time, that while he drove them both to an explosive orgasm, his eyes had been fully shut. She assumed it was just how he made love. And he'd certainly hit all the right buttons.

But when they reached their pinnacle—an event that once joined hadn't taken very long—and pulled out, he'd flopped to his back, eyes still closed, and begun to snore. To this day, she wondered if he'd accomplished the entire sex act in his sleep.

Chapter Five

"You know her girlfriend's alerted her by now that we called, and she's probably back on the run as we speak," Wiley offered, sitting shotgun in the beige SUV they'd outfitted for all road-trip possibilities.

"If that's the case, then at least we have a hot trail to follow," Del answered confidently. He easily but aggressively maneuvered the large vehicle through the mid-afternoon Boston traffic headed north. "But I'm not so sure she'll run again," he speculated, causing his seatmate to regard him, and two additional pair of eyes to fix on his in the rearview mirror.

"And why is that?" Wiley smirked. Del knew he was about to get his ass roasted. "You told us you didn't exchange names on your one-nighter."

Wait for it. Wait for it.

Wiley continued. "So she doesn't know her pursuer is the totally harmless dude who's so incompetent that he can't even get it up when the occasion presents itself."

Del flashed him a one-fingered salute. "Keep talking, Wiles. I might not have scored, but at least I'm not the asshole who tossed my cookies on a conquest's belly." They'd had a laugh over that old story, and had whipped it until it was beaten. Wiley had caught some horrible bug in the tropics a few years earlier, and completely grossed out his civilian fuck-mate—post-coitally—one night.

"Right. But it looks like I'm not the only puker here, boss-man. You just waited until after she'd left to barf. Or so you think. You might have lost your lunch as soon as you got her in the room, and that's what turned her off for sex. At least I showed my honey a good time before I spewed."

Prez interjected from the back seat. "Will you guys shut up and quit bickering? I don't need to hear anymore about who screws or pukes the best. I'm trying to get some sleep. If we need any munitions action on this job, you don't want my hands to be shaky."

As if, Del thought. He'd seen Prez setting detonators and fuses—tremor free—on a three day recon with no z's. But he wouldn't argue. If cranky Prez wanted nap-time, far be it from Del to get in the way.

He continued softly for Wiley and Sarge. "Back to my original summation. I'm of the mind that our quarry has come to roost. If she takes off from here, she'll have to run blind without the help of her friend. Her money will disappear quickly, and eventually she'll have to surface again, which you know is not on her agenda." He paused. "On the other hand, if she sticks with her buddy, she can stay in any backwoods hidey-hole, completely secure, until they both think we've given up." He laughed. "Of course they don't know that we won't quit. Eventually we will win."

"So we win," Prez groused again. "And the next step?"

"Once we find her, we confront her. Find out why she left. Then it's only a matter of containment so she doesn't disappear again. Piece of cake," Del finished. What he didn't say was that he'd be damned if he let her get away from him again. Three months was an awfully long time to be fixating on one, sassy blonde. He needed to keep her around long enough this time to work her out of his system.

"Yeah? And then what?" Sarge grunted. "You don't exactly trust this Blithe guy now that you've caught him withholding information, and the job seems pretty easy for the amount of money we're being paid. Do we tie her up and hand her over, or just let him know we've found her?"

"I guess that depends on what Ms. Capadella has to tell us. We'll hear her side of the story, then decide whether to deliver her, or simply report back to her boss. She's of age, and we're not obligated to force her into anything. The best case for everyone would be for her to call Reynold voluntarily and let him know she's all right. Then we talk to him, and if he insists we bring her in, he'll need to have a damned good reason why."

"Sounds like a plan," Prez added from underneath the cap he'd pulled down over his eyes to nap. "So why don't I believe it'll go down that way?"

"Because you're a negative human being, Prez," Wiley snarked. "I'm not sure why we put up with your ass. If rainclouds could talk, that would be you."

"Sleeping here, Wiles," Prez snorted in answer. "Not caring here, either." The cap got adjusted down a little farther and the guys grumbled, but took their cue from him and settled in for a snooze while Del drove.

The miles ticked by and Del couldn't get his brain to shut down. He'd purposely kept himself—for months—from fully reliving that night at the bar, but now his mind refused to hit "off" regarding the smart and snarky blonde who'd captured his attention.

Why had Brina even walked into the bar that night? If she'd been the girlfriend of the rich and arrogant CEO of US AIM, should she have been out trolling the waters? Or had she been? Maybe it was his ego talking, but perhaps she'd only come into the lounge to drown her sorrows with a few, quick shots before heading off to bed. But then she'd spotted him. Maybe she'd been gut-punched with an instant attraction. The same one he'd experienced, first setting eyes on her.

Oh sure, he'd picked up the occasional woman in a bar before, but it wasn't normally a gut reaction that made his decisions for him. No. It was based more on whether the female in his sights appeared cheerful, clean, and footloose. With the emphasis on footloose. He wasn't ever looking for anything permanent.

All that aside, he'd been drawn to Brina the minute she'd turned her fathoms-deep, green eyes toward his. It was as if, even before the smile hit her lips, she held secrets he needed to know.

Del shook his head. Now who was being crazy? Clearly, the only secrets he'd needed from the woman had been those he'd anticipated sharing between the sheets. And because he'd somehow lost the battle of the shot glasses, he couldn't recall touching one inch of her bare skin.

And there lay an embarrassing concern for when he met up with her again. How did you approach a girl for whom you didn't perform, and still have her regard you seriously? She'd probably take one look at him, recognize his sorry ass, and laugh him right out of her sight. Wouldn't the guys just love that?

But something told Del she wasn't the type who would hold his non-performance against him. Because there *had* been another connection between them, something more than physical. Brina had seemed to find him as fascinating as he found her when they'd mentally connected and shared small tidbits of their lives. Normally reticent to bring up his past, Del had found himself regaling her with some old, but light soccer stories from high school. And after hearing her delicious, full-throated laugh in response, he'd also readily shared some of the comical pranks he and his team had pulled off in the jungles of South America while between missions; things he'd never shared with any woman before.

Yet after that, after all the humor, when the time came for more thoughtful and philosophical musings, Brina didn't shy away from those, either. Although what he'd pontificated about while well on his way to inebriation, Del couldn't recall. He figured he must have done okay, because there was sufficient evidence that she'd accompanied him to his room and laid in the bed next to him. He could clearly remember her unique lemon scent now, as he took a deep, cleansing breath. But that visceral memory, instead of comforting him, made him shut down. He needed to let the idea of Brina as someone special, go. Especially now that he'd found out she was the rich, entitled kid of some uber-millionaire. He knew her type. He'd cut his teeth on a trust-fund girl in high school, and he didn't like their ilk one single bit. He steeled himself to understand that Brina from the bar was gone now. *This* Brina was his job, and that was it. End of story.

Del drove for an hour and was approaching Portsmouth, New Hampshire, when he noticed a small, gray luxury sedan a few cars behind. One he swore he'd seen in Boston as they'd been leaving the city. Not a crime, Del pondered. Lots of traffic headed north. It just seemed that this particular car was keeping time with them. Del pulled from the middle lane and sped up in the fast lane to test his suspicions.

"Hey guys?" His team had fallen into slumberous positions, but popped up immediately, alert at Del's hail. "Keep an eye on that little charcoal two-door behind us," he instructed. "I think we might have a tail."

Del hung in the high speed lane until he gauged that the small vehicle was darting in and out amongst the now sparse traffic, trying to keep up but also remain unseen.

"Good call, boss," Sarge commended, staring backward out the window. "I can't tell definitively how many are in the vehicle because the windows are lightly tinted, but I think only one."

Del grunted. "That's one to lose," he confirmed. "Hold onto your hats, gentlemen. We're going to have a short tour of the Portsmouth Rotary." He cut sharply across two lanes of traffic and dropped down exit five with two tires just clearing the grass.

"Yes!" Wiley called triumphantly. "The tail missed the turn." The sedan sped by on their left but Del didn't let up. He hit the gas, approaching the traffic circle, and took the long, slow curve at a fast clip, going almost fully around before speeding up the onramp and back onto the highway. It was a good thing he'd had his foot in it, because the car that had been following them was just veering off on exit six, hoping to intercept them.

"Faster, Del," Wiley urged, slapping at the dashboard. "I can't see the plate yet."

Del punched the pedal and all but flew the few hundred feet that would make the difference. He didn't dare follow the car down into Portsmouth, but hoped from their vantage point, still on the main route, that the guys could ID the tag.

"Got it!" Sarge yelled a few seconds later. He'd kept his cool, leaned out the window and snapped a picture at the last moment before the car disappeared down the ramp. Del held his breath. Would the snap be clear enough to make out numbers? Sarge let out a triumphant howl. "Oh yeah," he preened. "And here it is, looking good."

Del didn't ask what came next. He knew. Sarge tapped away frantically on his laptop, quiet descending upon the car until Sarge spoke again.

"Well, I'll be," Sarge mused. "Who do you think was our friend?"

"Reynold Blithe," Del, Prez and Wiley said in unison without a moment's hesitation.

Sarge blew air from between his pursed lips. "Ah, you guys are no fun. Of course it was him, but couldn't I have had just a second of glory?"

"We don't want to stroke that already oversized ego, Sarge." Wiley grinned. "Besides, who else could it be so early on into our investigation?" He turned to Del. "You were right not to trust him. He's obviously after this woman for something other than just a boyfriend's concern. What do you think? Do we drop this whole thing and turn around? Without us, he hasn't got a chance in hell of finding her."

Calling Reynold and declining the job was the smartest option, but by this point, Del was not feeling smart anymore. He was running half on curiosity and half on emotion, neither of which was particularly bright, but he couldn't seem to help it. Now he needed to be honest with his guys.

"If you want out," he told them, "I'll drop you off and you can get a bus home, but I need to keep going," Del admitted. "This lady is under my skin." *Wait. Had he just said that out loud? Fuck. Note to self: Keep a lid on the emotional crap.* He took in the guy's smirks, glared, and changed tacks. "She's gotten herself into something bad with this guy, and I need to find out what is is. If Reynold, who doesn't take a key-stroke if a secretary can do it for him, got into his car and followed us, someone's ass is on the line. If Brina doesn't come back, I'll bet it's his. He said as much when I asked if he'd notified her dear old dad."

"Which means that Brina Capadella must have found something out that she shouldn't have, and Blithe needs to shut her up, perhaps before she gets to daddy?" Wiley returned.

"That's one guess. But then why didn't she run to her old man?" Sarge pondered.

Del might have the answer to that one. "I remember her saying that their connection wasn't the greatest," he recalled. "They stay in touch, but he's not a doting father."

Although hadn't Brina mentioned an aunt? Something to ponder, but he turned his mind back to the patriarch of the family. Considering that Brina's father and Reynold Blithe dealt with each other, the government, and arms contracts, Blithe's transgression could be that he'd been skimming off the top on Mr. Capadella, or... Del refused to speculate beyond that. He needed more information, but either way, Brina seemed to be in big trouble, and he couldn't let her shoulder it on her own. He looked at each of his guys who by this time had settled back, comfortably in their seats. "Well?" he asked.

"Well, what?" Prez returned. "Like we're going to leave your sorry ass to deal with this alone," he scoffed. "Give us a break, man. Shut the fuck up and drive."

It was the second time Del had been told to zip it by his munitions expert, but this time he did as he was told. Besides, being quiet gave him more time to think about his imminent meeting with the gorgeous Ms. Capadella.

Chapter Six

Nearly three hours later, just after noon, Del pulled up in front of a white, two story farm house just outside of Orono, Maine.

"Do you think anyone's home?" Sarge asked.

"I sure as fuck hope not," Prez growled. "Knocking is for sissies. And there's only one way to find out. Come on." He opened his door and emerged from the vehicle, stretching his legs. Del followed.

"Let me do the talking," Del cautioned the every-ready to verbally spar, Prez. "I think we need finesse here, not aggression."

"Whatever you say, boss." Prez's quick answer gave Del no comfort. Given provocation, Prez never stayed out of anything.

The four men walked up to the front door and knocked, despite the sissy comment. When no one answered, Del knocked again. He gave a nod to his crew, and they spread out to walk the perimeter of the home and peer into windows. Del tried the doorknob, but it was locked. Yeah. That would have been too easy, and he wasn't about to do a B&E since he was trying to gain trust, here.

Within two minutes, his guys had reconvened.

"Anything?" Del asked.

"Not a sign of life," Wiley answered. "Dishes drying on a rack beside the kitchen sink though. Two coffee cups." He raised a brow. "Could be more than Ms. DePalto lives here?"

"Not according to town records," Sarge answered. "I did some poking around about our target's host, and she's lived here alone for the past year since an elderly DePalto died. Probably her grandfather."

"So that might say that Brina came here. Perhaps early, considering her time-line, or maybe after she'd waited and tracked her friend down at the college," Wiley speculated.

"Either way, let's see if we can find something that places her here." His eyes traveled the property and he nodded toward the back. "Let's check out the barn."

Four pairs of feet trod down the dirt driveway to the front of the large, white structure where a huge, rolling door encompassed a large portion of the face. Del knelt in front of it. "Quite a lot of footprint activity here," he noted. "Small feet. Child or female." He raised his head.

"Yeah, but there's been no rain in the past week, so it could be an accumulation."

"Perhaps," Del granted, but his gut told him differently. "I think we need to get into this barn." It would still be breaking and entering, but since it wasn't the woman's actual house, he didn't feel guilty about it. He reached for the iron handle to slide the door, and gave a satisfied grunt. Unlocked. He eased it open just far enough so they could all slip in, then closed it behind them. Weak light filtered in from a window up high, and *bingo*. Brina Capadella's car.

"So we have her car," Wiley stated the obvious, "But no girl, which leaves a few possibilities. She's either hiding inside the house, she went back to the University with her friend, or they've stashed her someplace else altogether."

"Scenario number four," Sarge interjected, running his hands over a sweet looking vintage Indian. "She continued running, took off in her friend's car and is hundreds of miles away already."

"All of which just means we have to speak with Maygan DePalto." Prez gave the leather seat *he'd* been caressing one last pat and cracked his knuckles.

"In a nice way, Prez." Del wasn't putting up with any of the guy's baloney, even if he knew Prez just liked to do things to get him riled. "What do you think?" he asked everyone. "Lunch, then a visit to Ms. DePalto at school?" His stomach was hitting his backbone, and at this juncture, he was pretty sure things would remain status quo for the time it took to eat.

"I'm in," Sarge yielded easily. "We passed a good looking diner a few miles back."

"And local diners are a hot-bed of gossip and information. Maybe we can find out more about Brina's friend. Something that will point us to where our quarry might be hidden," Del added.

"It's a plan," Wiley smacked his lips, clearly anticipating lunch.

They left the barn, pulled the door fully shut behind them, and strode back to their SUV. The possibility of food made them move in synch. Del had to chuckle. It didn't matter the time or the situation. The stomach called and it got answered.

"When we get there," Del said, driving back the way they'd come. "Take my lead. Depending on who we meet, I'm not sure what story I'll tell."

Sarge nodded, while pecking rapidly on his ever-present keyboard. "Cranky old guy, and you're a long lost friend of the family. But a cute, young waitress? You play the love-struck boyfriend. Got it."

"Smart ass. But yes. That about covers it," Del huffed.

"Okay? Then what about a cranky older waitress, hot-shot?" Wiley invited. "What then?"

"Then we'll let you take care of her, Wiles," Sarge answered. "I hope she's eighty. That's about your speed."

"More than you could handle, sweet cheeks," Wiley came back.

"Will you two cut the shit," Del blistered as he pulled in. "We're here. Just behave yourselves." He dropped the SUV into park.

"As if that's possible," Prez snorted, pushing the door open. "And you worry about me." He shook his head at Del and kicked his long legs out of the vehicle.

"Oh. One last thing, boys. If I nudge you, I want flirting and smiles. Catch my drift?" Del kept walking. He didn't need an answer to know they'd do what was required.

Len's Diner. Del looked up at the sign which had seen better days. It might have once held neon tubes, but what was left now was the wooden frame. Still, the parking lot was full, and the silver siding shone brightly in the afternoon sun. Not to mention the smell of foods frying in heavy grease that permeated the air had his mouth watering. Del smiled. This was going to be a great lunch.

The four of them stepped into the diner and immediately traveled back in time. Gray Formica with a pink and white boomerang print graced the counters and table tops. The spinning stools that remained unoccupied, showed patched wear and tear. Burgundy naugahyde reinforced with duct tape. A classic.

There was one booth open far to the right, and Del quickly turned his feet in that direction. A chipper waitress, neither young nor old, quickly intercepted to stuff four menus into his hands. "Have a seat and I'll be right with you, honey," she said, her down-Maine accent thick and delightful.

Being dutiful boys, Del passed the menus around, and they did what they were told.

"Damn. Meatloaf," Wiley expounded, his menu already open as he slid to an inside position in the booth. "I haven't had that since I visited my Elisi."

"Your grandmother makes meatloaf?" Prez's mouth actually fell open. "Last time you had me there, she was shoving all kinds of corn and buffalo meat down my throat. Even for breakfast."

"That's only because she wanted you to take our Native American roots seriously. It's what she always brings out for company. The rest of us get meatloaf and American chop suey," he grinned.

"I've been had. I believed I was getting an authentic experience."

"Oh, you were. Just not a twenty-first century one." Wiley put down his menu, clearly settling on the meatloaf.

"What about you, Del? Anything look good?" Sarge asked.

"Yup," he said, just as the waitress arrived. He turned his request to her. "Big burger with everything. Rare." He smiled.

The waitress, whose name tag read Hazel, nodded and jotted it down on a small pad. "A man who knows what he wants. And how about you, sweetie?" She turned to Prez.

"Four hotdogs. Buns grilled," he stated, without blinking.

The waitress stared right back. "Only way we do 'em here." Although her "here" sounded more like "heah". Del didn't have time to ponder that as she continued. "And you want chips with those, or fries."

"Fries," the men said at once, and Del, seeing her pencil paused, took the lead. "Lots of fries for all of us," he told her. "A half dozen larges."

Now she laughed. "You boys are cute, you know that? What's got you visiting our little town?"

Here was the opening Del had been waiting for. "We're passing through on our way to Canada, but stopped to visit an old school chum on the way north."

"Oh? And who's that?" Del could tell she was ripe for a little gossip.

"Maygan DePalto," he said, looking her straight in the face. "We haven't seen her since before her grandfather died."

Hazel put on a sad face. "Yup. Art. He was a good man," she sighed. "Left Mayg all alone in that house now that he's gone. But she's a strong one. Hell, you must know that. So. You staying long?" She skipped back to glean more tidbits off their agenda.

"Depends," Del hedged. And now he went out on a limb, hoping he wasn't making a grievous error. "We never did get to go hunting with Art like he'd promised us. Didn't know whether Mayg still traipsed around in the woods." Del held his breath. Didn't all old guys in Maine, hunt?

Hazel let out a crackling laugh. "Oh Lawd, yes," she slapped her notepad on her apron-covered thigh. "You can't keep Mayg out of the woods. She was practically raised in that little hunting cabin."

"Right," Del agreed, but put a puzzled look on his face. "She told us about that, but we've never been. Is it someplace nearby?"

"Near enough," Hazel shrugged. "But I'm sure she'll show it to you before you leave." She picked up her pad, clearly through with the chit-chat. "Now. What can I get you other two fellas?"

Del didn't push. He wasn't about to set off any alarms by asking more. Instead, he kicked Sarge to have him turn up the charm. "What do you like best on the menu, ma'am? Because that's what I'm having."

Good. With Sarge's big smile, Hazel would forget about the questions that might have been a little too probing. When looking back, it would seem natural to the friendly waitress.

She put him down for a fish and chips, and smiled her approval at Wiley's hearty request for meatloaf, before crisply taking her leave to put up their order.

After a short wait and a little chit-chat, their meal came to the table, piping hot. The food was outstanding, and once stuffed to the gills with the extra fries, each man sat back to rub a lean, but replete, abdomen. Hazel clearly wanted them to stay for pie, but Del begged off, knowing they needed to get moving. "Next time, Hazel. We're too full right now. Besides, it'll give us something to look forward to."

"Great," she beamed. "Have Mayg bring you back for supper before you leave town. Our pies are made in the late afternoon, so you'll be getting them hot out of the oven."

"Sounds like a plan," Del agreed, and grabbed the tab off the table. As the waitress turned with a final wave, he threw a couple of bills down. The good sized tip would go a long way toward making her feel better if she caught Del and his crew out on their lies.

"Let's go," Del herded the group from the diner, Prez still interested in the spinning glass carousel of pie. "Hey. Bottomless pit. You can have more to eat, later."

Prez grunted, but obediently turned away.

Sarge yawned. "Yeah? How about a nap. When do we get one of those?"

"You guys are getting soft," Del griped, forcibly stifling a yawn of his own in response to Sarge's. "As soon as we get finished with this, it's a twenty mile, heavy-pack run for us."

Wiley groaned and cranked him the middle finger. "Fuck that, slave-driver." But Del knew he didn't mean it. They liked working up a sweat, and loved proving to each other that their physical stamina ruled.

They piled back into the vehicle, set the GPS, and headed off to the college. Sarge brought up a picture of the campus and quickly located the soccer fields. Finding Maygan would be easy. Convincing her that they weren't there to hurt her friend would definitely prove more difficult.

Two o'clock and there were athletes everywhere as they strolled across the various courts. Del could feel eyes—mostly female—glued to his group as they walked, but he supposed they made an impressive sight.

They all stood over six feet tall, with Prez coming in at freaking six foot-three. And they filled out their T-shirts with broad shoulders and hard-won muscles, carrying themselves with a military precision that couldn't be mistaken. Del's dark skin, and Sarge's swarthy complexion made a startling contrast with Prez's Scandinavian blondness. And Wiley's cheekbones pronounced his Native American heritage as surely as if it had been stamped on his forehead.

In the city, they blended in pretty well, but here on a Maine campus? Not so much.

Sarge poked him in the back and pointed a finger at a woman staring at them with a little more intensity than the rest. Del recognized her from the pictures they'd pulled up. Here was Maygan DePalto, and she didn't look like anything like the pushover they'd hoped.

As they continued their march toward her, she crossed her arms over her ample chest and spread her feet in a ready position. Del wanted to grin, but didn't. Shit. He liked Brina's friend, already.

"Maygan DePalto?" he asked, imbuing his voice with warmth. She didn't melt one bit.

"Who's asking?" she countered.

"Delancourt Songen." He stuck out a hand. "We spoke on the phone, but I believe we got cut off."

"No we didn't." She shook her head and refused his outstretched digits. "I hung up."

"Yeah, well," Del hesitated, trying to decide what to say next, when Wiles took over.

"William Prancing Deer." He stepped forward introducing himself with a smile. Del was surprised he'd used his real name. Maygan blinked. So she wasn't as immune to charm as she pretended. He nudged Sarge forward.

"And I'm Serge Montverre," Sarge picked her hand up from where it clenched her bicep, and gave it a short squeeze.

What the hell? Had that growl come out of Prez's throat? Del shot him a glare, but Prez refused to smile.

"Lucas Balshir," he muttered. And hands clasped behind his back, his eyes dropped to his feet as his cheeks grew red.

What? Who the hell was this guy and what had he done with Prez? But there was no time for Del to speculate. Maygan had started to speak.

"So if you're looking for Brina, you've come a long way for nothing," she stated, not giving an inch.

Del couldn't let her get away with that. "We know she's here," he said gently, "and we know you're helping her." He played his trump card right away, before Maygan could retreat behind her cold mask any further. "Just tell us where your grandfather's cabin is, and we'll leave you alone."

An unintended gasp slipped from Mayg's mouth. She quickly covered it up with her hand, but it was too late. She had to know she'd given the game away.

"Forget it," she said, moving her hand down to make a fist. "I'll never tell you. Do what you have to do, but know that if you try to hurt me, I'll end up putting a world of pain on all of you before I go down."

Del didn't doubt it. Maygan was one solid human being. Shaped to absolute perfection, she had highly muscled legs and arms that carried more flesh than most athletic females he knew, but it was packed solid, making her a formidable opponent. Before Del could speak, Prez, oddly, stepped up to the plate.

"We're not here to hurt you, Ms. DePalto," he said smoothly, in probably the most gentle voice Del had ever witnessed coming out of the guy. "We really need to find Ms. Capadella because we feel she's gotten into some trouble."

Maygan looked wary, narrowing her eyes to nod. "I'm not saying I know where she is, but how do I know you guys aren't part of that trouble?"

"It's complicated," Del took over. "If you'd just get her on the phone, I can explain things to her, faster. And then you can point us in her direction or tell us to get lost, depending on the way she receives us."

Maygan narrowed her eyes, taking a fucking long time to make up her mind. "Fine. I'll call her, but you stay over there," she warned. "I don't want you seeing her number."

Prez put his hands up in the air and took two steps back. "We'll do anything you want, Maygan," he complied. "Gentlemen?" He gave them a quick look, with an especially withering glance at Sarge.

What was Prez's problem?

At the moment, Del didn't particularly care because Maygan was dialing a number. He held his breath.

"Bri? Hi. I don't know what you want me to do. That guy who called earlier is here at the field and he wants to talk to you." There was a short pause. "Are you sure?" Another silence. "Okay. I'll put him on." She proffered the phone to Del. "She says you have one minute."

Del grabbed the phone and put it to his ear. "Brina? This is Delancourt Songen," he offered, but Brina cut him right off.

"I know. And I need to find out just why the hell you're here, Del? Are you looking for a do-over on our one-night-stand, or completing a job for Reynold?"

Del's mouth dropped open. *Fuck.* She knew him.

Chapter Seven

"You…you know who this is?" Did his voice just squeak? Well why wouldn't it? He hadn't expected recognition until they'd done a face-to-face.

"Duh." She mocked, not sounding in the least bit contrite.

Del shook his head and took a few seconds to regain his equilibrium. Somewhat. "Do you mind telling me how?" He kept his tone steady. Perhaps it was something she'd just found out. Maybe she'd looked him up on the internet when he'd given his name to Maygan earlier, but wouldn't it have sent a ping to Sarge if she'd used her internet?

"I knew who you were that night at the bar." She cleared things up, sounding a bit defensive, but Del didn't care about the attitude she was throwing at him. He was too busy being blown away. She'd known who he was when they'd met? He didn't know if that was good or bad. But it suddenly hit him hard that, even though she'd occupied a good deal of his brain after their encounter, she'd known who he was, and he hadn't made a good enough impression on her that she'd looked for him. His stomach sank.

She was still talking. "And if you hadn't been so falling down drunk, I probably would have ended up confessing that you weren't a stranger."

Oh, yeah. That cinched it. He'd been a loser with a capital "L", that night. *Damn.* And how much more embarrassed was he now for his black-out, non-performance? But no matter how mortified he felt, he had to let it go and get back to the business at hand.

"Fine. Then you know who I am. So if you've done your homework, you should also know you can trust me."

There was a succinct snort in reply to that. "Why would I trust you? As far as I'm concerned, you worked with Reynold before our, uh, meeting."

Del experienced a little satisfaction when Brina stumbled over the memory of their one night tryst.

"So I assume you're working with him now," she continued.

Del wondered how to answer that. Technically he had been hired by Bri's boss-slash-boyfriend to find her, but that didn't mean he danced to the man's tune. He went on the offensive to throw her off guard.

"You know, when Blithe showed me your picture I was surprised, and a little disappointed to find out that you were dating him when you picked me up in the bar."

An outraged gasp hit his ears, and a certain satisfaction settled over him as he persisted. "I'm not someone who condones cheating."

"I…" She tried to interrupt, but Del wouldn't let her.

"No need for apologies," he goaded, quickly changing the subject. "You're right. My firm has been hired to locate you." He gave a significant pause. "But we uncovered some questions during our search. Questions that beg answers. So we haven't told him we've found you. Yet." Del added the last word as a blatant warning that if Brina didn't open up and give him the intel he wanted, right the hell now, Reynold would be informed.

There was a very long pause, and Del was almost certain Bri had cut their connection, until she finally spoke. "What do you want to know?" she asked belligerently.

"Why did you run?" Del gave her carte blanche to either answer fully and honestly, or hang herself.

"Reynold was never my boyfriend, and he was getting too possessive," she answered far too quickly.

Damn. Get the rope, Del seethed. Coming clean was clearly the last thing on Brina's mind.

"Pardon me if I don't buy that," Del shot back. "Reynold seems like the type of guy who only gives a shit about himself. And if a girlfriend left him high and dry, he'd snap his fingers and find another one. Not to mention that he's spending a lot of money for me to track you down." Del waited.

"Okay. Fine. My assignment to US AIM, and in particular my attachment to Reynold comes from an agreement he made with my father," she allowed, then clammed up.

Good. They were getting closer. Not that the idea her father had used her as an incentive in some business deal made him feel all warm and fuzzy.

Del cleared his throat. "So why not just call your dad and tell him the guy's a jerk? Or better yet, when you left Reynold's ass, why didn't you run away home?"

"It's complicated," she clipped again.

"Then make it simple," he returned, keeping his voice as devoid of emotion as possible.

She sighed. A long, deep, heart-rending sound, and he suddenly wanted her to trust him with whatever had her tied up in knots.

"Listen. Bri," he hesitated, stepping away from the group, not knowing precisely what would come out of his mouth once he got started, but he went with his gut. He lowered his voice. "I thought we had a nice connection that night at the bar. Despite the fact that you knew my name and didn't let on, I perceived an honesty between us." He ran his free hand back through his military cut, and gave a self-deprecating laugh. "Hell, I told you some things from my past that I've never shared with anybody." It was true. Some of the high school stories he'd pulled up were one's he'd like to forget. And God only knows what he'd shared after he'd blanked out.

"I felt that, too," Brina whispered. Had there been a slight catch in her voice? Her vulnerability nearly did him in. The put-together woman at the bar hadn't been one who would easily show weakness, so something pretty bad must be going down.

Del kept talking and went for broke. "I'm going to give it to you straight, Bri. The reason I know that you didn't just up and take off on Reynold unannounced, is because we have footage of you leaving two envelopes for him, and when I interviewed him for details on your disappearance, he didn't share that piece of information."

"Not surprising," Brina's defiance came through again. "Although nothing in either of those envelopes was damning," she advised.

"So that remains a mystery, but there's another bothersome event you should know of. On our way here, we caught someone tailing us. It was our boy Reynold, and I get the feeling he doesn't normally put a hair out of place to maintain the status quo with a girlfriend."

"He followed you?" Del caught the immediate panic in Brina's voice. "Oh my God. He didn't. How could you?" He heard fumbling over the phone. "Goddammit. I have to leave. Right now. Please don't try to come after me."

"Brina, no." Del commanded, yelling into the phone to circumvent her obvious fear, and getting a look from those waiting. Mayg would have charged him had Prez not put a hand on her arm.

"Calm down, Bri. We lost him in Portsmouth. I promise," he pledged.

All the shuffling noises stopped, and her raspy breathing slowed. "How can you be sure?" she finally asked.

"It's my job," Del soothed. "And I'm good at it. We lured him to take an exit, then we sped up and continued on the highway." Her over-the-top reaction scared him. What had she gotten herself into? "He never knew where we drove after that. Believe me."

"Okay. Let's say I trust you. What now?"

He pictured her dropping to a chair as her voice deflated.

"Tell me what was in those envelopes, and why you are so worried he'll find you?"

"The envelopes are easy," she divulged. "One was my resignation, and the other told Reynold that despite what he believed, I could never be his girlfriend. He'd started becoming too demanding of my time, wanting me to be on his arm for parties and galas," she huffed. "He'd even started to get aggressive, physically, even though I let him know there was zero attraction. Every time I pushed him away, he backed off, but I wondered how much longer that would happen. He was becoming too insistent. "

Del saw red and his hand clenched the phone he held to his ear. He had no time for the type of man who wouldn't take "no" from a woman. He'd show the bastard aggressive. How dare he shove his unwanted attentions on Brina? Next time he saw Reynold, he would gladly put a fist in the man's smug face.

Del swallowed. He blinked. *What the hell?* Where was this protective crap coming from? He barely knew Brina, and perhaps she'd been a tease with Reynold, the same way she'd come on to him at the bar. How could he know all of the particulars? Del shook off his unaccustomed cave-man feelings and cleared his throat. He had a job to do, and he needed to focus.

"And that's it?" Del let his skepticism show through. "You quit and blew him off, and he's spending thousands of dollars to get you back? I don't buy it."

"Are you going to call and tell him where I am?" Brina asked, changing the subject and meeting his hard tone with belligerence of her own. "I need to know."

Dammit. Del wasn't doing it. He stepped back to his team and went for broke. He held the phone out to get a consensus, and let Brina hear his question and their reaction "What do you think, guys? Are we going to out Ms. Capadella's location to Blithe?"

"Not feeling it," Sarge answered first. "There's something not right about the guy."

"We need more info before we act," Wiles agreed.

Prez put it most pithily. "Fuck, no."

Del put the phone back to his ear. "Did you get it? That was my team," he told her.

"They sound like a good bunch. But what about you?" she sent back. "I haven't heard your opinion, Del."

He loved hearing his name spoken thoughtfully through lips he remembered as being soft and lush.

"Ah, hell," he grumbled. "I have no intention of handing you over unless you insist on keeping the rest of the story from me, Bri."

"I…"

"And I know there's more to this than what you've divulged," he cut her off. "So what do you say? Shall we meet, and you can tell me what kind of trouble you're in?" Del held his breath. It was make or break time.

"Okay," she finally said.

He let the air out of his lungs, slowly.

"But put Mayg on the phone," she challenged. "I want her to get your identifications so in case anything happens to me, she can call the police."

"Bri," Del answered as politely as he could without giving in to the relieved chuckle that moved up into his throat. "You're not thinking straight. If we were the bad guys and we did that, wouldn't that make her second on our hit list?"

"I'm not stupid, Del," Bri shot back. "Having seen you, she's in danger anyway. Just hand her the phone, please."

Del shook his head. She had him, there.

****

"Mayg, listen," Brina gave a sigh that burned up from the depths of her stomach. "First of all I'm sorry I dragged you in to this."

"Forget it, Bri. If you ask me, these guys look harmless," Mayg quipped. Did Brina hear a sharp bark of laughter from one of the men?

"Someone find that amusing?" she asked.

"Yeah. Big ugly dude they call Prez." There was a snarky quality to Mayg's voice that told Bri her friend might be enjoying the opportunity to razz one of the group. Well good for her. Still, she wanted Mayg to be careful.

"Mayg? You're cousin, Mason. You told me he's a cop in town. Do you trust him? I mean, like, with your life?"

Mayg grunted. "More than you can possibly know, Bri. Why? Do you want him to get these guys off your case?"

"No. It's more like I want you to be safe. Tell Del that the only way I'll agree to see him is if you can take a picture of him and his guys. If he agrees, send them on to Mason before Del has a chance to stop you. That way if anything happens to me or you, there will be a place for the cops to start."

"Smart thinking, Bri. Hang on." The phone came away from Mayg's mouth because her next words were muted. "She wants me to take a picture of each of you to save in my phone in case anything happens." Mayg didn't give the rest of the plan away.

"Not a problem," Bri heard Del agree. "Line up, guys."

Mayg came back on the line after a short pause. "All taken care of," she assured. "But now what?"

Brina didn't know whether it was the right thing to do, but she had to trust her gut. Her gut where—right now—Del's baby nestled comfortably. She gathered her courage. "Now you give them directions to the cabin."

"Okay, Bri. But I'll be calling you every half hour to make sure you're okay."

"Thanks Mayg. I think it will be fine. I hope it will be fine. Will you let me know when they're on their way?"

"Absolutely."

Brina hit the button and hung up. *Damn.* She cradled the phone next to her chest, her hand shaking. She'd either done the stupidest thing of her life, or she'd enlisted some much needed help. Only time would tell.

She paced the cabin, ten steps in one direction, ten steps in the other, waiting for Mayg to call back. Alternately, she cursed and prayed. When had her life gone so out-of-control? Was it when she'd finished college and let her father dictate where she would work? Or was it before that, when she'd given in, eschewed the art career she'd wanted, and gone for the business degrees instead to try and please him. She laughed bitterly. In truth, since her mother's death and his ascension to the top of the family business, she'd never been able to make him happy. She counted herself lucky when she simply gleaned his approval. And now? Now it looked like—because she'd stumbled onto something, most likely illegal—she could become disposable. That said a lot for their relationship. *Shit.*

Bri kicked herself with twenty-twenty hindsight. If she'd been more prepared, had more time to think over her reaction to that damning email, she would have played it differently. The minute Daddy knew she'd run from Reynold—a rash act quite unlike her—he had to have known she'd been alerted to something sinister. That she didn't know what it was, probably didn't matter to him one way or another. The cold line he'd written kept coming back to haunt her. *She's as good as dead.* Yeah. Right. The time for believing in daddy was over.

Now to see if the danger she faced would have Del stepping up to the plate. Oh, not for her. She had no illusions that her gorgeous one-night-stand had any feelings for her. But for a son or daughter? She was playing a long shot here, but Bri only had this single hand to play. Once Del knew she had a baby on the way, would he care enough to keep her and his child safe?

Chapter Eight

The call came in. "They're on their way," Maygan told her. "I hope you know what you're doing."

"Did you get the pictures off to your cousin?" Bri worried her lip.

Maygan huffed. "Yeah. And of course your Del noticed and acted as if it was a riot. He demanded Mason's name, so he could calm him the fuck down when he shows up."

Bri's mind caught that Mayg had called Del, hers. And she didn't mind one bit.

"Not to mention," Maygan continued, "that my cousin Mason has called about a dozen times since to find out what the hell's going on. I'm going to get back to him now and fill him in. Don't be surprised. He *will* be at the cabin to check things out."

"That might not be the worst thing," Bri pondered.

Mayg snorted. "Well it might take a half hour or so, because if I know him, before he heads to you, he'll attempt to put *me* in protective custody 'for my own good'."

Bri gasped. "You're joking, right?"

"Sort of," Mayg snickered. "But you've met Mason and my other macho cousins. They're big, fearless guys, and if they think little Maygan or any of her friends are in trouble, they go to any lengths. But don't worry about me," she added quickly. "I've been dealing with them for years. Just watch out for yourself, and answer your phone when I call, or I'm going to think the worst."

"I will, Mayg. I promise." Bri's voice caught briefly. "And Mayg? Thanks for all of this. I really owe you one."

"Fine. I'll decide whether I want a new motorcycle or a month's vacation on the Riviera," Mayg quipped. "Will that make you feel better?"

Brina laughed, as she knew Mayg intended. "Yes," she approved. "It will. Bye for now."

Brina disconnected and resumed her pacing. Her conversation with Mayg had momentarily loosened her up, but now she continued fretting.

How would she feel, seeing Del again? She remembered him so well. His warm, dark face, his thick hair that had proven as soft as she'd imagined, and his killer body which had proven as hard. And those dimples, popping out when he laughed, kindling his molten eyes into a state capable of melting an iceberg. Remembrance brought an upward twinge to her lips.

She conjured the way he'd looked in bed, sleeping so innocently after he'd brought her body to the moon and back in ways that still made Brina's toes curl. When she'd given in and snuggled up to his rising and falling chest just before leaving, Bri had inhaled a scent that was all man; part musk and part coconut shampoo. That potent combination had been stored and retrieved from her medial temporal lobe many times in the past three months, fueling some pretty hot fantasies. Would the man live up to her imagination in the light of day?

She looked at her phone. Ten minutes had gone by. Another ten and he should be pulling in. Should she meet Del and his men outside, or stay protected until a last minute knock? *Screw it.* Bri squared her shoulders. She was no coward, and the late afternoon sun would feel nice. Decision made, she marched determinedly to the door. Yanking it open, she pushed through the screen and plunked herself down on one of three enormous wooden rockers that sat on the rough, planked porch. *There.* Now let them come.

Ten minutes later, as if on cue and with Bri's foot tapping, tires cracked over small branches in the long, dirt road that approached the cabin. Her breath quickened and her pulse raced. She rested a quick, reassuring hand on her belly and came to her feet. *Damn.* If only she'd remembered her sunglasses. Then she would have had some protection from Del's sharp gaze. But it was too late to retrieve them from inside. A large, beige SUV rounded the final corner, and came to a stop next to Mayg's car.

Bri raised her chin. As much as she was shaking, she wouldn't show them any weakness or fear. If there was one thing she'd learned, being a relatively solo person, bluff went a long way toward keeping people at arm's length and fending off unwanted questions.

The passenger side door opened first, and from the front seat stepped a tall, dark haired man whose cheekbones looked like a slab of chiseled granite. *Smiling* chiseled granite if that was any comfort. Bri quickly turned her eyes to the second to emerge from the right side. Another smiling face, this one dark like Del, also sporting an impossibly big body. Where did men like this come from? In the colleges she'd attended and in the financial industry where she'd worked, men buffed up by going to the gyms, but none of them had the natural size and girth of these drool-worthy specimens.

The driver side door opened, and images of the first two men fled her mind. She vaguely registered a large blond getting out behind Del, but her eyes were all for the male who'd tipped her world upside down and left her with a whole lot of something to remember him by.

"Bri," he said, rocking that deep, resonant voice that had caused goosebumps to rise on her skin as he'd growled over her most sensitive parts. Her skin pebbled now.

"Del," she managed to get out. She was in big trouble. He looked even better in the light of day—dressed in a tight white T-shirt and jeans—than he had in his Armani business suit the night she'd picked him up. Why couldn't she just have imagined his killer body, his large, oh-so-capable hands, and that grin?

If the sky had been cloud-bound, it wouldn't have mattered. Del's smile still would have lit up the whole clearing. And as she watched, he held both hands out, away from his body to the sides, palms up. "Guys?" he gave a jerk of his head, and his three men followed suit.

"What's she going to do, frisk us?" The cheek-boned one smirked. "Me first."

Del actually growled. "No need for that. Everyone give a slow turn so she can see there are no places for us to hide weapons."

As the group pivoted in place, Bri knew she was supposed to check out all the men, but her eyes were glued to Del. His ass and flexing lats were a work of art as he presented his back. She had to swallow back the drool that threatened. How could one man take her breath away so completely that she barely noticed his buff friends? *Uh, barely.* She wasn't dead, after all, just knocked up by the hunk who, if she wasn't mistaken when he turned around, sported a little more up front in his jeans, than he had before he'd taken his spin. So maybe he was remembering her, too?

Never wildly adventurous in bed, she'd cut loose with Del and done a few things that night that still amazed her. He'd brought out the animal in her, and he must have loved it. Oh yeah. *If* he remembered.

"I trust that you don't have any guns." Bri was amazed at how steady her voice emerged. "But knives kill, too. I'm pretty sure I've seen enough TV and read enough books to know that most of you bounty hunter types strap something to the inside of your ankles, or tuck a blade into your boots."

"Bounty hunters?" Del's face registered amused distaste. "Is that what you think we are?" He took a few—slightly more aggressive than she would have liked—steps forward. "Search and rescue is our job," he told her. "We find and we save. End of story."

"Well pardon me for not wanting to be found and saved," she returned.

"She's got you there," The blond, not smiling, came forward to plant himself next to Del. "And," he pulled up his pant leg to reveal a knife. "She's dead on about the blades." He reached down and caressed it with his fingers.

Bri held her ground, but braced herself. If he flung it at her now, she could be dead in seconds. Why hadn't she thought that one through? But instead of whipping the six-inch, lethal looking thing in her direction, he withdrew it slowly and laid it on the ground. Amazingly, the others—including Del—followed suit.

When they stood, divested of weapons, Del shot her that sexy grin again. "So are we good, or do you want us to strip down?"

"Uh. Not necessary," Bri managed, although she knew her eyes probably said something else, fastened as they were to him. "I guess you can come up on the porch now and have a seat. Would anyone like water? Cookies?" She had a box of chocolate chip confections, store-bought, but the soft kind that always proved to be good.

"Cookies? Hell, yeah," the blond one, who so far had looked bad-ass, cracked his first smile. If you could call it that.

Del barked a laugh. "That's Prez, by the way. He's got a ridiculous sweet tooth, and we denied him pie at the diner, so I hope you've stocked up. And some water would be nice," he added.

"I have enough to keep you happy, Prez. It's nice to meet you…I think." Bri nodded in his direction, got a nod back, then glanced quickly at the other two unknowns. Del filled her in.

"The loud mouth who got out of the front is Wiley, and the guy with the laptop attached to his hip is Sarge."

"Well, you already know who I am." Bri gave a shrug. "Make yourselves comfortable while I get some refreshments." She walked back into the cabin, shaking her head. Why did these guys seem more like protective, big brother material—besides Del—than hired kidnappers or assassins? She could only hope her gut was right.

****

Del watched Bri scoot through the screen door, clearly uncomfortable. He'd wanted nothing more, upon seeing her, than to rush to her side and fold her into his arms. He'd had a difficult time reigning back his desires. She looked even better than he remembered. Softer somehow. Rounder. It was probably the difference between her being in jeans and a tank top, rather than the uptight, formal evening wear she'd had on when they'd first met. Damn, she looked good enough to eat. And if he read things correctly, her eyes had devoured him in equal measure.

That bolstered Del's confidence. Normally when he was out with the guys, a woman ogled the offerings equally, kind of like being one in a box of chocolates. But Brina had pretty much ignored his questionably flavored crew, and gone right for him. *Sweet.*

Without conferring, the group took the couple dozen steps to the porch, where Del gestured for his guys to take seats. Wiles and Sarge plunked down into two of the rockers, Del balanced on the railing, and Prez dropped to the steps, effectively both guarding their girl and cutting off escape. Not that Del worried about that. Clearly there was nowhere for Bri to go, way out here.

"So what do you think?" Del asked quietly, fully aware of the screen door and Bri's proximity.

"Hot," Wiley winked. "I can see why you wanted to nail her."

Del shot him a look to kill. "That's not what I meant, Wiles. And don't even be thinking about Bri that way."

Far from acting contrite, Wiley's smile just grew wider, and Del flipped him off. "I meant," Del clarified, "What action do we take if she isn't forthcoming?"

"You don't have to worry about that." Brina, quiet as she pushed the screen door open with her hip while balancing a tray, gave him a quelling look. "I've invited you here, and I'll tell you why I ran." She handed a plate of cookies to Prez and continued. "Although I'm probably signing my own death warrant. After all, I have nothing to assure me that you've quit working for Reynold, other than your word. So I'm inclined to be skeptical, if you'll forgive me."

"I get it," Del reached for a glass of water. Bri recovered as her tray momentarily shifted off balance. "But you're still going to tell us what happened. Right?" Del needed to know, unsettled deep in his gut to think Brina could be in big trouble.

"Yeah. I am," she concurred, handing out the other waters. She placed her tray on the railing nearest to her, and took a seat in the remaining chair. "Give me a minute to figure out where I want to start."

Del waited, not so patiently. He yearned to solve whatever it was. Get it out of the way, so he could see if Bri might be interested in having another go at whatever they'd started at the bar. This time he wouldn't get drunk. This time he'd make sure to satisfy her every need. This time he wouldn't let her slip away in the night.

He leaned forward and caught a whiff of her elusive, lemony fragrance. He hadn't imagined it. His fucking libido sucked it in, only to render him painfully perched on his railing, needing to adjust certain anatomy but not wanting to call attention. *Cripes.* She needed to start her story, fast. And it damn well better be a sad one.

Chapter Nine

"I guess I'll start where I remember things beginning to go wrong." She drew her eyebrows together, accentuating the furrow that she knew had grown deep in the past year. She wondered what Del would think of her and her family when she was through.

"Going wrong with US AIM, or before that?" Del questioned with just enough sincerity to give her confidence.

Bri snorted. "Oh. Before. Long before. I'd just turned twelve, and it was a birthday to forget. My parents had spent most of the morning arguing until my mother stomped off, slamming the door on her way to work…"

Bri sighed from the staircase where she sat, silently witnessing the fight while hidden behind the ornate railing. She thought maybe today would be different. That perhaps her mother would forego the office and do something fun with her and her dad, as a family. Not only were her hopes being dashed, but her special day became the reason for all of the harsh words.

"You have to start taking more of an active role, Bennet." Her mother's voice rose shrilly. "In typical male fashion, the people I'm dealing with are reluctant to deal with a woman."

"Helena. Calm yourself. Please. Bri might hear you."

"Bri," her mother scoffed. "She's the real problem here, isn't she? If you hadn't been so picky choosing that

last overly sensitive nanny, we'd have someone able to watch her right now. And about that. She's twelve, for God's sake. She doesn't need constant care. She should be off at boarding school right now. I'd already been out of my house for two years at her age."

"She's still too young." Her father's voice became hard. *"I want her to have more time with us before she loses her family life."*

"Listen to yourself." Her mother's brittle laugh grated on Bri's ears. *"The only family life she has is when you neglect your work to come home and be with her. Detrimental to everyone, I might add. Move on, Bennet. In another year she'll be a teenager and have no use for you."*

Bri knew that wasn't true. She loved spending time with her father, and she'd never give up on their special hours together. But what would her mother know of that? The last time Bri had seen her mother for more than five minutes was when Bri had sneaked downstairs and out to the pool in the middle of the night to watch her mother take her customary swim. When her mother spotted her, she'd received a five minute lecture on children being in bed and the evils of spying, before being given a swat and sent back to her room.

"All the more reason I should spend time with her while I can," Bri's father replied, to which her mother huffed, swore and stormed out the door, slamming it behind her.

Her father opened the back door to the kitchen, and Bri's dog, Buster, a pure-bred boxer came prancing in. His nails clicked on the floor as he refused to pause for a pat from her dad, but headed straight for her position on the stairs. He spotted her instantly, looked up with his big, soulful eyes and gave a happy *"woof"*.

"You can come down now, Bri," her father called from the kitchen, across the vast marbled foyer to where she hid,

having been alerted to her presence. "Your mother's gone to work."

Bri rose to her feet and skipped the few steps down to Buster, hugging his enormous head before running into the kitchen. She launched herself at her father, wrapping her arms around his middle.

"Good morning, Moppet," he gave her a squeeze and a kiss on the brow before moving away to the vast, kitchen island, ducking down behind it. "Today wouldn't be anything special, would it?" he teased.

"You know it's my birthday, Daddy." Bri rolled her eyes with much exaggeration. "Do you have something for me?"

Bri squealed when he stood up and brought a beautifully wrapped box out from behind him.

"Did you think I'd forget?"

She shot over and grabbed the box from his hands, quickly bringing it to the table where she tore off the paper, hurriedly, a broad smile on her face.

"I knew you wouldn't," she told him. Her dad always remembered, even if her mother was too busy to put it on her calendar. When the present was revealed, Bri screamed again. "It's just what I wanted," she cried, attempting to rip the end of the box open, but failing miserably.

"Here. Let me." Her father came close, extracted his pocket knife from within his suitcoat, and slit the cardboard seam. It was then that Bri noticed her father's attire.

"Wait. You're dressed for the office." Her mouth turned down. "I thought we were spending the day at the museum, and the zoo, and my favorite ice-cream..."

"I know, Bri. I know." He cut her off. "But something has come up at work, and your mother insists I go in. I'll make it up to you another time. I promise."

The joy leached out of opening her present as the realization of one more day—home alone since nanny number a million had flown the coop—settled into her brain. "Yeah. Okay Daddy." Bri tried to school her face to remain impassive, stood dutifully up on her tiptoes as her father bent, and gave him a kiss on the cheek. "I'll see you around." She took calm, measured footsteps back to the stairs and trod slowly up, Buster at her heels.

"Bri," her dad called. "You forgot your present."

But she couldn't bring herself to turn around. The day had lost its previous joy.

Later, after she'd heard her father leave, Bri shuffled back to the kitchen and carefully opened the box. She'd been having a phase—her father liked to say—where she was into everything that had to do with spying. Perhaps it had been triggered by the use of her mother's words several months before at the pool, but whatever, she coveted all of the paraphernalia she saw on TV. It looked like her father had done one better than the nineteen-ninety-five special she'd pointed out in the ad. This spying periscope looked professional. Leave it to her father to get her the best.

Bri spent the day using her new toy to look over the fence, undetected by her neighbors. First on one side, then on the other. The houses in her gated community were far apart, and private, so she saw nothing except one pool-boy and a couple of teenagers, a boy and girl, out for a swim. That the swim turned into a kissing, make-out fest between the pair held her interest for a while, but she soon became bored.

"That was yucky," she told Buster, climbing down from the patio chair she'd used. "Let's go inside." He immediately heeled and dutifully followed.

Bri snagged a smock from a peg in the kitchen, and without pause, headed to her art room. She'd spend the rest of the day painting, she decided. That way, at least, the day wouldn't be a total loss.

Late that night, Bri couldn't sleep. She was excited to try out her new periscope. The directions had said she'd be able to use it in the dark, and she'd heard her mother go out the back door to the pool a few minutes before. Maybe she'd watch her do laps and not get caught this time.

Bri sneaked down the stairs. Buster wouldn't give her away. Her best friend and companion was outside, always relegated to front yard duty at night. Her mother was obsessed with the idea of burglars. Bri couldn't imagine why. Nothing exciting ever happened in this neighborhood.

She eased the back door open and slipped out into the shadows. There was barely a moon, but that didn't deter Brina. She knew every inch of the back patio. Silently, she positioned herself behind a chair, and gently raised the end of the periscope up and over. Her eye went to the sight. She blinked once. She screamed.

And screamed and screamed until she was hoarse and shivering. Until she remembered a blanket being wrapped around her and being held in someone's strong arms. She was brought into the house and within what seemed like seconds, the house was filled with police. Emergency vehicle lights strobed through the room from the open front door, round and round, blue and red. They mesmerized her, making her think it was all a dream. But it wasn't.

What she'd seen was true. Her mother had lain, face down, in her white bathing suit, unmoving and surrounded by a pool of something dark. Something that Brina had understood immediately was blood. It was shocking more than anything else. Bri couldn't get the picture out of her head.

When she eventually overheard someone mentioning that Buster was dead, that he'd been fed something poison that the authorities were packing up for analysis in their lab, Bri had broken down. Buster. Poor Buster. Tears leaked from her eyes. Her only friend was dead, and it must have had something to do with her mother. Bri's heart hardened, although her tears continued to flow for her dog. But not for her mother. Her mother always ruined everything. And now she was dead.

"Geezus, Bri," Del had listened to her sad and gruesome story. *Damn.* His own young difficulties paled in comparison. At least he'd been given a healthy dose of love from his folks at one time or another. And he hadn't witnessed any of his family violated. "Nobody should have seen that, let alone a twelve year old kid." His heart bled for her, but she shrugged.

"It is what it is," she told him, her normally animated face closed and cold.

"So did it work out anyway, the bitch dying?" Wiles asked in his normally blunt way. "Did you get to spend more time with your dad?"

Bri laughed, a bitter sound. "No, actually. He immediately took over her position in the family business, and his sister, my aunt, came to watch me for a few years before I finally got shipped off to boarding school. So the bitch, as you called her, got one of her last wishes granted."

Bri blinked, and Del could see her physically shake off her immersion into the past. "But that was a long time ago," she flashed a big, fake smile. "I went on to play sports, make lots of friends, and get my degrees."

"And don't tell me," Del blew out a long breath. "Your dad became as remote as your mother had been."

"That about sums it up," Bri agreed. "From that point on I only saw him on holidays and vacations, things Aunt Celia maintained at our home to keep a semblance of normal family life." She laughed bitterly. "But even during those he'd be on the phone or his computer most of the time." Her face became perfectly calm again, and Del didn't like it. He wanted to kill the bastard for abandoning his daughter after the death of her mother. What kind of person did that?

"Is that why you didn't run to him when this threat arose from Reynold?" Del asked gently, wanting nothing more than to pull her into his arms. "I mean, I get that he might not be the most attentive father in the world, but surely he would have kept you safe."

Tears appeared in Bri's eyes, and Del bit down on his tongue. What had he said that set her off? Nothing else she'd revealed so far had caused her this kind of anguish.

"Here's where my story gets a little messy," she admitted with a bitter chuckle, dashing away the small amount of wetness that she'd allowed to escape. She hardened up again; a feat Del was beginning to recognize as the rollercoaster of Bri's emotions. "Reynold and my father are in business together."

Del shrugged. That didn't make her father evil. "I understand. But if you recall, Bri, I'm in business with Reynold, too."

She narrowed her eyes at him. "Which is why I remain unclear as to whether or not I can trust you," she said. "And whether or not you also dance to my father's tune."

Del quickly squelched that supposition. "I've never met your father, nor do I care to," he said.

Brina seemed to agree. "And the only reason I'm buying that you don't have that connection is because I didn't see any mention of you on the damning email I found from him on Reynold's computer, intimating that if I found out about something they had going on, I'd be eliminated."

Del felt gut-punched, and watched the same spine-straightening reaction hit his buddies. "You're shitting me? Your father said that?" he asked, stunned.

"He did," Bri revealed, "And that's why I ran."

"Tell me everything," Del ordered, and for a moment he didn't think Bri would comply. Her lips compressed and she stared him straight in the eyes, her pools of green holding so much suspicion. He huffed. "Listen. If we were going to kill you, or bundle you back to Reynold or your father, wouldn't we have done it by now?" he questioned, looking at his watch. "As a matter of fact, I give your friend Maygan's cousin, the cop, another ten or fifteen minutes before he shows up. So if I were a bad-guy, wouldn't I be long gone by now?"

"Point taken." But she refused to look away, and Del didn't flinch. *Fuck.* He needed her to trust him. He put his bottled up feelings for her into his eyes, and it must have shone through because she eventually dropped her defensive glare. Her shoulders slumped and she inched her way back to her chair, sitting down, hard. "Okay. I'll give you everything I know, but I don't have much," she finally told him. "So you may think I overreacted."

"Let me be the judge of that," Del replied gently. He doubted she'd exaggerate anything. The way she'd so calmly articulated her childhood, led Del to believe that she was very good at separating emotional reaction from fact. Only that one small lapse, where tears had gathered unbidden, had shown that she wasn't as unaffected as she wanted them to believe.

Brina inclined her head. "When I visited Reynold's office to leave him my resignation and my dear Jane letter, I accidently bumped into the mouse and woke his computer." She paused and took a deep breath. "Normally I wouldn't have been interested. I've worked at US AIM for several months, and most of Reynold's correspondence gets forwarded to me for reply or filing. But as I was about to walk away, I saw my name."

Del tried to keep his muscles from tightening up with the need to punch something. His suspicions had been valid. Bri had been being used as some kind of a pawn.

"So I read it. Most of the letter talked about business dealings, using very vague and general language. But the part about me seemed very clear." Brina paraphrased. *"You'll only get to keep her as long as the dealings between us remain under wraps and go smoothly. Brina isn't stupid. If she gets any inkling of what our business involves, and you screw up, she's as good as dead, and you along with her. Do you understand? If not, let me be clear. If you sign Brina's death warrant, yours will be executed right along with it."*

"Holy hell," Sarge barked. "Your father is one cold dude. And I thought hearing about your mother was bad."

Brina blinked up at Sarge, and then around at the crew, ending up with Del. "So you don't think I'm imagining things?" she asked.

"No, Bri." Del ran a hand over the top of his head, angry and distracted. Every protective instinct in his body roared to life. "That was an out and out threat on you, and on Reynold's too. Now it makes sense how hot he became when I asked about coming clean to your old man. No wonder he wanted me to find you fast."

"Oh." Bri scowled and bit her bottom lip. "I didn't even think of the danger to Reynold when I left." That persistent worry line showed up between her brows again, and Del wanted to reach forward with his thumb to smooth it away. He had to grip his hands on the railing to keep from following his impulse.

"Don't give him a second thought," Del answered gruffly. "Reynold is an ass. And whatever he's gotten himself into via your father, is his own doing. Let him worry about his own skin while we worry about yours." Del couldn't help but ask another question that had been bothering him throughout this whole conversation. "So if you are fairly estranged from your father, and not working for the family business, why were you at US AIM?"

Brina sighed. "You have to understand. Even though I don't see much of my father, he makes no bones about being proud of my business acumen. And because a part of me still remembers the man who loved me so much and had my best interests at heart when I was little, I've let him recommend me for a number of temporary jobs over the past few years. Very lucrative jobs," she added, almost daring him to call her a spoiled child. His understanding of Bri remained far from that.

"It looks like you may have been in danger from the get-go, so I'll say you've earned your money." This time he gave in to the impulse, leaned forward and touched Bri's shoulder before quickly restoring himself to his previous position so as not to grab her up into his arms. He needed to touch her that badly. And to think, he scoffed inwardly, he'd had her pegged as a debutante, being groomed for a life of spoiled bliss married to a rich CEO. Instead, she was more like chum in a tank of sharks. He raged. *Fuck that.* He wouldn't let bait be her reality anymore. "We'll just have to make damn sure you never have to swim in Daddy's waters again," he told her, not sharing his shark analogy, but knowing he'd be first on the front lines wielding the largest harpoon.

Chapter Ten

Bri had tried hard to keep her demeanor impassive during her story, with pretty good success. But when Del touched her shoulder. *My God.* Her whole body had lit up from inside, fire licking through every nerve ending. What had he just said? She played back—in her brain—what sounded an awful lot like assurances, and gulped. "So you're going to help me?"

She didn't want to let her guard down, but so far Del's words and actions pointed to him not only being innocent of any involvement with Reynold's dirty dealings—whatever they might be—but also willing to help her disentangle herself from her current situation.

Now Del's brilliant white smile cut across the distance between them, and it stole her breath. "Damned right we are," he assured her. "Although this is out of our normal wheelhouse of search and rescue, we have a few skills." He glanced around at his friends and they smirked.

Yeah. Skills. She bet they did. She actually knew a few of Del's more intimate ones, but she couldn't think of those now, or a blush would give away her naughty fantasies.

Bri cleared her throat. "And you'd use them for me, why?" she questioned, wiping her mind clean of everything sexual and raising her brows. Bri had to wonder at Del's motives. He certainly didn't know she was pregnant, something that—if she judged his character correctly—would give him incentive, so why would he go out on a limb to help her? She was almost a stranger.

When Del looked to be tongue-tied, his friend Prez spoke up. "I think I can speak for us all," he told her gruffly. "It's because we've seen too many people victimized for simply being in the wrong place at the wrong time." His eyes clouded over with memories. "And nothing sucks worse than an innocent being tangled up with assholes."

Bri heaved a sigh. She could believe that. And considering his obvious sincerity, it was clear his words cut deep. But she also needed this group to understand that she wasn't as naïve as they believed. "Before you agree to help me, I have to admit that I'm not totally without guilt. I figured out a long time ago that the crazy overseas family business my mother, and now my father is mixed up in, couldn't be the simple import/export enterprise they led me to believe. The older and more educated I got, the more my eyes were opened." She paused here for significance. "But that's also why I firmly and stubbornly refused to work for the company and closed my eyes again. I don't want to know what the family business entails. I purposely kept myself from finding out."

"And yet your father used you. He sent you to Reynold. You were to be wooed into Blithe's world and made his wife." Del didn't look happy as he worked the puzzle. "Your father clearly found value insinuating you into US AIM. We just have to figure out why." He probed deeper. "Where did you work before dear old dad set you up there?" His synapsis seemed to be firing rapidly.

Bri named three companies, all government backed weapons industries, and knew it was time she pried the lid off her reluctance and dared voice her fears. "I've thought about this for months, and with that email, I can only come up with one thing." She swallowed the lump in her throat and spit out her supposition. "Illegal arms dealing."

There. She'd said it. Now Del would either have to, A: kill her if he'd been lying this whole time, B: walk away from the danger she would bring to him, or C: help her.

"Yup. That was our first guess." Del rubbed the bridge of his nose, preoccupied with whatever was in his head, barely paying attention to what had cost her a lot to reveal.

"Wait. You knew?" Her voice became shrill, but Bri couldn't help it.

"We had our suspicions," Wiley interjected, "But..." His head suddenly came up, and before Bri could even blink or wonder, both he, Sarge and Prez exited the porch, slipping into the trees. If she hadn't known they were there seconds before, she would have completely missed them as she lost track of them both within seconds.

"What...?"

Del held up his hand to shut down her question. "Get inside," he ordered. "Now."

Bri didn't stop to argue. The Del she was beginning to know had instantly turned into a stranger. A hard and unyielding stranger. Someone she didn't know and although this side of him scared her, oddly enough, it also gave her a chilling kind of thrill. It made her feel protected...and just a little bit turned on. The tough attitude looked good on him, and thank God, not once had he looked at her with that guarded, lethal edge he held now. She scooted inside, moving to a position behind a curtain where she could peer outside without being seen. Or so she hoped.

When a police car drove up the dirt road, she let out her breath and slid from her hiding place. She was just about to push the door open when Del growled. "What about stay inside didn't you understand?"

"But it's obviously—"

"It's obviously nothing," Del snarled. "Take nothing at face value or you might find yourself dead."

She skittered back inside to take up her position behind the curtain again. Of course Del was right, but Bri had never found herself in a situation like this before. She sucked in a breath. She hoped never to be in anything similar, again.

Del's voice rang out. "You can stop your car right there," he roared. And whoever was in the vehicle, complied. The cruiser came to a halt and the door opened slowly. Two hands appeared in the air, both empty.

"I'm not looking for any trouble."

Bri recognized a broader, more muscular Mason from the one she'd met years ago, and now he was dressed like an officer. "The name is Mason Sothard. I'm with the Orono Police Department, here to check on the well-being of Brina Capadella."

Bri saw Del give a nod of his head, and his three men ghosted out of the woods behind the officer.

"Put the gun down on the ground," Wiley requested in a pleasant, how's the weather kind of voice.

"Like hell," Mason rumbled. "I'll be turning around first to make sure you haven't got yours pointed at my head."

Prez rumbled darkly. "I always like a good stand-off," he snarled. "Odds are we win."

"Prez. Behave," Del called out, turning his attention to the man who was clearly Mayg's cousin. "Nobody's weaponed up," he assured the officer, calmly. "We dropped our gear in the grass when we got here to assure Brina we meant no harm." He waved at the small pile of knives resting innocently on the ground.

"I don't see any guns," Mason replied, equally as casually.

"Because if we have knives, we don't need guns," Del came back. From somewhere behind Mason, Prez snorted. While everyone paused in a stand-off tableau, Bri noted that Sarge had taken a seat in the open door of the SUV and was frantically tapping on his keyboard.

Seconds later he gave the thumbs up. "We're all clear," the computer geek hit one last key, then closed his laptop with a flourish. "He *is* Mason Sothard, Sergeant with the OPD and cousin to Maygan DePalto. And don't piss him off too badly. He's got six brothers. Two police and four military, so they might feel like kicking our asses if we rough him up."

"Shit. How'd you do that so fast?" Mason had stepped out from behind his open door, hands still in the air.

"Trade secret," Del chuckled. "And you can put your hands down now that we know you're a friendly."

"Yeah. About that. Where exactly is Bri? If I don't get a twenty on her right the hell now, my cousin's going to have my head."

Again, a grunt from Prez. "Scared of that little spitfire?" he mumbled.

"Damn straight," Mason agreed, turning to nod but not even cracking a smile.

"Bri?" Del called, but her feet were already moving. She exited the screen door with a flourish.

"I'm here. And I'm fine," she stated to Mason. "It's nice to see you again." She pushed the blonde curls back from her face. "These guys are just being protective." She didn't know why she had the sudden urge to defend Del and his men. But she did. "There's someone who's looking for me with a less than honorable intent, so we can't be too careful."

"Yeah. About that," Mason frowned. "Mayg gave me a little of the back-story. Do you want to fill me in on the rest?"

Bri turned to Del. She'd defer to him since he'd clearly decided he was in charge. At least until he pulled something she didn't like. And then all bets were off. As much as she believed she could trust him, she'd gotten herself this far. She could easily disappear again.

"I'm not sure you need to be involved," Del speculated. "We've got this covered."

Mason nodded thoughtfully, but didn't back down. "You may have this place buttoned up tight." He waved an arm behind him to indicate the pair of rear flanking guards. "But wouldn't it be nice not to worry about visitors at all?" he questioned. "Fill me in on what's happening, and I can make sure there's a patrol watching this road; the only way in to the cabin."

"Could be helpful," Sarge supplied from his perch, raising one eyebrow in Del's direction.

Del made up his mind in an instant. Bri liked that he always seemed to know what he wanted. "Fine. Come join us on the porch. We're headed for a brainstorming session."

No more than half an hour later, with all known details regarding Bri, Reynold, and Bri's father having been put on the table, a plan of action had been hammered out. Not that Bri was too thrilled with it. Or maybe she was. Talk about totally conflicted.

Mason would go back to town, and without actually giving any information about her and her troubles to anyone higher up, would order a patrol at the turnoff for the cabin, looking for "poachers".

Sarge, Prez and Wiley would take the SUV and go back to Boston. From there, they would branch out and keep a covert eye on Bri's nemesis, and whoever or whatever else

Sarge uncovered with a wide-net computer search. He'd be digging into Reynold's past, as well as that of her father, and her father's company. They'd stake out Bri's old home where her aunt still lived.

Bri interjected any number of times for them to be careful, but other than a few chuckles from the men, they hadn't paid much attention.

Del—*no duh*, because she knew they needed to clear the air—opted to stay behind as her bodyguard. She just wondered how close he expected to get to her body, and whether or not she'd let down her guard to allow a repeat performance. Since that one night with Del, Bri hadn't been with anyone else. Del had imprinted himself on her, and the idea of another man touching her, baby or no baby, had become unimaginable. He'd been everything she'd ever wanted in a lover: kind, passionate, caring, wild. The few men who had approached her in the past few months, Reynold included, couldn't begin to compete and left her cold.

"Take good care of her, Del," Wiley winked as he clomped down the steps. Just how much Del had told his men, Bri didn't want to know, but the answering smirks from the others told her that their hook-up hadn't stayed completely under wraps.

"Call me with every new detail you come up with," Del answered, clearly choosing to ignore the innuendo.

"Wait," Bri interrupted. Something had just occurred to her. "If Reynold has anybody as good on details as Sarge, he'll be tracking you, too, and they'll find me through your cell phones," she worried.

Del held up his phone and wiggled it in the air. "No worries." He grinned. "Auto-scramble on any number, name or coordinates that come up. One minute I might be Edna

Snoopinger in Sheboygan, and the next, Forrest Gumblethorpe in London. Pretty cool, huh?"

Bri caught Mason's eye-roll, and why not. Del, for a moment, had sounded more like a kid with a new toy than a reckoning force. *Damnit.* Score another point for him on the cute but lethal scale.

"Besides," Prez put in. "There's no one as good as Sarge, unless it's one of the guys he cut his hacking-teeth with, and they're on our side."

"Nice to know," Bri acknowledged. "If I ever need tickets to an event that's sold out, I'll know who to ask." Her attempt at humor was met with smirks.

"Been there, done that," Sarge snarked, giving one last wave and scooping up the knives from the ground before dropping what had to be Del's duffel out of their vehicle. He hopped into the back seat while Mason entered his cruiser. It looked like Wiley would drive the larger vehicle this time while Prez rode shotgun.

Mason left first, backing into a small turn-off before pointing the nose of his car back toward town. Bri watched the last barrier between herself and Del leave as Wiley followed, close on Mason's tail.

"So," Del cleared his throat, looking much less at ease than he had with the possibility of an approaching threat.

"So?" Bri challenged. She leaned forward on the railing, two feet away from the position he'd taken up. This was going to suck, but she wasn't about to start the conversation which was certain to be awkward. Let Del have that honor.

"I, uh, guess we should talk about what happened," he suggested.

Hah. Little did he know *all* that had happened. And Bri wondered how he would take it. Del seemed like the principled sort, but as much as she wanted his protection, the last thing she wanted to do was have him proposing marriage in order to give their child a two parent home. She was fully capable of raising this baby on her own. Well, at least—with Del's help—as soon as she got herself out of her current troubles. But she could never be cruel or unreasonable to Del, either. He had every right to a vested interest in their baby's life if he wanted it. Really, once she let him know of her condition, it was his call. Involved or not involved. Whichever way it went down, Bri could handle it.

"I know what I have to say," Bri led. "But I'm interested in hearing your thoughts, first."

"Fine then." He drew a hand over the short hair on the top of his head in a gesture she'd witnessed a few times before. An easy tell when he was nervous or rallying his brain-cells. "I guess I'll start off with an apology."

Bri snorted. "No apology necessary," she assured him. She could only imagine he felt bad about passing out and not being able to say goodbye, or call her a cab, or whatever else a gentleman did after a one night stand. But Bri was of a different opinion. Since he'd satisfied her a good number of times, and in a myriad of ways, she figured conking out wasn't a major sin. Her mind spun with future possibilities.

Del looked a little stunned at her confident declaration. "You don't want an apology?" he queried, a glimmer of disbelief appearing in his eyes.

Bri shrugged. "No. Of course not. Why should I?" They needed to get these "niceties" over with so she could fill him in on what really mattered.

"I don't know." There went that hand again. "I guess I didn't realize you would be so magnanimous. Forgiving me for non-performance after the foreplay at the bar. I would have me labeled as a dud."

Bri's mouth dropped open. "Non-performance?" she repeated, his words sinking in. *Oh God.* Del figured… Del thought… *Shit.* She was in such trouble. He didn't remember they'd had sex.

Chapter Eleven

"Yeah." Del squirmed, damned uncomfortable bringing up his lack of stamina, but what else could he do? And if she'd been relieved he'd been a no-go-er, what was with the shocked look on her face? *Wait.* Maybe she'd passed out, too. Perhaps she believed he'd enjoyed her body while *she* was unconscious, and that's why she'd never tried to contact him afterward. It made sense. She didn't know him. She had no idea he wasn't the type of guy to take advantage of a comatose woman. Hell, he'd label any male who did that as a huge asshole. His shoulders loosened. His educated guess felt right. That had to be it. So now all he had to do was assure Bri that her body had remained untouched, and that he'd passed out, too. It seemed like a hell of a lot easier job than defending his masculinity.

She cleared her throat. "Del, you need to tell me everything you remember once we left the bar," she demanded.

"Oh, no, sweetheart. You first." Now that he stood on firmer ground, Del was beginning to enjoy himself.

Her eyes narrowed. "Uh, uh. No way. You're not getting off that easily. Tell me your version of what happened after we finished our drinks."

This Del remembered, if vaguely. He could give her their trajectory. Certainly in his fantasies, he'd relived those few semi-lucid minutes, making them a vivid, technicolor reality on the otherwise muddled screen of his brain.

He grinned. "Okay. I'll go first. I handed you my key at the bar, and you slid off the stool looking all sexy in that tight, white dress that you were poured into." He was pleased when a flush worked its way up Bri's cheeks. "I happen to recall every man in the lobby watching you walk from the bar to the elevator, and every damned one of them was thinking how lucky I was to be the guy with my hand on your back."

Now she scowled. "Is this fiction or reality, smart-ass?" She moved closer and poked a finger into the center of his chest. "As I recall, there were two people in the lobby. One was the concierge, and the other was a woman who had to have been in her seventies."

Shit. She remembered that? Del amended the picture in his head, but it was his turn to frown. They had both been drunk, and this was his illusion, right? What business did she have messing with his daydreams? He huffed. "Well I say there were at least five young execs in suits watching." His glare dared her to argue. Which she didn't. Instead she rolled her eyes and visibly clamped down on her tongue. *Good.* He continued.

"You pushed the button for the elevator, and while we waited, I could barely keep my hands to myself. I wanted nothing more than to touch every inch of you."

Had a spark of desire ignited behind Bri's semi-lowered lids? She cleared her throat. Was she feeling it, too? Talking about that night was making him as hard as a spike.

"When the doors slid open, you sauntered inside, and leaned up against the wall, mentioning that your feet hurt in your heels." Funny how that hadn't been part of Del's dream before. Maybe he was remembering a few more things.

"That's right," Bri concurred. "So I bent my knee to take off one shoe, and—"

"And I asked if I could do it for you," he interrupted, the picture suddenly becoming clear. "I took off your left shoe, then the right, but didn't stop at your ankle after removing the second one. I dropped it and ran my hand up your leg instead, pushing your dress higher and higher."

Del's mouth dried up, and he could see that Bri's mouth had dropped open, her breath escaping in fast, staccato puffs.

Damned if he didn't remember the smoothness of her thigh and her soft moans as he'd raised her skirt up over her hips to reveal a white silk thong that did very little to hide the blonde curls nestled at her apex.

He brought his eyes to Bri's. Her lids had lowered and her gaze had definitely heated.

"I made you stop because I was sure someone would get on the elevator and see us," she said breathlessly, and licked her bottom lip.

"But not before I kissed you," he added, so certain of that detail that he didn't hesitate to say it.

She nodded, looking at his mouth intently. "It was quite a kiss," she whispered.

Del got up off of the railing slowly. He didn't want to scare her, but he needed his mouth on hers this very moment. As much as he needed air. Thank God she didn't flinch as he halved the inches between them. Her pupils dilated as he closed the gap. When there remained only a whisper of space separating their mouths, he spoke, his rasping tone almost unrecognizable to his own ears. "Kind of like this one?" he asked, and lowered his lips.

Bri's whole body sighed against him, and he had to call upon all of his strength not to grab her ass and grind his aching cock into her warm, soft belly. He fought to keep the contact light, teasing. He was being given a second chance and he didn't want to blow it.

When they'd first started discussing that night, Del hadn't planned to kiss her, but he couldn't deny himself. He'd been drawn in since his first glimpse of her earlier, posturing boldly on the porch, demanding they lose their weapons.

Weapons. Del nearly lost it. The only weapon in his head right now; the only one of any danger to Bri, lay hard and throbbing behind his zipper. He needed to back off before he plowed through any boundaries she might have. *Yeah. Right.* In a minute. Now he needed just one more gentle nip of her lips.

Thank Christ Bri seemed to agree, reaching up to wrap her hands around the back of his neck as his teeth engaged, but she pulled back at the last minute, dragging her plump bow away from his bite, giving him mixed signals. He held himself still, waiting for some kind of cue. And fuck, she better make it fast.

"Oh, Del," she breathed. "Harder." Bri whimpered, searing him with the heat of her demand. She rose on tiptoes, digging her nails into his skin. "More."

Mixed signals unscrambled, Del yanked her roughly against him, mashing her lush breasts between them. "My pleasure," he managed to growl, getting a hint of lemon before he crushed her eager mouth beneath his once again.

He deepened the kiss. He plunged his tongue, and she answered him back, stroke for stroke. Del shouldn't have worried that Bri would fear the proof of his ardor, she ground her heat against him with a fervor that had him worried about his endurance. He had become so hard and inflamed that he feared combustion and incineration at any moment. And if he lost it in his jeans, wouldn't that say "loser" about someone who'd batted an enormous goose-egg once before.

He needed to take things down a notch. He needed to regain some of his control. Attacking her wasn't what he'd had in mind when…oh hell, who was he kidding? This was exactly what he'd had in his head since the moment Reynold slid the picture of Bri across his desk. If that made him an asshole, then so be it. He wanted to finish what they'd started in the elevator at his hotel, and he wanted to do it now.

Del scooped Bri up into his arms, and hauled his lips away from hers. He managed to snarl, "If you don't want this, tell me now. Because as soon as I go through that door and find your bed, all bets are off."

Bri smoldered up at him, then buried her head in his neck, biting the skin just under his ear and insinuating her warm little hand into the neck of his shirt to pinch his skin. That was answer enough for him. He strode to the screen door and shoved it open with one foot, giving them room to pass through before it slammed behind him with a finality that fit his mood. He would make Bri his, and he would do it now. It was way past time.

One quick glance around the small cabin told him where the bedroom lay. He crossed the main room, quickly tearing off her shoes and dropping them to the floor as she balanced in his arms. Part of him feared that despite her early capitulation, Bri would put a stop to things. If she did, he'd have to honor her wishes, regardless of what he'd said. Which only proved that he'd be a fucking idiot to give her time to think.

He lay her on the bed, immediately covering her body with his, propped up on his elbows above her but touching from chest to hips. Her emerald eyes watched him languorously under hooded lids, and she didn't demur as he shifted his weight to the right and lowered his now free hand to the hem of her tank top.

Del inched it up slowly, scraping his knuckles over Bri's silken skin until he encountered a barrier of lace. He followed it around to the left and behind, the pads of his fingers encroaching between material and flesh until he found the offending clasp. Del sprung it easily, at which both he and Bri gave a simultaneous sigh. His hand moved around front, and flicking the bra away he filled his palm with her abundant breast. He suppressed a shudder. Her erect nipple poked hard into the center of his palm.

"Pink, or brown?" He asked, his voice nearly useless.

"You don't remember?" Bri volleyed, not shrinking with embarrassment that he'd asked the first thing that popped into his mind.

"Nope," he admitted, bringing his fingers together on the peak that had him fascinated.

"Pink," she gasped, and colored slightly, not unaffected by his ministrations.

"Lovely," he murmured. He slid his hand away from his initial target and she gave a cry of dismay. "Don't worry Bri," he soothed. "I'll be back there soon enough." His eager digits headed for recon-two; the zipper on her jeans. And when she realized his intent she shivered and wiggled her hips in anticipation.

So fucking responsive. Del couldn't wait to feel all of her skin, sliding silkily beneath his thrusting body, but before that happened, he had a plan. He had things he needed to take care of first. He drew her zipper down.

"Lift," came his gruff command, and she complied without argument, her eyes still fixed to his, searing him with their intensity. "Good girl," he praised, tugging the material down. Del allowed his roaming fingers to pluck at the little bow he encountered gracing her panties, then bobbed his head for one more scorching kiss on her mouth before leveraging himself away. "It's time to get you naked."

If he wasn't so consumed with lust, Del would almost have laughed. Bri's fingers competed with his to remove her clothing as fast as possible. Where he pulled off a leg, she'd already shed her shirt. When lowering the scrap of lace off her long, toned legs, she hooked her toes into the elastic and ripped it off with a sigh.

Del sat back on his heels when all barriers were gone and gazed at fucking perfection. God, she was beautiful naked. And she smelled delectable. He couldn't wait to get his mouth on her hot pussy, which might be in Bri's mind too, because she let her legs drop open, giving him a view of heaven. He groaned. "What you do to me." He shook his head, stunned at the depth of his need.

"No." Her blonde curls shimmered on the pillow behind her head. "What you do to me," she corrected.

He could see the evidence of her desire, an abundance of glistening wetness on her nether lips as he drew near. Del breathed her in and nuzzled her thigh. He gave a small love bite, and she widened her legs even more, allowing his broad shoulders just the room he needed to insinuate himself into paradise.

Del started slowly, swiping delicately with his tongue at her hidden clit. Once thoroughly teased and appropriately taut, he lowered his sights and blew across the moist flesh of her pussy, causing a tremor of need to ripple over her abdomen.

"Don't torment me, Del," she begged, squirming closer.

"What do you want, Bri?" he asked. "This?" He drew one finger firmly down through her folds, then eased it up inside her.

"Yes," she hissed, arching grandly. "Like that, Del."

He spared her nothing. After his initial breach into her wet channel, he teased, licked and plunged, stretching her welcoming pussy with two fingers when her inner muscles unclamped to give him room. He could feel the tension inside of her building, could sense that she approached her goal in the way her heels dug into his back. Yet he pulled away, prolonging the moment, knowing that the ache he built would only increase her pleasure once he sought to carry her over the edge.

"Bastard," she laughed, a strangled sound. "Finish me now," she demanded.

"And if I don't?" he chortled against her swollen flesh.

"Ahh." She lifted to feel more of his vocal vibrations, but he pulled back again.

"Then I'll have to take care of it myself," she threatened, playfully, with an ache in her voice.

Del growled. "Hell, no. As much as I'd like to watch you do that, we'll save it for another time." He dropped his head back into position between her thighs, and this time gave no quarter. He melded his mouth and fingers into a maddening staccato, and had her reaching the precipice of her orgasm with the precision of a planned assault.

She gripped his head, she cried out his name, and as the inner walls of her pussy contracted, Del experienced a surge of satisfaction such as he'd never encountered before. He loved hearing his name on her lips as she came. And in that moment he knew he never wanted her to utter any other. Bri was his, dammit, and from this point on, he needed to make sure she understood that. He didn't know where the possessiveness was coming from, but it felt right. And damned good.

Several seconds after her body grew limp in his arms, he crawled up to hold her. And dammit, she'd regained a certain degree of lucidity. He'd wanted to bask in her afterglow, but she pushed him aside to sit up before he could protest, and tugged at his shirt. Understanding dawned and he grinned. "Say it, Bri," he chuckled.

"I need these things off you. Right now," she ordered.

"No ma'am." Del waggled a finger in her face. "Not quite yet." He smirked. Although he was damned uncomfortable with the unrelenting stiffness behind his zipper, his jeans were all that stood between him and where he'd ultimately find his nirvana. But it wasn't his turn. *Yet.*

He looked up to see Bri narrowing her eyes. "Yes, Del. Right now," she groused, reaching a hand down to stroke his hardness. "And don't give me any of your bullshit."

Del blinked and gritted out a smile. "What bullshit, sweetheart?" he purred, loving that he was making her crazy.

"You know, that 'three before me' crap you spouted in the hotel." She shook her head. "Not happening today."

Del gasped in shock. Now it was his turn to come upright, pushing her hand away, a jolt of disbelief rocketing through his system.

"Wait. How do you know about that?" he spluttered. Damned if Bri hadn't just thrown back at him a long-term motto that he lived by. But he'd never uttered it to women whom he expected to be more than a one-nighter, or unless he was too drunk to keep a lid on it. *Ah, hell no.* His sloppy drunk mouth must have said it out loud to Bri. How could that have happened? He'd known at the bar that he didn't want her to be a one and done.

Del groaned and covered his face with one hand. His inner credo to which she referred had always been, three orgasms for his partner before he let himself go. "I didn't—"

"Mmm, hmmm. You absolutely did." Bri crossed her arms over her flushed breasts. And yes, they were tipped with the loveliest of pink nipples, just as he had imagined, but he couldn't focus on them right now. He had to come to grips with what Bri had revealed.

"I said that to you." He swallowed past a nasty lump that had risen in his throat.

"Yup. Said it, and did it," she informed him, giving a succinct nod.

"And after you…then did we…?" Del lowered his head into his palms. Did he want to hear this?

A soft hand glided over his back. Not at all what he expected. Bri began to rub small, comforting circles on the muscles that had bunched there.

"Yeah," Bri said, gently. "We did. So now you know why I was a little freaked out when you mentioned 'non-performance'."

Chapter Twelve

Del groaned and looked utterly miserable sitting there. "How is it that you have such a good memory of that night, and I don't?" he asked, head cradled, staring at his jean's clad knees.

This wasn't necessarily a conversation Bri wanted to have while she sat, naked, and he remained fully clothed. She gave him an option. "Do you want me to get dressed or do you want to join me under the blankets?" she propositioned.

He turned his head to look at her, and she could feel the damnable blush coming up again. She dragged one pillow over her midsection and scowled. That seemed to break Del's wretchedness. "You can't hide, Bri." His smirk was wry. "I've seen everything up close and personal." He frowned again. "Apparently two times now, although the first still hasn't made an appearance in my head. And *you* haven't answered my question."

"You haven't answered mine," she groused pointedly. "Dress?" She indicated herself. "Or undress?" She gave his body a nod.

Del stood up, keeping his eyes glued to hers, and toed off boots. Bri tried to keep from drooling as she anticipated his striptease. The T-shirt came next, grabbed from the back of the neck, then up and over his head in a purely masculine move that Bri had always loved. His dark chest, devoid of hair, looked massive in the daylight. Far larger and more impressive than she'd remembered. And those pectoral muscles twitched in an erotic dance as he reached for his fly.

Oh my. Had she remembered the rest of him correctly?

When she scooted back on the bed, flush up against the headboard feeling suddenly shy, a short barked laugh emerged from his throat. "This was your call, Brina. Tell me now if you've changed your mind and the clothes stay put."

She bit down on her lip and pondered. They needed to have the conversation that had been bottled up inside her since the moment she'd found out she was pregnant. Naked was probably a better way to do it because they'd be equally vulnerable.

"No. Go ahead. Undress." She dropped her eyes and scooted the comforter out from under her bottom, slipping beneath it just in time to look up and see the magnificence that was Del's ass. *Holy hell.* He'd turned to give her his back, and what a back it was. Bri didn't remember seeing him from this angle before, and the sight of his muscled rib cage, tapered waist, and hard, delineated ass-cheeks were enough to set her whole body on fire. The man was exquisitely built, and if they didn't have an important conversation pending, she'd be content to lay here and look at him all day. *Damn.*

When Del turned, he was fully erect, his shaft bobbing high and proud against his abdomen. And yeah. She hadn't imagined the magnificence of his cock. And he was at full staff. He'd just been between her legs, and hadn't reached his own release, so that made perfect sense. She licked her lips, instantly knowing what she'd rather be doing than talking, and he groaned.

"Is this conversation, or action?" he queried. "Because I need to be in the right mind-set."

Bri sighed. As much as she'd like to sample his impressive wares, she knew they had to get other stuff out of the way. If he was still amenable to act on their obviously mutual attraction after she broke the news? Well, she wouldn't say no at that point.

"Talk." She pursed her lips into a moue of disappointment that made him laugh, just as she'd intended. He stalked to the bed and flipped back the covers, lowering himself to the sheets and cocooning both of them inside the comforter once he settled.

They turned at the same time to face each other, and his gaze fell to her breasts, which seemed to swell at his perusal. Certainly her nipples had never tightened to such diamond points, or hurt so wonderfully before. It had to be because of the pregnancy. Maybe that would explain her shortness of breath, too?

"They look bigger than I remember," Del marveled at her cleavage.

Bri wasn't quite ready yet to spill the reason for her size change, so she sought to keep him off balance. "Eyes front, soldier," she barked, hoping for his compliance. Del might not remember everything about their evening together, but Bri recalled every last detail she'd pried from him, including his military career.

He laughed and kept his eyes right where they were. "You don't look like any drill sergeant I've ever had," he chuckled. "And thank God. Because right now I'd be doing push-ups for insubordination."

Bri couldn't help her giggle. This was going pretty well so far. Her comfort level was way better than she'd imagined, especially with them both baring their assets again. But unfortunately it was time to start nibbling away at what had happened three months ago.

"So you joined me at the bar," she tapped his shoulder, calling his attention back to her face again. "And it was very unlike me not to just get up and walk away. I mean, I don't succumb to guys in bars, ever, and your line was extremely cheesy," she teased.

"What?" A nearly perfect pout appeared on his sculpted lips. "I simply told the truth. That it was sad you were drinking shots alone."

"Yeah. Right," Bri returned, and watched his eyebrow do a little dance in response.

She snorted. "And that." She brought a hand up from under the covers and pointed at his brow. "That's what actually got me going," she admitted. "If I'd gone on your charm alone, you would have come up empty. But that damned thing," she shook her head. "It seems to have a life of its own."

Del rolled to his back and laughed so hard it sounded like he nearly choked. The joyful reaction caught Bri off guard. Even drunk, Del hadn't allowed himself such an uninhibited display, and the sound flooded her chest with delight.

"What?" she poked him as he wiped a tear from the corner of one eye.

"Oh God," he caught his breath. "You're not the only one. My guys call it my evil twin," he clucked in amusement. "They complain that even when I'm not saying a word to them, they can always figure out my mood by the actions of that eyebrow."

Bri couldn't help it. She reached out a finger and smoothed it over the dark hair in question. "Well, it won your case with me that night," she confessed. "While you talked and fed me more corny lines, it was doing a little dance of its own, and completely dragged me in."

"Remind me to thank it, later," he said, going back to his side. He leaned in for a soft, but lingering kiss.

"What was that for?" Bri asked.

"For making me laugh," he stated, then became serious. "And for trusting me." He swept a hand down, indicating their position in bed. "I didn't expect this."

"I didn't intend it." Bri told the partial truth. She really had no idea of how she'd approach Del, but had she still wanted him? *Hell, yes.* And she certainly wasn't upset that the warmth of his big body was stretched out next to hers under the covers.

Del brought them back to their original discussion. "So that night..." he prompted.

"I'd had a bad week," she recalled. "A bad month, actually. You know all about Reynold, so I don't have to extrapolate." She rolled her eyes. "I was only looking to get a little drunk at that hotel to ignore my troubles, when you appeared. And that damned eyebrow let me know I could be in for a whole lot of dilemma-forgetting if I loosened up a bit." She chewed her lip again. "So I went for it."

"You certainly did," Del chuckled. "Let me tell you, I've never met a woman who could pound down alcohol like you did that night, let alone keep up with me shot for shot. I still can't believe I was on my ass, and you remember everything."

"Yeah. About that." Bri swallowed, sheepishly. "I have a confession to make." She walked a couple of fingers up and down Del's chest as he waited, patiently. "After the first couple of rounds, I might have asked the bartender to switch mine out for water."

Del looked at her blankly, clearly stunned.

Oh, shit. Was he pissed off? Would he get up and walk out, leaving her to fend for herself?

Del's shoulders squared. They quaked. His face drew together as if pained, and then laughter spewed forth with such force that it shook the bed beneath her. A smile lit her from within. *Hot damn. Not pissed.*

"I wondered..." he attempted. "I wondered..." Bri watched as Del tried to reign in the grip of his amusement. Finally, words became coherent around his chortles. "I had no idea how you could drink so much." He gave a long, keening breath out. "You're half my size, and after the fifth shot, I was in trouble. Except you kept ordering, and I didn't want to appear like a wimp so I had to keep going." He flexed his whole face as if the laughing had caused it to cramp up.

"I realized that," Bri confessed. "And kept you going on purpose. I'd already had enough after the first few to give me my courage, but I wanted to make sure that if I changed my mind, I'd be in control, and you'd be harmless."

A gleam came into his eyes. "Oh sweetness," he divulged, looking wolfish. "That's where you made your biggest mistake. I'm never harmless." His lips twisted wryly. "At least I never had been before. Which is why passing out and not, uh, culminating our time together, baffled the hell out of me."

Bri figured it was a good time to stroke his ego. He certainly deserved it. "Actually, there came a point in the elevator where you couldn't quite string two words together and I thought maybe I'd gone too far. That you'd had too much. But by that time I'd totally committed to going back to your room, and you somehow gained a second wind." She ran a finger slowly down the space between his two prominent pectoral muscles, and felt him twitch. "Was I ever surprised when you kept going. Like the Energizer bunny, you just wouldn't quit."

Del groaned, but in a good way. "I know. I know. You can call me all kinds of a dork. But I aim to please. And three before me has always been my rule."

"It was pretty funny," Bri giggled. "Trying to get you to stray from your policy was like hitting my head against a brick wall. You kept repeating that mantra every time I tried to get you to…you know."

Bri became aware that Del's fingers had begun to play across the bare skin of her hip, and her breathing hitched. Warmth pooled between her legs, but she couldn't let herself become distracted. She still needed to get the whole truth of that night off her chest.

Del clearly had different ideas. "So now that I know you tricked me into getting drunk to sleep with you—"

Bri slapped at his chest, causing that devilish grin to appear again, along with the dimples in his cheeks, and a lift of that evil brow.

"Well, you did," he told her smugly. "You just admitted it. And I'm not upset at all," he continued magnanimously. "It's not every day a woman goes to so much trouble to seduce me. Most times I have to make a little effort. Why just last week…," he teased.

Bri leaned in and bit Del's nipple.

"Ouch!" He rubbed the spot after she drew away. "What was that for?"

"Bragging," Bri chastised. "And you happen to be naked, in bed with me. So I don't need to hear about your other conquests." He used the hand on her hip to pull her closer, and she swallowed excitedly, feeling the solid length of his arousal against her thigh.

"I'll be truthful with you, Bri." All humor left his face and his dark eyes bored into hers. "I haven't been with anybody since I met you that night. I've had plenty of opportunity, but nobody seemed to be as sassy, or as beautiful. I haven't been able to imagine anyone in my bed who doesn't have blonde curls and emerald green eyes." His free arm dragged her in so her breasts plumped into his chest. "I kept calling myself a fool for not staying conscious enough to get your name. Your number. I even prowled that bar every night for two weeks after, to see if you'd come back."

Now he sounded hurt. Even though he had to know that his business connection to Reynold was the reason she hadn't sought him out. "You understand that I hadn't completely disentangled myself from Reynold at that point," she explained. "But honestly? I planned on contacting you as soon as I was settled in a job that didn't have 'conflict of interest' written all over it."

"I wish you would have let me decide that," he censured. "It would have saved us a lot of time. Although right now I seem to have you right where I want you." He leveraged up and over Bri, scooping her body underneath his, looming above her, dark and powerful. She shivered when he prodded against her with his hard cock, reminding her of his formidable brawn.

"What happened to 'three before me'?" she murmured against his lips as he landed small kisses from one edge of her mouth and back.

"Screw it," he muttered. "I'm turning over a new leaf. It's all about me from now on."

Her body relaxed with laughter, and her legs fell open, welcoming his weight between them. She had one quick pang of guilt about waiting until he knew everything before engaging in sex, but shoved it back. Once she broke the news, he might not want to fuck her. Ever again. Or worse, he might hate and reject her. Didn't she deserve just one more piece of heaven? And this time Del would be able to look right into her eyes and show her everything he was feeling. As good as it had been before, she had missed those dark orbs which had been hidden behind closed lashes for their entire sexual encounter.

Yeah. She was going to go for this, and she refused to feel guilty. Del was far too potent a drug for her to deny herself just one more taste.

Bri arched up and brushed the wetness of her pussy onto the bulbous tip of his cock, urging his fast entry.

"Shit." He pulled back with a curse, and practically leaped out of bed.

"What?" Bri flew up to her elbows and regarded him with wide, worried eyes.

He turned to his pants on the floor, and picked them up, rummaging through his pockets. "Protection," he grunted, dropping them back down. Bri sagged back, but before she could say a word to admit it wasn't needed, he'd marched his naked ass right out of the bedroom. And what a sight that was. She fell flat on the bed and fanned herself. The man's ass should be outlawed. Why, exactly, hadn't she sunk her teeth into that delectable piece of flesh yet? Bri couldn't wait to check *that* box off her to-do list.

The screen door slammed behind him, and less than half a minute later, slammed again. She caught a distinct thud, and the scrambling of something being undone. She grinned. He must have packed condoms in his duffel. Not that he needed them, but she'd let him go through the motions this one last time.

Del appeared in the doorway, triumphant, his sex at full-mast, and a square of foil in his hand. He ripped it open with his teeth, dropping the package to the floor. He'd just begun to smooth it on, when a look of consternation came over his face. His eyes darted from his shaft to the discarded package and back again. "Wait."

His eyebrow looked worried, and Bri didn't like it. Not one bit.

"That night," he frowned. "I didn't find any used condoms in my hotel room. No discarded packets, no nothing." He remained vexed. "It was one of the reasons I was sure we didn't do anything." Now his voice became anxious. "What exactly did we use for protection that night, Bri?"

He waited and watched, while Brina attempted to school her face and her racing heart. Disappointment zipped through her. It looked like she wouldn't get "last-ies" after all.

"We didn't," she told him. "I'm pregnant."

Chapter Thirteen

"What?" Del's whole face, not just his eyebrow went berserk. His scowl darkened and his hand immediately left his shaft to quickly snatch his jeans from the floor. The condom dropped, forgotten. He plunged his feet into his pant-legs, fuming. "You wanna let me in on the joke?" he spat. "I've never once, no matter how drunk I've been, made a 'mistake'," Del snapped.

Bri regarded him without blinking. "It's my fault," she admitted. "I want to lie, Del, but I have to own this. I told you that I was on the pill."

Before he could interrupt—which seemed impossible at the moment since the word "pregnant" kept scrambling around in his brain—she held up a hand and continued. "Which I truly believed I was." Her voice remained low and level. "And since you said you'd been tested and were clean, and I hadn't been with anyone for a really long time, it was only birth control that was an issue. And I've been on the pill for years due to monthly problems."

That was an interesting thing to share, and Del cringed. It seemed far too intimate, even after what they'd just done together. Del didn't have any sisters, nor had he ever lived with a woman, so periods weren't something he was used to hearing about.

He crossed his arms over his bare chest and waited for the rest of what she had to say, uncomfortable and glowering.

"Apparently that wasn't good enough," she snorted. "I looked up the statistics. Sometimes if your system is screwed up, and you take them erratically, which I've been known to do, there's a nine percent chance of pregnancy." She gave a self deprecating laugh. "Leave it to me to win the lottery."

By this time she'd lifted the pillow up again, covering her nakedness. And that helped, how? Del wanted to howl. She couldn't possibly think that the barrier aided the situation. Her new posture actually added to her fucking allure. And screw that.

Del shook his head. What was he thinking? He shouldn't still be enticed by Bri. He should be scrambling to get as far away from her as possible. His inner wariness-compass had lost its mind. The lady was clearly running some kind of a scam on him, yet for some reason he still wanted her.

Del's blood suddenly ran cold. Was it a trap of some kind? Had Reynold been in on it? Put her up to it? Was this some devious way to get him involved in illicit arms dealing?

"I didn't mean for it to happen," Bri added defensively, not knowing where Del's mind had taken things. He blinked. He'd pretty much stopped listening to her while formulating his own suppositions. Del waited another ten seconds to see if she was through, and then it was his turn.

"First of all, I don't know what you're trying to pull, but it won't work," he barked. Brina cringed and flinched back when he moved close and put a finger in her face. "I never would have taken your word for the pill thing that night. I've had that told to me dozen's of times before, and not been fooled, once."

121

Her eyes widened at this disclosure, but he moved back and kept on.

"I never trust a partner to take care of things. I *always* wear a fucking condom," he told her vehemently. And because he hadn't found evidence of the latex item, he couldn't have screwed her. He couldn't have.

Okay, maybe he'd given her three orgasms, and been so drunk he'd actually told her his golden rule, but that didn't mean he'd done anything more. And it certainly didn't make him a baby-daddy.

When Bri didn't move, didn't whine or cajole, he lost some of his posturing. When she simply shrugged and refused to try and convince him, Del became uncomfortable. Where was the blow-up? The drama?

"Will you leave the room now so that I can get dressed?" she asked finally, with a polite coldness in her voice. "Clearly this is not the place to have the rest of this discussion."

Aha. So there was more discussion. She still wanted to play her game. Just not while she remained naked, in bed. Del grabbed his shirt from the floor, and turning away, pulled it on and stomped into the living room.

He wondered what lies she was conjuring in her head as he listened to her getting dressed. But really, did he care? Nothing she could say would sway him. He wasn't going to be drawn in to any of the wild tale she spun.

But he couldn't help but feel puzzled. What could be her motive? That she'd pretend she was pregnant with his child and maybe…what, cry rape? That way his new career might be ruined, and perhaps Reynold could blackmail him into joining his illegal shit? Del ran a hand over his head. *Hell.* That made no sense. As soon as the baby was born—and proven not to be his—they'd have no leverage because no jury would convict him. And surely any legal action Reynold threatened could be held off until after the birth. So that theory was full of holes and out the window.

Wait. What if Bri had simply found herself knocked-up by Reynold, and hadn't wanted to tie herself to the jerk-off? That made more sense. She'd run from her boss, Del had shown up like a chump, and Bri figured she could pin the father badge on him. That sounded more like it. Did she think threatening him with paternity would make him more committed to helping her out of her sticky situation? If so, she was wrong. Once he learned about the email, he'd been on board to help her. How would adding paternity make things better?

Some time during his pacing of the small room, Bri had finished dressing and stood in the door regarding him. If he could say that her face showed anything at all, it had to be disappointment. But that was just crazy. This was *her* mess. Why would she be disappointed in *him*?

When she spoke, he focused on her carefully, ready to rebut anything and everything.

"It's only been a couple of hours. I'm sure you can call your guys and they'll turn around to retrieve you," she said levelly. "Or if you want, I can call Mayg and she'll have her cousin come back and get you. You can spend the night in Orono or rent a car and have a late trip back to Boston."

Del deflated. She wasn't going to rail at him? He grew uncomfortable; a little less sure of himself. Where was the arguing? The crying? Was she such a poor actress that she couldn't put on a few water works? If he was the pawn in some kind of game, her fast capitulation wouldn't get her anywhere.

"Maybe I *will* take one of those suggestions," he allowed. "But first I need to know why you'd try to pull this over on me?" Del didn't like it one bit, and needed to hear her motive, *if* she'd start being honest.

"I'm not pulling anything," Bri spoke softly but firmly. "I have no agenda here. Once I decided to tell you, I just went with it." She raised her chin. "I didn't know how you'd take it. But this was one scenario. So now that I'm clear on your reaction, you're free to go."

Del snorted at her easy surrender. "And your baby? If there is one. Who gets to be the father now?"

Her gaze became steely. "There will be no father. *I* will be this child's parent. As I've told you, mine didn't do such a bang up job, and I won't put up with an ass being an integral part of my baby's life."

There. He'd guessed correctly. The baby had to be Reynold's if she was referring to an ass as the sperm donor. She'd simply been looking to pawn things off on him to keep her boss from knowing. Maybe she'd wanted Del to stay with her until the birth, and keep her well hidden from Reynold for...how many months? Maybe she'd trip up in the telling. "How far along are you?" he asked.

"You can count," she told him with a sneer.

Okay. That hadn't worked out well.

"But, oh yeah. This baby couldn't possibly be yours, so any number of months will do." Her eyes narrowed to slits. "And what do you care, anyway?"

Del tried to tell himself he didn't, but something about Bri's demeanor got under his skin, and dammit, liar or not, he still wanted to keep her from Reynold's clutches if that's what she needed. "I want to know how long you planned on using me to keep your child's real father at bay."

"Well pardon me." She shook her head. "Again. Since you're so sure it's not yours, my baby is now none of your business." She picked up a sweater from the back of the tiny couch. "Please make arrangements to be gone within a couple of hours. I'm going for a walk, and when I return I don't want to see your face."

She said her piece evenly, without yelling, and without tears. Del didn't get it. She'd let him off the hook far too easily.

"What about your safety issues?" he asked.

She shrugged. "I'll take my chances. I've made it this far, and if you don't give me away, I think I can disappear even further."

"And what will you do for money?" Del asked. "I know how much you withdrew before you ran. You won't be able to live on that for long."

Now he saw her anger. "What do you care?" she asked again, practically snarling this time. "We're done here."

She held up her fingers and counted off. "You were hired by Reynold to find me." Her thumb bent down. "You tracked me despite my precautions, but only because of our previous association." Another finger dropped. "You decided to take my side and help me once you heard my story because you obviously wanted to fuck me again." Del winced as finger three went south. "And I believed I owed it to you to confess that your DNA is swimming in my womb." Finger four. That left her middle finger standing tall and proud, which she thrust forward, aimed in his direction.

"Now I'm telling you to screw off. There's no point in prolonging our association. I've worked it through, and if I'm found, maybe my father won't be inclined to kill me if I'm carrying his future heir. That should make you feel better. Good enough that you can take your misplaced chivalry, shove it up your ass, and get lost." She turned in a huff of blonde curls and stunning outrage, grabbed her sneakers off the floor and slammed out of the screen door.

"Don't go too far!" Del yelled, before falling heavily onto the miniscule couch. *Wow.* Her tirade and its intensity had him baffled. Unless she was a really good actress, there was no way she could have faked that amount of fury. And it was pretty clear she actually expected him to be gone when she returned. Where did that leave him?

A tiny crack appeared in his certainty that the baby she carried wasn't his. What if he'd been so turned on by her, and so equally drunk, that he'd let his rules slide. He sat still for a few moments and regarded an ant, crawling relentlessly in and out of a crack in the wooden floor. What if, let's say, just for a moment he believed that Bri really carried his child. *His child. Holy shit.* A baby boy or girl, with his dimples and Bri's golden hair. The possibility made him shiver. A child with Bri. A lifetime with a woman who had become of endless fascination to him. Even as he'd accused her of lying, he still couldn't help but admire her conviction, her fight. Del took a deep breath. And really, *could* she be telling the truth? He had to consider the possibility.

That this was a turning point in his life, suddenly occurred to Del. He'd barely admitted to himself—even though his guys seemed to see it—that Bri meant something more to him than a one night stand. That she'd stayed in his mind for months after one drunken encounter had been sign enough, but when he'd seen her picture on Reynold's desk, it had felt like coming home. In truth, he couldn't take the jerk's case fast enough. The fact that Bri would be at the end of the trail he followed had made every nerve ending in his body twitch with anticipation.

And when he'd finally seen her again? He'd almost lost it, holding onto his sanity by a mere thread so as not to run, drag her into his arms and refuse to ever let her go.

So why had he reacted like such an ass when she'd hit him with her news? She hadn't made any demands. She'd simply stated facts. And when he'd loudly protested, she'd taken it in stride and let him off the hook. Immediately. Hell, it was only when he'd pushed at what her next move would be that she'd gone on the defensive. Del actually chuckled.

He should have seen her little finger trick coming. It was something one of his superior officers used to pull all the time. He just hadn't credited that Bri had it in her. Another point in her favor.

As far as Del could figure, he had one of two choices, and neither one had him abandoning Bri.

He could either remain aloof and keep her safe until she delivered the child, demanding a DNA test be done after the birth. Or he could apologize, tell her he would accept the child as his own until proven otherwise, and try to reestablish the trust they'd been building.

In the first scenario, a cold war would ensue for the next six months. Del would be hard pressed to fight his attraction, and Bri would hate his guts. In that situation, even if the baby turned out to be his, the best he could expect would be partial custody and weekend visits. He'd never have a relationship with Bri, *or* a full-time connection to his child.

With choice two, once she got over being angry with him for his initial, reasonable mistrust, they could attempt to work towards building a long term relationship. And when the child was born, perhaps they could live together as a family, whether the baby was his or not. If marriage came into things, it wouldn't be so bad. On the contrary, a lifetime of Bri and children instead of an empty apartment actually sounded damned appealing. There was no denying the sparks that flew between them, and if they could blow the embers into a long-lasting flame, the fire could last a lifetime.

Del felt better. He always did after analyzing his options. He yawned and rubbed his stomach. It was getting late, and it would be dark soon. Bri would be back. She knew the dangers and probably huffed and stomped not too far away. Maybe she would have thought it through like he had, and calmed down. Even if she was still spitting mad,

Del would make sure that they talked it out. They'd sit down over a nice supper and together they would form a plan.

He got up, happy with himself for figuring it out, and pulled open the refrigerator. Del chuckled. Fresh fruit, vegetables, eggs, milk, and a package of hotdogs? Didn't she know that mystery-meat was bad for a pregnant woman? He'd learned that on the news sometime in the past. Del grunted. While he cooked, he'd have to check his phone's search engine for a list of no-no's with pregnancy. He didn't want Bri doing anything to hurt herself or the baby.

Eggs and broccoli came out of the fridge. An omelet would surely make Bri more amenable to conversation when she returned.

Chapter Fourteen

Two days had passed since Bri walked back into the house after pacing off her anger about their baby discussion. She'd gone back to find Del cooking...and smug. The arrogant bastard had magnanimously offered a truce, where, under his terms, they would continue their mutual admiration for each other. Clearly he planned that to include a shared bed, which was not *remotely* happening. He'd also offered—quite nobly, or so he'd believed—to take full responsibility for her and her unborn child until such time as the baby was born. A paternity test would follow.

Bri had fumed, and let him know that until he trusted her, and took her word for whose baby this was, he wasn't laying a hand on her. And as many times as she calmly told him, or screamed it to the rafters that she hadn't slept with anyone but him, he figuratively patted her head, maintained an unruffled demeanor, and wouldn't commit to believing her. Apparently he imagined that by remaining serene, he'd win her over. Instead, he found himself sleeping on the too-short couch. Served him right. Bri hadn't had a moment of remorse, alone in her big bed. Sleeplessness, yes. Regret, no.

It was late, and Bri headed out for one of the many walks she'd managed lately, despite Del's warning that she made it difficult for him to keep her safe. She picked the path she'd found that wended its way from the back of the cabin to a stand of large boulders. If she squeezed between them, a lovely, wide space lay between, hiding a deliberately placed pile of smaller rocks that acted as stairs.

She'd shown it to Del the second time he'd protested her going out, and he'd looked it over carefully before approving it as safe. Which also made her fume. She'd known it was a secure spot, so how was it that his opinion made it okay? Men were so arrogant. They imagined that not only could they be in charge of everything, but they could dictate the outcome. Like imagining that she'd go back to sleeping with him when he still believed she was a liar.

Without hesitation in the gathering dusk, Bri climbed the steps until she found herself perched on top of one rounded outcropping, a view of the valley below just visible through the trees. It was nice. Peaceful. Bri sat down and attempted to calm herself for the umpteenth time. Really? Couldn't Del, for just one minute, believe this child she carried was his?

It sucked, him having no memory of their sexual encounter. And yes, it irked her that she'd been the one to cause his alcohol induced amnesia, but still, considering how well he'd performed, she'd had no way of knowing how far gone he'd been.

Heat moved up into her cheeks. And damn it, even after she found out he didn't remember a thing, he'd managed to get her naked again. Which was the real crux of her anger. She'd tried so hard, but she couldn't ignore her attraction to Del. And as days ticked by, her resolve slipped farther and farther. Even when she tried to provoke a fight so as to renew her resentment, his dimples and that damned eyebrow did their darndest to deflate her anger every time.

As foul as she got with Del, he always returned her bad behavior with a smile and patience. When she threw surly complaints at him, he showed a tolerance and fortitude that made her want to scream. And every now and then when she caught him peeking at her ass with that shit-eating grin on his face, she kicked herself for wanting him to make good on the implied promise in his eyes.

And it wasn't just the man himself who made her crazy. It was his habits, too. He was, by far, the easiest roommate she'd ever had. He cooked, he cleaned up after himself, and due to the lack of technology in the cabin he'd even coerced her into playing—mostly silent—games of Rummy when boredom took over.

His presence was so stress-free it was ridiculous.

Which begged the question, why couldn't he just believe her and be done with it? Why not go the last step toward building back their fledgling relationship? What was he afraid of, and why wouldn't he trust her on this one thing? It wasn't like she wanted to trap him into a domestic situation. *Hell no.* Not that she wouldn't mind playing house with Mr. Hot and Sexy, but it would be from a mutual decision, not from entrapment. When a DNA test proved that the child was his, it would be his call, completely, whether he wanted to stay or go.

If she was honest with herself, she wanted him to stay, even though it irked the hell out of her that she wasn't one hundred percent trusted.

It was times like these that Bri wished she had someone she could talk to. A mother to confide in. A close friend. Her heart yearned for Mayg, but she immediately dismissed it. Her one-time teammate had already helped her immeasurably. There was no need to heap her woes on top of what Mayg had already done.

She stared off into the lowering sun of what was her third day at the cabin, and succumbed to weakness. She would call her Aunt Celia.

Bri pulled the disposable phone from her pocket and glowered at it, before laying it on the rock. Should she? Aunt

Celia was the closest thing Bri had to a confidant, and she already crawled with guilt, running away and not letting Auntie Cee know. But dare she call?

She'd initially worried that her aunt might be in on any plot that was afoot between Reynold and her father, but having mulled that over, she now rejected it. Celia had been under the same arm's length from Bennet Capadella as Bri herself had been. When Bri looked back, she could easily see that both of them had merely been pawns on her father's chessboard.

She glanced back down at the phone, coming to a decision. Bri would spare her aunt from becoming involved, but she wanted...no she *needed* to be selfish just this once, and talk about her emotional upsets. Surely she could contact her aunt without divulging any details of her overall predicament *or* her location. Bri bit her lip. She picked up the phone and dialed.

One ring. Two.

"Hello?" The female voice on the other end of the line sounded hesitant, suspicious. Bri realized that caller ID would show a number unknown to her aunt.

"Auntie Cee, It's me. Brina."

"Oh, thank God, Bri!" Her aunt cried. "I've been so worried about you."

Bri sighed. There dissolved the idea of a nice, chatty phone call to air her dirty laundry. "How long have you known I've been gone?" she reluctantly asked.

"Since early today when your father called," she scolded, sounding more like herself. "He's quite upset that he hasn't been able to reach you at your job. He's called three times since this morning, wanting to know if you've been in touch."

Bri panicked. This was not good. "Listen to me Aunt Celia," she said, using the more formal name she rarely uttered. "If you love me, you won't tell him I called."

When her aunt made sounds as if to disagree, Bri continued. "I'm going with my gut here, and trusting you. Things aren't what they seem right now." she said. "I'm in danger, and if you let Dad know I called you, it could be bad." She took a deep breath. "I uncovered something at the office where I worked that showed me I can't trust him any more. Do you understand? If you say anything to him and he finds me, my life might be in danger."

"Bri," her aunt chastised. "You're over-reacting. You can't really believe that your father would hurt you. As far as he's concerned, the sun rises and sets with you. He would never do anything to cause you harm."

Funny, up until a few days ago, Bri might have agreed. "Auntie Cee, the man you're thinking about, the man I thought I knew as well, disappeared a long time ago. Once, when I was small, he doted on me. But after Mother died, he changed. We just never knew how much."

"You can't really think that, Bri," her aunt countered. "Outwardly perhaps he's changed." The defense was natural for the woman's only brother. "But you know deep down his feelings for you have remained the same."

"That's the lie I've been telling myself all these years, Auntie, but I can't hide from the truth that's right in front of me. He set me up to be foisted off on my boss as an arm-piece-wife to further his company ties with US AIM, or to keep my boss quiet about something. I'm not sure which, but he warned Reynold that if I got wind of what they had going together, I would be expendable."

"Oh, dear." Her aunt faltered. "I knew he'd become remote with me, but I never considered…"

"I know," Bri comforted. "It's a lot to swallow, but believe me, it's the truth. So do you see why you can't tell him I called?"

"I do, Bri. And I'll honor your wishes. But I can't help believing it's all a misunderstanding, and as soon as you talk to your father, it will be cleared up."

There was the aunt she knew and loved. The eternal optimist. Bri's inclination to trust Aunt Cee hadn't been wrong. "As long as you keep our conversation secret, I'll work on how I want to handle it with Dad," Bri soothed.

"That's all I ask, sweetie." Her aunt sounded much calmer now. "And thank you for letting me know you're okay. I was so worried." She gave a bitter laugh. "Not that I won't be worrying even more, now that I'm imagining problems where there probably aren't any." She changed tracks. "Are you certain you're safe, wherever you are?"

Bri wasn't about to disclose her location, but she could give her aunt the comfort of knowing she was protected. "I have a group of people looking after me," Bri told her. "They seem to be taking my safety pretty seriously."

"I'm glad." Her aunt fell silent, and Bri couldn't help the next suggestion the sprung to her lips.

"Auntie Cee, you might want to pack a bag, take some money and make yourself scarce as well. I don't know what Daddy's capable of, or how far he'll take things now that he thinks I've found him out."

"Oh, honey. That's not necessary," Auntie Cee scoffed. "And besides, you know I have no money of my own. Your father has provided me with everything since the day I walked in here to take care of you. But even if I had the wherewithal, he's my brother, and I trust him. You and Bennet are my whole life."

Bri squeezed her eyes shut against the stunning sunset that crept through the trees. It hurt that the hidden ugliness of her father existed alongside such beauty, and that her aunt was trapped by it. "Then I'll send for you as soon as I can, Cee," Brina barely kept the tears out of her voice.

The knowledge that her aunt still trusted her father hurt doubly so because Bri had called for a shoulder to cry on, but now she couldn't. If she burdened her aunt with the details of her pregnancy and the man who confused her so much, she had no doubt that her tender-hearted aunt would feel it necessary to share with her father. She terminated the call before emotions swamped her.

"I've got to go, Auntie Cee. I'll call you soon, and please stay safe."

"I will, Bri. And think a little harder on this, will you?" she pleaded her case. "I'm sure you mistook something, somewhere along the line. Bennet could never hurt you."

"I'll think about it," Bri promised, crossing her fingers at the lie. "I love you, Cee."

"I love you, too, honey. Good bye."

"Bye." Bri punched the button and the phone dropped from her hand, unseen, to her lap. The sun's final rays had almost disappeared below the horizon, and Bri knew she had to move soon. Del would be out looking for her any minute, and she needed time to compose herself. At least if she showed up to pace the porch, he'd give her the space she needed to appear calm when she finally went inside.

She pocketed her phone and scrambled down from the boulder. Del might have her under his thumb, but he totally didn't need to know she'd called her aunt and become upset. As screwed up as their situation was, weirdly he'd been looking up things about pregnancy on his phone. He was sure to bring up the fact that getting distraught wasn't good for the baby. Although why he cared, Bri didn't know. Already he'd stopped her from eating certain foods, hotdogs and bacon, and warned her not to sleep on her back. Oh, and that the left side was better than the right. Geeze. *Bossy much?*

Chapter Fifteen

Del let one arm flop down over his face. *Dammit.* Another night where he wasn't going to get any sleep. And it was his own fault. The problem had nothing to do with the small, lumpy couch, where his six-foot two frame refused to fit. Hell no, he'd slept in much worse places. The problem lay right behind that partially opened door to the bedroom.

Every night the cabin seemed to get smaller and smaller, to the point where he knew—after lights out—the instant Bri sighed, or turned over. He knew for a certainty that she wasn't asleep tonight. Her movements were too erratic. He wanted so much to march into her room, push her aside and move next to her under the blankets, holding her up against him until her body relaxed into slumber. *Right.* Like that was going to happen. He gave another huff and draped one calf over the back of the sofa. This sucked.

He knew exactly how much time had passed since they'd turned in. He'd checked his phone about every five minutes, and now the glow of his cell told him it was after midnight.

"Del?" Bri's tentative voice breeched the darkness.

"Yeah, Bri?" He was surprised to hear from her. His voice when he answered sounded gruff, even to his own ears.

"Why don't you believe me?"

Del wanted to groan. It was just like Bri to cut right to the crux of the problem. Couldn't she leave it alone?

He paused before answering. *Why didn't he believe her?* Because of his screwed up past. His formative years hadn't been any picnic. Maybe it was time for him to spill his reasons for caution. Perhaps it would keep her from asking anything of him he was unable to provide.

"It's a long story," he answered.

That got a short laugh. "Well it doesn't look like either one of us is going to sleep tonight, so unless it's a several volume saga, we have time," she cajoled sarcastically.

"No saga," he returned. "Just some regular bullshit."

"Then let me hear it." Her voice became serious. "I want to understand why you're being so pig-headed."

"You won't like it," he countered.

"Let me be the judge of that?" She didn't back off from his challenge.

"Fine. But can I come in and lay down beside you?" he asked. "I don't feel like talking loudly to the ceiling for the next hour. And I'll keep my hands to myself. I promise."

Did he just hear a muttered, "too bad"? *No way.* His mind had to be playing tricks.

"Come on in," she groused.

Del tried desperately to discourage the sudden cock-stand that sprang to life under his sweatpants. He didn't want to get sent back to couch-jail, so he needed to behave himself. "Down boy," he growled at his crotch.

"What was that?" Bri called out, clearly catching the sound of his voice.

Damn. She had ears like a cat. "Nothing. I'll be right in." Del tried to conjure the grossest dead animal he'd ever seen in the jungle. Complete with maggots. *Nope.* Still hard. Well at least it was dark. He'd try to keep the damned thing

138

away from her. He snorted. There'd be no spooning while he told his life story.

"Well? Are you coming?" Bri sounded impatient, and Del liked that. She wanted him next to her. He could tell. She wasn't as immune to him as she pretended.

He peeled himself off the couch and padded on bare feet to her room, making sure to take his firearm with him. He'd retrieved it from his duffel days ago, and travelled no place without it, even with the censorious raised eyebrows of Bri trained on it every time it was in the open.

"Permission to enter?" he asked from the doorway, studying the shape of Bri's body under the covers, in the dim moonlight.

"Permission granted," she returned.

He moved to the unoccupied side of the bed, and rested his weapon and phone on the bedside table. "Is it okay if I get in?" The night air was cool here in Maine, despite the fact that it was summer. As good an excuse as any.

"Of course," she replied with a humorous edge to her voice. "I'd hate for you to freeze anything off."

He lifted the blankets. Two could play at her innuendo game. "Believe me, with all of my important parts right now? Freezing from weather isn't an issue."

"Good to know," she answered, snickering. Not the reaction he'd been looking for.

Del flipped back the sheets and slid into the space previously heated by her body. Her lemon scent filled his head and he turned his nose into the pillow to drag it in even farther. God, he'd missed her smell.

"So where are you going to start?" she asked, dragging his mind back from the carnal. "Birth? Early childhood?"

"Nothing to report there," he replied gruffly. "Well, almost nothing," he admitted. "I grew up in the projects in

Boston and as early as elementary school I found trouble, hanging with the wrong gang."

She turned onto her side to face him. "Makes sense. You seem like the type who thrives on danger." She tagged him astutely.

"Yeah. I've always been a magnet for messes." Del wanted to smack himself. Now she'd think he meant her.

"Is that right? So that's why your radar targeted me the minute I walked into the bar."

"That's not what I meant," he huffed.

Del was surprised when she reached out a hand to lay on his shoulder. "I know it's not. I'm teasing. Can we get to the good stuff now?" she questioned.

"I thought you didn't want me to get physical," he quipped back.

"Depends on the story you tell. Look at it like singing for your supper," she taunted. "If you do a good job of making me feel sorry for you, I might be swayed in your direction."

There twitched his cock again, responding to her slightest encouragement. He covered it with a hand and held it down. "I'll get back to my story, and I'll try to make it juicy."

"Oh, good," she settled deeper into the mattress. "I've been bored."

Del ignored that and cleared his throat to start again. "So my parents, who aspired to be missionaries and didn't like their only son running with a gang, found a program for me that—starting with middle school—would bus me out to the suburbs to an affluent community. Since my grades were good, I qualified, and beginning in sixth grade, I was shipped off before the crack of dawn every day to the south shore of Boston."

She nodded before interjecting, "I've heard of that program. Metco, right?"

"Yup. Metropolitan Council for Educational Opportunities," he rattled off. He'd been asked enough times that he knew it by heart. "The longest running voluntary school desegregation program in the country."

Another nod. "So you hated it," she stated.

Del barked a laugh. "No. I actually loved it," he said. "The school was clean, the classes were challenging, and I discovered soccer."

"I remember," Bri mused. "You told me you became an all-star in high school."

Del was pleased she'd held onto that piece of information. "That's right. Our team made it to states my senior year."

"So what *aren't* you telling me?" she asked, astutely.

Del blew out a long breath before answering. "As soon as I was deemed 'safe' by my parents—which was the beginning of my freshman year—they left me in the care of my grandfather, and traveled to South America to pursue their dream."

"A dream that didn't include you," Bri sent out, softly.

"No. It didn't. But they figured I'd be okay with Gramps, and I was. Really." He said it as much to convince himself as her. He'd always understood that his parents believed they had a higher calling. With twenty-twenty hindsight, he just wished they had waited until he was through with school to fulfill their aspirations.

"They called whenever they could, and they wrote a lot," he assured her. "In the meantime, I built an impressive GPA and played soccer."

"What did your grandfather do?" Bri asked curiously. "He didn't resent having a grandson foisted upon him?"

"Hell, no," Del let a smile break free. "Gramps and I were two kindred spirits. He owned and ran a diner on the outskirts of the old neighborhood, and when I wasn't busy being a suburbanite, I helped out all I could. He loved the attention and the accolades of having a successful sports figure in the family, even if it was at the high school level." Del remembered every one of the newspaper articles his grandfather carefully cut out and framed, hanging them on the walls of the diner for everyone to see. His heart ached just a bit, remembering that love, and missing Gramps.

"So what happened next?" Bri sounded impatient.

"Who's telling this story?" Del teased.

"You are," she pinched his shoulder. "But you're damned slow at it. I'm still trying to figure out where the stubborn, bull-headed Del comes into it, and what that has to do with trusting me."

Ignoring her taunts, he pursed his lips. The next part of his life, he'd rather forget. "In the middle of my junior year, calls and letters from my parents stopped. We waited. We contacted various groups and embassies. But no matter how hard we pushed, no formal investigation was ever made. They simply vanished."

"Oh my God, Del. That's terrible." Bri moved closer and he could feel the warmth of her leg against his thigh. But he couldn't allow himself to get distracted. Now that he'd started his story, he needed to get it all out before he lost his momentum.

"You'd think that was the worst of it." He swallowed the lump in his throat. "But it wasn't." Her hand came out to rest on his arm this time. "Despite being blindsided by my parents going missing, I kept my grades up and continued to thrive with the love of my grandfather. I applied to colleges in my senior year, and got a full ride to Stanford."

Bri gasped. "Wow, Del. That's not bad, that's amazing." He waited out her significant pause. "But wait. I don't remember you telling me that you played soccer there. I would have remembered." She lowered her voice, clearly bracing for the hard news. Del didn't disappoint.

"Two weeks before my graduation, Gramps suffered a stroke. A severe one," he added, and shrugged. "What could I do?" he asked rhetorically. "The diner he'd owned had kept us going for all those years, but hadn't made us rich. There weren't any savings. If I'd gone off to school, he would have lost everything and been put into a state home. I couldn't let that happen."

"So you didn't go to school," Bri supplied, her voice filled with understanding.

"Not for a while," Del told her. "I took over at the diner, and made just enough money to have a woman come in and care for Gramps during the day. We only served breakfast and lunch after his stroke. But I got the hang of it, and managed to make time for myself a few nights a week to attend the community college a couple of T stops away. I took as many courses as I could, hoping that there would come a day when Gramps would get better, and I could go back full time."

"But that didn't happen." Again, Bri was ahead of him.

"It didn't," he confirmed. "A couple of years after the initial stroke, Gramps had another. That one proved fatal."

Now Bri sat up in bed, her eyes shining down at him in the ambient light of the moon. "What did you do?" she asked.

"I sold the diner, banked the money, and joined the military."

"Just like that," she intoned with wonder in her voice. "So young, but so grown up. Can I ask why the military?"

143

Del had believed the telling would be easy, but he'd underestimated how it would feel to have her compassionate gaze fixed on him. Tears welled in his eyes. He struggled to continue. "Without Gramps, I could finally do something I'd contemplated for a long time; the only thing other than school that had been my dream. By joining the military, I could look for my parents. I found out about a branch of the army, a special operations unit that performed search and rescue. I put all of my energy into proving myself good enough to join a team located in South America."

Bri got it, just as Del assumed she would. "And you spent every free minute looking for your parents."

Del grunted. "That was the reasoning. But my inquiries never panned out. I had three deployments, and couldn't uncover anything about them, even though I spent an enormous amount of my down-time investigating."

"I'm so sorry, Del." Bri brought her knees up to her chest and he caught the flash of bare skin. She was wearing some kind of shirt, but no pants. His immediate need, however, seemed to have disappeared with his story.

"So how did you become involved with Reynold?" she asked, her voice curious again.

He chuckled at her quick change of topic. It was so like her to try and make him feel better. "While in the jungle, I discovered a compound secreted by caterpillars that, with the right kind of night-vision goggles, could be seen much farther and more dramatically than body-heat with regular infrared."

"Huh?" The noise was cute coming out of her normally smart mouth, and Del could just make out her nose wrinkling up in consternation.

He grunted a laugh. "Think bright, fairy rainbows as opposed to fuzzy green light, and you'll get the picture."

"Okay. Got it," she hummed in amusement. "So how is it used?"

"Before a recon, a task force drinks it and becomes highly visible in the dense jungle to his partners wearing my goggles. No more fumbling around wondering who's a good guy and who's a bad guy. Rainbow good. Green, suspect. And if one of the good guys gets taken by an insurgents, he's much easier to track."

"That's amazing, Del." He could almost see her smile. "So even without Stanford, you did well for yourself."

"It worked out," he admitted, but not with as much enthusiasm as she probably expected. To Del's mind, it would have been so much nicer to have Gramps or his parents alive to share his success. He glanced over at the silhouette beside him in bed. If he was honest with himself, Bri was the first one he'd ever imagined—outside of his long-gone family—partaking in the joy of his achievements. How screwed up was that?

"So…" Bri seemed hesitant to continue. He wondered what could possibly be on her mind.

"Spit it out, Bri," he commanded curiously.

"So I'm really honored that you shared this with me, but what exactly does it have to do with you trusting me?"

Del laughed. He'd deliberately skipped over a few pertinent facts, and leave it to Bri to call him out on it. "Don't worry. I'll tell you," he chided.

"I'm all ears." She settled back onto the headboard.

"When I was in high school in that rich suburb I mentioned, I fancied myself a star." He knew he wasn't bragging. It was how he was treated by his coaches. "I got told all the time how smart I was, how talented, how good looking," he scoffed. "You can imagine my head swelled, and I always had a girl on my arm."

"Not hard to picture," she said with a wry edge.

"Right," he grinned, liking the censure in her voice. "So I dated a lot. Hung around the town on Friday nights to party with different groups and make my moves. But I never let any girl get close, until…"

"Ah, hah! I knew the problem had to be a woman." Bri sounded smug.

"Yeah, but this wasn't just any girl who captured my heart. This was the captain of the dance team, a valedictorian. She was a stunning brunette with a tight little ass that set my body on fire."

"Down boy," Bri laughed, unaware that she said the same thing to him that he'd said to his own cock, earlier. "You've doubled in age since then. Surely time has warped your sense of how perfect this girl was."

"Maybe," he chuckled. "But I was just about to get to her witchy qualities if you'd give me time." Damned if Bri hadn't done it again; made him amused at something that had always, during a rehashing, been painful.

"Ah. So the paragon of virtue wasn't without flaws."

"Hell, no," Del snorted. "But she led me on for a long time before I found out. And that's why my heart got broken."

"Tell me," Bri demanded. "Then I'll Google her, creep on her, and bitch-slap her for you." She remained silent for about one second before snapping upright. "Wait! You're not going to compare me to *her*, are you? It just occurred to me that we were attempting to tie your mistrust of me to something fucked up in your life. If this chick is it, I might have to bitch-slap *you*." She'd come up on her knees, glaring at him as if itching for a fight.

"Calm down, Rocky," Del teased. "Are you going to let me tell this, or not?"

"Okay. But watch yourself. Pregnancy has left me feeling very vulnerable." She settled back on her heels.

146

Del choked back a snarky reply, barely able to continue, his amusement was so strong. "So everything is going smoothly…"

"Wait. What was her name?" Bri interrupted again.

"Does it matter?" Del asked, entertained at the interruption yet again.

"I want a picture of her in my head, and a name makes her more real."

"That's screwed up on so many different levels, you know," he countered.

"Okay. How about this? Let's make sure I hate the name so I don't inadvertently name my child after her."

That made him shut up. But before he could stop the process, he pictured an adorable teenage girl with a pouty face surrounded by blonde curls, looking scarily like Bri, but with his dark skin and brown eyes.

"Fine." Del finally got his mouth working, forcibly dissipating the disturbing image. "Her name was Regina."

"Regina?" Bri chortled. "Oh no it wasn't. That's the name of the alpha bitch in *Mean Girls*. You made that up."

Del crossed his heart, and knew she could see it in the moon-dappled room. "I swear it's the truth," he promised. "Can I keep going now? This is taking far longer than I imagined."

"Go ahead," she nodded.

"I saw Regina every Friday night for months during the second half of junior year. We were quite the item, but when I asked her to the junior prom, she hedged shyly, not giving me an answer. I thought she was doing it to be cute."

Bri made a scoffing noise, but otherwise kept quiet.

"Up until this point, she hadn't asked me anything about my family, and I hadn't offered. But one night while making out on the grass at a party, I pressed her for a decision on the prom. Out of the blue she demanded to know where I was from."

Tension filled his shoulders, even though as Bri had said, the memory shouldn't affect him this many years later. "I believed we were in love, and that being from the projects wouldn't matter. So I told her everything; about my missing parents, and the diner. I didn't realize until she was sitting up tugging her shirt back into place that she hadn't said a word in response.

"When I asked her what was wrong, she jumped to her feet and told me that her parents would never let her go to the prom with someone like me. I felt like I'd been punched in the gut.

"'A person like me?' I asked, still not getting it. All this time," he continued, "She'd told me my color wasn't an issue. That she was the envy of her friends." He gave a bitter laugh. "I found out pretty quickly that she was envied like the kid who brings a rare and ugly bug to school. Fascinating to have for shock appeal, but nothing anybody would ever want keep."

He kept going to get it all out. "So not only did she reject me for what was my 'screwed up background', but she spread my not so lily-white, inner-city, working class life to the other girls. None of them ever looked at me after that. Not that I would have trusted it if they had."

"Well shit." Bri chewed on her nail. "What about your teammates?" she asked quietly.

"Oh, my teammates were fine. None of them seemed to care about me being poor because we worked together like a well-oiled machine on the field. Their parents even let me in their homes because I helped win trophies they could brag about." His ire petered out. There really was nothing left to say. He'd spilled the worst.

"So you think," Bri breathed out, "that because I came from a rich, suburban background, I'm treating you like a bug to show off?" Her voice raised a slight bit. "That it's a game to me, bringing you into my life, luring you in with the idea that this child could be yours, only to knock you down?"

Del bit back his programmed response to watch as she slowly shook her head back and forth. "That girl really messed with your brain," Bri stated flatly, holding his eyes prisoner with hers. "And the guys did one better, really. If I prove to be like one of your teammates, I'll only want to wave our child around like a trophy...showing off that I got lucky with a guy who made it big."

She leaned down to within a hair's breadth of his face and he smelled the mint of the toothpaste she'd used hours earlier. Somehow it soothed him.

"Damn, Del. You have a screwed up view of humanity. I feel sorry for you, but I get it. So I'll cut you some slack and tell you this just one time. You can believe me or not. That's on you. I have no problem with your color, or where you came from. I don't care if you have parents, or a bank account. I find you amazingly intelligent, incredibly patient, surprisingly humorous, and as gorgeous as sin. I slept with you that night because I knew all that about you after five minutes of sitting at the bar. I hadn't had sex with anybody for four years before that night, and I haven't slept with anybody since." She paused to take a breath. "You can choose to believe me or not, but if you don't, it's your loss."

Chapter Sixteen

Bri tiptoed from the bathroom and stood in the bedroom doorway, looking down at Del stretched out on his back. What an anticlimax. She couldn't believe they'd both fallen asleep last night. Some time after her tirade, Bri had gone from her haunches to ease back down under the covers wondering how Del would respond. But before she could hear any epiphanies? Click. She'd been out like a light. So much for the drama of the moment. According to the soft little snores emanating from Del's mouth now, he probably hadn't lasted much longer.

Sliding back into bed, Bri took the opportunity to lean over and study his face. Although he wasn't shy about posturing and smiling, there was something about his features in repose that had her heart pounding louder in her chest.

His snarky brow lay calmly, resting while it could. And its sleek softness, at least for the moment, exactly matched the other—non-aggressive—brow. They both arched over nicely spaced, perfectly matched eyes, closed now, but Bri had already memorized their melting chocolate brown. Weren't people supposed to have features that were slightly lopsided? As far as she could tell, her bed-mate didn't. Which made him model material. Of that she had no doubt.

His nose was straight and smooth. Probably never broken. But he'd been a soccer player, not a hockey jock.

She moved her gaze sideways, over to the nearly silky cheek closest to her. One scar lay high on a cheekbone, and another ran up into his hairline. They looked thin, and silvery. Funny how she hadn't noticed them before, but the force of his eyes and his smile had obviously drawn her completely away from any imperfections. Not that his scars were that. On the contrary, they added a bit of understated dash to what otherwise might have been a too-pretty face. She'd have to ask him how the marks came to be.

Bri had saved Del's lips for last, but let her eyes devour them now. Pink and lush, they lay slightly open as she listened to air pass through them. She remembered how those plump bows felt on all parts of her: urgent against her mouth, latched hard onto her nipple, or whispering softly against her pleading pussy. A gush of heat spread between her thighs. Why did she torment herself so? Until he could tell her, with sincerity, that he believed everything she said, there would be no repeat performances.

"Are you through staring yet, or do I still have to pretend to be asleep?" His morning voice sounded gravel rough, and set her even more a-tingle.

"You jerk," she smacked him on the chest. "How long have you been awake?"

"Since you got up to use the bathroom. You aren't exactly stealth material," he smirked.

Bri huffed, flopping onto her back. "I wasn't interested in your face, you know. I was plotting a way to subdue your eyebrow," she toughed it out. "I wonder. Would it attack if I came at it with a razor while you slept?"

"I wouldn't risk it if I were you," Del teased back. "The other one might feel compelled to come to the rescue."

Bri giggled. Del was witty. And not at all reticent to make fun of himself. As far as she could tell, mistrust was his one and only flaw, and that reminded her. She needed to know. "So. Did you give any weight to what I said last night?"

His face lost its humor as he turned his head to regard her. "Yeah. I have," he scrutinized her carefully.

Damn. She wished she'd at least checked for eye-sleepies or pulled a comb through her hair before she wilted under his laser gaze.

"Don't keep me in suspense here, boss-man." She'd taken to calling him that, liking how it had sounded off the voices of his crew.

He brought his hand out from under his pillow and eased it up to her chin, gripping it firmly but gently. "I…"

Intent on his answer, Bri wasn't sure, at first, why Del stopped talking. But when he fumbled to the bedside table, she realized that his phone vibrated, sending it dangerously close to the edge. His big hand scooped it up.

"Yeah," he snapped, his face showing displeasure at having been interrupted.

Bri couldn't hear what was happening on the other end of the line, but as she watched Del closely, his expression went from shock, to anger, to closed off hardness all within the space of his several minute conversation.

Somewhere during the one sided dialog, he sat up. Bri followed suit.

"Stay on it," he finally barked into the phone, indicating to Bri with one upraised finger that he was nearly finished. "I want every detail as soon as you get it." His suddenly cautious eyes traveled to her. "Yeah. I'll be ramping things up here to defcon two. Keep in touch." He punched his thumb to disconnect, and drew a hand over his face. "Dammit all to hell," he snarled, mashing his orbital ridges with deep strokes.

"What is it?" Whatever the call had been about, it had clearly superseded their petty trust issues. That was for sure.

"Your boss. Reynold. He died last night." Del moved his hand away from his face, but didn't blink, watching her.

"What?" Her voice came out a mere whisper. As much as she'd detested Reynold, she'd never wished him dead. "How?"

He stared, as if gauging whether or not to disclose all, before speaking. "At first it looked like he died in a flash fire," Del revealed. "The entire suite of offices at US AIM had gone up in flames, and everything in it destroyed."

Bri could only nod for him to go on. She didn't trust her voice, thinking about the destruction.

"When they came across Blithe, sitting at his desk, they assumed he'd succumbed to the smoke before the fire got him."

Bri knew what Del wasn't saying. Reynold's body had burned in the conflagration. She shivered.

"But then they found the melted remains of a gun in his right hand. Now they're assuming he spread an accelerant, and dropped a match before putting a bullet in his head."

Bri's head shook back and forth. Her mouth opened but she was unable to push words out. Words that Del needed to know.

"What is it, Bri?" Del's hand came to her back and rubbed in small, concentric circles.

She tried again. "He…" Bri coughed to clear her throat. "Reynold…he…he was left handed." She dragged in a deep breath.

"Shit," Del removed his hand and quickly punched a number on his phone. "Wiles?" he bit out. "Supposition confirmed. Reynold wasn't a suicide. Bri says he was left handed. Which means it can only be… Yeah. I know. Later." He clicked off again.

"That it can only be my father. Right?" Bri didn't need confirmation. She'd already come to her own conclusion.

"Which means that somehow dear old Dad found out that you went missing, and made good on his threat," Del stated.

"Made good on half his threat," Bri corrected. "The other half is me. Remember?"

"I know. Which is why you heard me tell Wiles that we're stepping up our readiness. Not that I think he'll figure out where you are. But the chances are better now. Especially if, before Reynold died, he was pressured into telling his killers about us, and they traced us to the north. I have every faith that Sarge can stay one step ahead of any computer genius your father might have, but eventually we might be traced."

"So what do we do?" Bri asked, looking around with another shiver. The cabin, which up to this point had seemed so remote and secure, now seemed too far away from civilization.

"We ramp up security with a few goodies I have packed away, and then sit tight until my guys come up with more information. If Sarge can open up small parts of our file on you and lure them in, he might be able to sneak in their cyber-back-door. The more information we have about what they've uncovered, the greater the possibility of making a next move that is secure. We've already covered our tracks and dumped the technology that makes us traceable."

Bri looked guiltily at her phone sitting on her bedside table. Was it possible that Aunt Celia had broken her trust, and told Daddy that she'd run away? She couldn't imagine it, but before this happened, she couldn't imagine her father as a coldblooded killer, either. That her carelessness might have been responsible for Reynold's death, hit her hard, making her normally handleable morning nausea rise. Bri bit her lip to tamp it down. It wasn't her fault, she reminded herself. Reynold and her father had been playing her for a long time, and her dead boss had clearly known what he was getting into.

After calming herself somewhat, one question remained. Should she tell Del that she'd made a phone call? How important was it, at this juncture? If Auntie Cee had told on Bri, the worst had already happened. Reynold was dead, as threatened. And Bri was safe with Del. She decided to keep her mouth shut.

"I'll make us some breakfast." She slid her feet to the floor before Del left the bed. No need to have his nearly naked physical self distracting her before the day even started. She grabbed a pair of jeans off the top of the single dresser on her way out.

Heading into the bathroom once more, Bri peed for a second time, and quickly performed her other morning ablutions. Pulling on her pants, she stepped brusquely into the main room, and stopped dead. Holy hell. Del knelt in a pair of beige boxer-briefs, leaning down over his duffle. His ass was thrust out, his every hard muscle delineated under the sheer fabric, and Bri's mouth watered at the sight.

For his part, Del didn't even seem to notice. "I have some trip wire the guys threw out of the truck, and some micro-video night vision surveillance cameras in my bag," he said, matter-of-factly. "I'll get started setting them up. Just give me a call when you have food on the table."

She stood rooted to the spot, and stared.

"Okay, Brina?"

No answer.

"Okay?"

"Yeah, yeah. Right. Food," she finally managed. Dammit for still being so attracted to Del. And they'd almost made things right before the ill-fated phone call.

"Hey." Del got to his feet and moved to take both of her arms in a steady grip, holding her above her elbows. "I know it's upsetting, Reynold getting killed. But he was a big boy. If he played out of his league, it was his own fault."

Just the reasoning Bri had already used to talk herself down off the ledge. Del didn't need to know that this silence was for him and appreciation of his fine body. She snapped to. "Right. I know that," she acknowledged his attempt at comfort. "I'll go make us some food." She risked a glance downward at the front of his briefs. "You should get dressed." *Damn.* Even soft, his package was impressive.

Del chuckled and strode for the bedroom, subtly adjusting himself. Maybe her quick peek had him interested. "You're right. I'll get my ass chewed by mosquitoes if I go outside like this."

Or get it chewed by me, if you stay inside, Bri moaned to herself. How amazingly inappropriate after the information they'd received this morning. But Bri couldn't feel remorseful. Nothing with Del had followed a predictable pattern. Not their first encounter, nor anything that had happened since. Maybe when this whole thing was over, they'd have a shot at normal. Whatever that was.

The day moved quickly, contrary to what she'd anticipated. Del mounted four mini cameras, one on each face of the cabin, pointed off into the woods. They fed to his cell phone, and as he showed her, when a wind gust came rustling through the trees, the movement triggered an alarm which alerted him to pull up a video on his screen. Pretty genius.

After they'd eaten, he had her help him with the next project, which was stringing a small, thin trip wire around the perimeter of the property, approximately fifty yards from the house. He'd explained that he hadn't felt the need to use it before now, because it could be triggered by any one of an unknown quantity of animals. Which would have presented more of a pain in the ass than not, until their danger level had increased. Bri understood. But when she questioned the distance he was putting it away from the cabin, he assured her that one hundred and fifty feet would give him just the right amount of time to respond to any intruder. Bri sure hoped so.

Del had one more call from Wiley. This one to let him know that in a time period consistent with Reynold doing it himself, all the computer records of US AIM had been destroyed with the detonation of a prearranged kill package. Reynold must have had an inkling that he was in trouble, and did away with any evidence of his company's or his wrong-doing before he'd been immolated. Self serving or protective of others, they'd never know.

Bri and Del ate lunch, continuing with their project after they'd finished. Bri pretended not to notice when Del stripped off his shirt in the mid-afternoon sun. Sweat trickled down his back, between well-defined lats, and she longed to trace the path of his perspiration with her finger. It was a testament to her own fortitude that she resisted the temptation.

Finally, as the sun descended, their precautions were firmly in place. If anyone breached their boundaries, they would know. Unfortunately, it would also be a night of many false alarms, or so Del warned. They'd probably get little or no sleep.

After their evening meal, and just as Bri got up for the deck of cards, Del deviated from their normal game of rummy. Going to his duffel, he pulled out what looked to be a couple of pieces of solid black clothing, and a small vial. His demeanor changed from one of mild-mannered roomie—something he'd maintained all day—to intense soldier, which made a thrill ripple down her spine. Did he know how hot his take-charge attitude made her? He motioned Bri forward and put the pile of clothing in one of her hands, and the vial in the other.

"What's this?" she asked, more curious than suspicious.

"This," he said, pointing to the black material, "is what you'll be wearing from now on at night," he told her. "And this," he indicated the bottle, "is a single serving of my magic elixir."

"Which you want me to drink?" Her nose wrinkled in distaste at the idea of drinking bug juice.

"Not until you think you might be in danger," he instructed. "There are a few things I haven't told yet. First of all, the chemical compound that emits the colorful array only lasts for forty-eight hours before being flushed from the system through natural secretions. Secondly, this particular mixture is a newer version we're working on. It contains a water-soluble tracking compound as well, which unfortunately will be gone from your system even faster. About ten hours faster. We're working on longevity for both, but right now this is what we've got."

Bri nodded. "Got it. Rainbow forty-eight hours, tracking thirty eight. Is it safe for my baby?"

She could have sworn that Del blanched. "It's undergone all of the necessary safety testing, and yes, you're good." He changed the subject quickly. "If anyone tries to locate you in the woods using infrared night vision goggles, they'd normally get the regular green heat signature or low level radiation off of your body. But wearing those clothes, they'll get nothing. The material absorbs heat, electromagnetic radiation, and perspiration so as to render you invisible to any abductor."

When she looked panicked he added, "Hypothetical abductor, of course. What we really hope, if it comes down to it, is that Reynold didn't sell any of our technology to your father yet, and that the destruction of his records kept any of it from getting into the wrong hands."

Bri totally got that. "What are the odds my father already has it?" She needed to know.

"Fifty-fifty," Del admitted. "Reynold didn't have access to manufacturing yet, so if he sold something, it was in concept only and chances of the recipient developing it so soon are slim. Also, I like to think Reynold was stringing a number of companies along, holding out for the best offer."

"Like a deal that might include marrying the daughter of the owner of the company he got into bed with?" Bri answered.

"Yeah," Del concurred with a frown. "Like that." He took her shoulder in one hand and stared earnestly into her face. "But since your relationship with Reynold was never cemented, I have every hope that they didn't consummate a deal yet."

"Funny word to use," Bri snorted sarcastically. "Consummate."

"I know. Right?" Del gave her a good-natured jostle. "Little did he know that you'd tip the scale by doing that with someone else first." He gave her a shove. "Now go put your new clothes on."

Bri walked to the bathroom, closing the door behind her and unsnapped her jeans.

Wait. *What?* Did Del just... Damn the man for his sneakiness. Without batting an eyelash, he just admitted that he believed her. That she'd had carnal relations with him before she'd been sold off to her boss. She leaned against the wall and smiled. *Sexy, smart-mouthed bastard.*

Chapter Seventeen

"Now what are you doing?" Bri exited the bathroom in her tight-fitting, new black clothing, and Del nearly had to pick his tongue up off the floor where he knelt, and put in back in his mouth. She looked like Grace Kelly in that 1950's, cat-burglar movie.

Holy shit. He'd had fantasies about that woman in his younger days, watching old flicks with Gramps. Bri was his young man's fancy come true. He wanted to throw her down and strip her clothes off with his teeth. *Shit. Engage brain.* What had she asked?

Del pried up the floorboard he'd worked on the day before when Bri had been out for her customary walk. "I'm stashing my duffel, just in case we have visitors."

Bri frowned.

"Not that we are," he placated. "I'm only playing it safe. This bag is full of my glowie compound, and several pairs of high-def photomultipliers, so it needs to be safe."

"Okay," she allowed, but she certainly didn't look comforted. Del moved the large plank off to the side and indicated the space below.

"Don't worry," he grinned. "All my guns are where I can get a hold of them."

She rolled her eyes. "Such a relief." Coming over to where he knelt, she ran a finger slowly across the back of his

160

neck. "And a total turn on. There's nothing quite like a man with a lot of big guns."

What the fuck was she doing? Del's nipples tightened and his cock sprang to life. Bri really knew how to derail him. What surprised him was that she gave off an "I want to play" signal before referencing the comment he'd made before she'd gone into the bathroom. He knew she hadn't missed it. She was too smart for that. No. If he figured her correctly, she'd probably stored it away to torment him once all danger had passed. And for now, it looked like she had put it aside. *Thank Christ.*

Her mouth came down to rest a hair's breadth from his ear. "And I know how big your favorite weapon is," she tormented.

Del nearly groaned. Why hadn't he shelved his distrust, and had the benefit of her teasing days ago? Hell, she knew just how to turn him on. As a matter of fact, right now it would be a piece of cake to use the hardest part of his anatomy to hammer that board back into place. He drew in a breath through distended nostrils.

"Didn't have you pegged for a gun-bunny, Bri." Del hissed, but then regretfully pulled away. "However, as much as I'd like to play, it's time for us to turn in. Separately. I'll be keeping watch from the couch tonight."

Did he catch a pout? *Score.*

"And we need to talk about precautions if things go FUBAR," he told her.

"I'm already pregnant, Del," she smirked. "So I don't think…"

"Not what I meant," Del groused, trying like hell to tamp down his rampaging libido. He finished up with the floor and pulled the area rug back into place.

"I know." She rolled her eyes and her cuteness factor shot up exponentially. "So do tell, Boss-man." She stood straight and saluted smartly, making her all the more adorable. "Orders, sir?" she snapped.

Del knew what he'd like to command Bri to do. He'd like to order her to bend over the hateful couch, transforming it into one of his favorite places, but once again timing was a bitch. He got up off the floor and sighed. "*You* are going to head in for some shut-eye, and I'm going to monitor our surveillance. But listen carefully. At the first sign of trouble, if we have any, I will wake you up. Depending on what I see on camera, you'll head out the most opportune window. Keep alert once you're in the woods, and don't stumble on our trip-wire. Head straight to your BFRs, where you'll stay until I come and get you. Got it?" He'd made sure—during daylight—that she'd been very aware of the wire's positioning.

"BFRs?" Bri squinched up her mouth. "I don't know that one."

"Big fucking rocks…grunt." Del kept the military slang coming. He could tell Bri liked it, and it took her mind off the potential seriousness of the situation.

She snickered. "Hah. Leave it to the military to have a name for rocks."

"Don't make fun. What else is there for a soldier to do on a boring-ass deployment? My bunch make up acronyms to see who can conjure one that sticks."

"Sounds like fun," she drawled. "Man who's GGLL."

Del snorted. "And I'm supposed to know what that means?" he asked.

"Nope," she said, turning with military precision and marching toward the bedroom door. "I just made it up…man who's gonna get lucky later."

Damn. She always managed to have the last word. Del chuckled, watching her disappear, then adjusted himself, trying to rearrange his cramped cock. After that impossible task, he whispered around the cabin and turned off the lights.

Settled in the dark, he tried to ignore Bri's lemon scent lingering in the air, and played mental games with himself, one's that he'd developed over the years to stay awake. It was going to be a long night.

Sometime after midnight, Del had just—virtually in his brain—re-assembled his assault rifle for the hundredth time, when he became alert on the couch. Something outside didn't seem right. The hairs on the back of his neck stood on end. But why? He palmed his phone and perused the screen looking for problems. Nothing showed up, but he refused to take the word of technology over his own instincts.

Carefully he rose to his feet, and picking up his standard issue infrared goggles, Del eased to the door. He put them on and peered out, keeping low and inside the screen. The earplug to his phone went into his ear. If someone was out there, he'd be ready.

The first "ping" came in, nearly shocking him with its loud insistence. He pushed the goggles to the top of his head and looked quickly at his phone. The west pointing camera showed one tango approaching stealthily, having stepped over the trip wire. *Dammit.* He must have seen it, which meant it had been rendered useless.

Del skittered back across the floor, stood up, and flew to the bedroom. He shook Bri's foot. "Up. Now,' he whispered.

Thank God she gave no argument and was out of bed faster than he could blink. There was no way she'd been asleep.

He checked the east side of the house on his phone. It looked clear.

"Out the window and head that way," he ordered, pulling up the sash and pointing. He'd done away with the screens, earlier. "And no noise." He could see her eyes, big, wide and scared, but she didn't speak as she pulled on shoes, only nodded. Del couldn't help himself. He dropped a firm kiss onto her parted lips. "Wait for me," he told her "I'll be there."

She bobbed her head again, and without hesitation, slunk left foot first out the window. He lowered his goggles to his eyes. *Good.* She melted into the blackness. He couldn't see her.

Grabbing his Beretta M9 from the small of his back, he crept out into the main room. His phone "pinged" one more time, and he could see another tango moving in from the south. His loaded H&K sat on the sofa and he snatched up the second weapon before hunkering down behind the couch. It took only five seconds to send a signal to his team. The cabin was under siege.

His heart pounded loudly, and he used every calming technique he knew to keep his cool. Usually he remained unshaken in these types of situations. But the presence of Bri, and the fact that her safety—and the safety of her baby—depended on him, made him oddly unsteady. He swore at himself. It would do neither him nor Bri any good if he lost his head and got taken out. Shaking off his uncertainty, Del quickly found his quiet center. He was ready.

The screen door opened slowly, and footsteps entered. One pace. Two. Del held his breath and counted to ten. His target stopped moving. A second set of footsteps joined the first, pausing at the screen. Both tangoes to whom he'd been alerted were now inside. Goggles in place, Del popped up from in back of the sofa, locked on one target, fired, and got a quick second shot off at mark two. Both went down before they knew what hit them.

Dropping his M9 and holding his other weapon with a two handed grip, Del leaped over the sofa, barrel trained on the downed enemies. He kicked one and then the other before letting out his held breath. They weren't going anywhere.

A noise from behind startled him. Del ducked and spun, but not before a stinging pain bit his left arm. *Fuck.* He'd been grazed. He got off a round of fire at his assailant who grunted, then dropped and rolled to his right, coming up to crouch behind the small wooden desk in the corner. Not much cover, but it sounded like he'd been lucky and scored a hit. He peered up. *Shit...* A figure came flying over the inadequate piece of furniture, tackled him bodily and flattened him to the ground, face down. In the struggle, his gun spun from his grip, sliding across the floor, while his back became the recipient of a hard, unrelenting knee. The air temporarily whooshed from Del's lungs.

"Fucking bastard," cursed a low voice above him as Del gasped for breath. The words were accented, but he couldn't place the dialect.

Del's lungs expanded while above him his attacker faltered; wavered as if about to fall over. Del, regaining oxygen, wrenched to unseat the invader, but damn, the guy weighed a ton. Wetness dripped onto Del's cheek, and he immediately knew why the guy swayed. The coppery tang on Del's face was blood. *Good.* His bullet hadn't been wasted. "Give it up, asshole. You're as good as dead," Del hissed, renewing his fight.

The man atop him growled, a hand digging into the back of Del's neck. "I may be dying. But I take you with me," he grunted. Del's blood chilled as the press of a cold barrel centered on the back of his head. *Oh hell, no.* This was not how he was supposed to die. Not before exploring things with Bri and witnessing the birth of his child.

Del bucked his hips, but heard the report. Pain ricocheted through his head. Blinding light flashed across his corneas. It was all he knew before darkness swallowed him whole.

****

Bri counted the gunshots. Five. She'd held back the screams that built after each one. What did they mean? She shivered where she crouched, hunkered down between the two large boulders, and tried not to worry. Del was bad-ass. He was good at what he did. All she had to do was stay calm, and he'd come for her. She waited. And waited.

Minutes passed. Long minutes. And no sound came from the direction of the cabin. No voice called an all-clear, and no footsteps crunched through the undergrowth. Bri bit her lip. She curled her nails into her palms. What should she do? She had to find out if Del was okay. Her heart seized that something might have happened to him.

Her knees cramped as she slowly unfolded to an upright position. She held her body snug against one rock and strained to hear anything in the night air. No sound reached her ears. *Dammit.* She needed to see what was going on. Carefully she picked her way amongst the smaller rocks, to the ones that led to the top of the biggest boulder. Perhaps from a perch up high she might be able to discern something.

Her footsteps were cautious, her demeanor wary, taking all Del's warnings to heart. If something had happened to him, she needed to stay alert and not fall. Damning herself for leaving her cell phone on the bedside table in the cabin, she wondered if she saw something bad, could she skirt the cabin and hike the several miles into town for help? *Hell, yes.* If Del needed aid, she would do anything.

Bri made it to the high perch without incident, and remembering Del telling her she was mostly invisible, she stood tall, hopefully impervious to anyone watching. She let her eyes adjust to the light levels from her new position, and saw the vague outline of the cabin several hundred feet away. Bri focused. She flicked her gaze to the left and right of the building, but could detect no movement. She held her breath for a very long time. *No.* She was sure that nothing down there moved. So what next? Bri bit her lip. She knew Del had told her not to move, but all she could think about was, what if he'd been hurt?

Half an hour had passed since the last shot, and to Bri's racing mind that meant one thing. Del was unable to come for her. He'd either been taken prisoner, or lay, injured. She refused to think of a worse scenario.

Surely the smart thing would be to avoid the cabin altogether, head to town and get help rather than put herself in possible danger, but in her heart she knew she just couldn't do that. She needed to see about Del.

Gingerly she made her way down from the boulder, and when her feet finally came to rest on the forest floor, she placed one in front of the other, as noiselessly as possible. Del had teased her about not being stealth material. Well not this time.

Remembering the trip wire at the last minute, Bri recognized the two behemoth trees that marked its passage, and delicately lifted each foot up and over. Once on the other side, she crouched down and waited again, listening again for any sounds.

Nothing.

Now came the tough part. She would have to approach the cabin. Should it be from the front or the back? Left side or right? Bri tried to think like an intruder, and surmised that the front porch would be her best point of entry. Anybody possibly watching or waiting for her would assume she'd sneak in through a back way. At least she hoped that was the case.

Bri stayed cautious. She moved from tree to tree, stopping each time she changed position, listening and pausing until she had a clear view of the front porch. She had to stuff her fist in her mouth to stifle a cry. A pair of legs lay across the threshold, a body half in and half out of the cabin. *Oh, Lord.* Could it be Del? Bri didn't want to move forward to find out, but she needed to know.

She remembered, even in her anguish, that there was one last thing she needed to do before she made this final move. In the event that she walked into a trap, she would need every advantage she could get. Bri wiggled the vial of bug-juice out of her pocket, took the stopper from the top, and chugged it in one huge gulp. It threatened to come up, causing her gorge to spasm, but she forced it back down until she was able to swallow without fear of it making a reappearance. She was going to have to talk to Del about the flavor, she gave a worried hiccup. It was hideous.

Lightly, she ran from the tree-line to the steps, and keeping her breathing shallow and noiseless, dropped to all fours, inching up the stairs, slowly, on her knees. When she reached the pair of unmoving feet, she gave a silent sigh of relief. Those were not Del's boots. His military style footwear had seen a lot of action, scuffed and worn. These were practically new. The deep treads that lay a few inches in front of her face, looked like they'd recently come out of a box. *Okay. Breathe, Bri.* One bad-guy down. But how many were there? Dare she look farther?

Remaining low, she crept forward, unable to skirt the body in the doorway on her hands and knees, so she resorted to a finger and foot crab-walk, giving a grimace of distaste as her digits brushed the dead-man's body. *Don't think about it,* she scolded herself. *Think about Del.*

168

She encountered a second still form, mere inches from the first. This one was thick through the torso. Again, not Del.

Inaudibly, Bri gave more thanks, and forced herself to become fully immobile again, listening for anything that would caution she wasn't alone. But the floor didn't creak, nor did breathing breach the quiet. Bri advanced again.

This time when she came across a boot, her heart nearly stopped. It looked more like Del's. She reached out a hand to encounter a jean's clad leg, and bit back a sob. It had to be him. The other pair of men she'd come across were in some kind of camo. She skimmed up Del's body, running her hand over the muscles of his back until she reached his head.

Now her sound of distress couldn't be held back. Dark wetness pooled on the floor around his upper torso, and for a moment, she flashed back to when she was twelve, and had seen the same telltale sign of death around the body of her mother. She shook it off. This wasn't her mother, dammit. This was Del. And his body was still warm under her hands.

"Del." she whispered, placing her hands on his shoulders to jiggle him gently. "Del. Wake up," she urged with a touch of hysteria in her voice. He couldn't be dead. He just couldn't be. She needed to call for help.

Bri raised her head and rocked back on her heels, trying to spot Del's phone, but before she could reach for it, harsh hands grabbed her from behind.

"No!" she screamed, immediately digging into the restraining flesh with her sharp nails.

"Bitch," she heard, and received a swift cuff to the head which sent her reeling.

Bri was pulled upright, and a cloth came down over her eyes, tugged tightly as someone knotted it roughly behind her head. Before she could react, another blow came out of nowhere, striking her hard on her cheek to send her sprawling downward, landing on Del's prone body. She cried out, stunned. Who was this, and what would they do to her?

"Don't kill her." An accented voice came from her right.

"It would be easier if we did," answered the one who was responsible for the blow.

"Our orders are to film before we make her disappear," the first one countered.

"What if we don't? What if we say she had accident," growled the second.

"You want to take chance? Go ahead." The owner of the first voice clearly walked away. Bri held her breath. Would she be killed, or kidnapped. Although neither scenario was good, the second could work in her favor. It she was given time, perhaps she could find a way to escape.

"We'll take her." The aggressive one didn't sound happy, but at least she'd be alive for a while longer. If only she knew Del's condition, but she dared not speak. Who knew what kind of horrible things these thugs could mete out? Better to bide her time.

A sharp jab hit her in the side of the neck.

"Sleep well, bitch." Laughter followed her down into a spiraling dizziness as she succumbed to whatever drug they'd given her.

Chapter Eighteen

Del didn't want to open his eyes. His head had clearly been blown apart and pasted back together again. But voices tugged at his consciousness, pulling him from the abyss. Good voices or bad? He lay still.

"Do you have to tromp around through the evidence?" A voice he recognized as Wiley's groused. "We're trying to put together a crime scene, here."

"Sorry, sir," a not-so-contrite male answered crisply. "We're trying to secure your friend."

Del moaned, attempting to get words from his mouth, but his tongue had grown too fuzzy and huge to move.

"He's got a hard head," Wiles squawked. "He'll be fine. And pissed off as hell if you compromise any evidence."

Even in his woozy state, he could hear the underlying worry in Wiley's voice. What had happened? So he wasn't just knocked out? Del struggled to remember. There'd been a guy on his back. A guy whom he'd shot. Then the cold press of a gun to the back of his head. *Fuck. He'd* been shot.

"How bad is it, Wiles?" Del managed to get the words out, though his physiology was uncooperative.

"Bullet grazed your head." A comforting hand landed on the middle of his back. "Lots of blood," he added. "Although some of it isn't yours. You must have nailed the bastard before he got to you. It looks like he was a goner even as he tried to do you in."

Wait. "Bri?" Del asked, his body filling with panic as he recalled what had happened.

"Not here," Wiley answered, adding a gruff, "Sorry."

Del struggled to sit, but someone held him down.

"You're not going anywhere until we take you out on a stretcher," a snippy male voice told him.

"Who…"

"Paramedic," Wiley answered. "We called them as soon as we got here."

"As soon as you got here… How much time did I lose?" Del was feeling stronger by the moment, and if the paramedic thought he was going to stay down, he had another thing coming.

"Four hours, give or take. We've been here for an hour, and made it in a record three from Boston. You scared the shit out of us, Del. When we walked in, we figured you were dead."

"Not dead," Del said, shoving the arm of the paramedic aside to struggle into a sitting position. His head reeled, and likely it would split open. He stifled a moan. That wouldn't get him anywhere. "How do you know Bri's not in hiding? That's what I told her to do." Screw his head. He had things to do that were more important.

"Her, uh, handprints were in your blood on the floor," Wiley coughed, clearly unhappy having to give Del that answer. "And there was some dragging going on."

Del worked at regaining his equilibrium. "Clean this up, will you?" he barked at the paramedic, pointing to his head. The man gave a "tsk-ing" noise, but picked gauze out of a kit and dabbed at Del's head while Del ignored the pandemonium around him and looked at the floor. Sure enough, there were small, bloody handprints near where he'd been laying, and then smears of blood leading away. He wanted to roar his frustration. Someone had dragged Bri off.

Taken her away. But why had she come into the cabin when he'd told her explicitly to stay put? *Fuck.* He'd throttle the woman next time he saw her. Del's heart skipped. He hoped with everything in him that he'd get the chance to see her again.

He puzzled over the whole scenario as a technician took blood samples off the floor and officers zipped bodies into bags before carting them off. Maygan's cousin, Mason, looked to be presiding over the dead guys. At least the officer knew the back story to this, so perhaps Del wouldn't be dragged into custody as authorities tried to clear things up. He looked around again. Sarge and Prez were nowhere to be seen.

"Where are the guys?" Del asked Wiley.

Wiles leaned down. "Sarge is doing a computer search for Bri's tracker that we assume you told her to drink. He doesn't want to share any intel with the locals, so Prez is standing guard in case anyone tried to bother him," he whispered for Del's ears only. "Thing is, with a four hour head start, Sarge says Bri's signal is probably out of range. So we need to be on the move. Fast."

Del grunted. Four hours was not good. "Anything else?"

"Well, as far as we can figure—since Reynold is dead—this snatch and grab must have been orchestrated by Bri's dear old dad, whose home base is New York City. The faster we can get on the road heading in that direction, the sooner we hope to pick up her marker."

"Got it," Del said, batting the paramedic's hand away and getting to his knees. "Help me up, Wiles."

Wiley got a good hold under Del's armpit and hauled him to his feet.

"Don't let go," he muttered, reeling due to his new altitude. The room spun and several sharp nails drove into his brain. But that wasn't going to stop him. Fuck, no. He needed to find Bri.

"Where do you think you're going?" A hard voice cut through his momentary fog.

Shit. Just what he needed. Mason.

"Gotta go, Mason." Del forced his eyes to focus on the officer. "You know they have Bri, and we have to find her."

"I get that, Del. And I'm on board. But we have a problem here." Mason drew a hand over his face in frustration. "Three bodies," he griped, "and the Fed's are coming in. They're not going to like it if I let you go."

"Are you afraid of them, Mason?" Del figured a direct challenge at the big down-Mainer would raise his dander.

"Hell, no," Mason growled, exactly as Del surmised. "I'm more afraid of my cousin, Mayg. If I don't let you guys leave to find Bri, she's going to have my head. It's just that the Fed's are going to be out of their minds when you're not here to question."

"Tell them I'll be happy to meet them in my Boston office after I've retrieved my client." Del dug in his pocket and gave Mason a card. "Songen Associates. Search and Rescue is what we do, and right now, finding Bri means a lot more to me than kissing some agent's ass." He looked Mason right in the eye, and let his emotions show. Not something he'd normally do, but valuable minutes ticked away, and he didn't want to waste a single one.

"Like that, is it?" Mason said. "Well get going," he added gruffly. "I'll figure something out."

"Thanks, man. I owe you." Del took a step, and swayed, but Wiley kept a firm hold.

Mason snorted. "Big time, my friend. If I'm fired over this, you're the first guy I'm coming to, looking for a job."

Del stuck out a hand and grasped Mason's proffered one. "And you'll have it. My word on that," Del promised.

He took two more steps, but before he could leave the room, the feisty paramedic got up into Del's face. "Here." He held up a package of gauze. "Direct pressure. Lot's of it. Since I cleaned the area, your wound started bleeding again."

"Stitches?" Del grunted.

"Nope. Superficial," the man answered. "You got lucky."

"Not feeling that way," Del declared. "Not until I get my woman back."

The paramedic sighed, but Wiley faltered next to him. Del knew he was going to get some shit for making his declaration, but at this point he just couldn't have held his words back.

"Now get me out to the car before I land on my face," Del growled. "And I know what you want to ask, but fuck it. We have hours ahead of us for you to grill me on my feelings."

Del got a snort from his pal, and if Wiley's hands hadn't been busy supporting him and opening the screen door, Del figured he might have been the recipient of a double bird. And he probably deserved it. *Feelings. Shit.*

Now was not the time to let emotions get in the way of their job. If he turned soft on the guys, their chances of rescuing Bri decreased exponentially. Not that his group couldn't function without him. They could. But he was the one who generally came up with the plan, and turning mushy wouldn't get the job done.

Still, Del let his insides churn for a moment. Bri had become important to him during their time alone in the cabin. And if he were honest, his attitude was more than a cave-man, "mine", taking charge. She'd wormed her way into his head and into his heart. He didn't want to think how life would suddenly lose its color if something happened to her.

And then there was the baby. Over the past few days, Del had come to the complete understanding that the child Bri carried was his. He'd been an asshole not to admit it, but really? It had scared the crap out of him. Now, all he could think of was rescuing Bri and his unborn child from the hands of a madman.

Sarge and Prez were already in the SUV by the time Wiley led Del to the back door of the vehicle. Nothing like walking old-man-speed, when time was of the essence. He eased up into the seat, clicked his belt on and snapped, "Drive."

Ignoring Del's bitter mood, Sarge opened his laptop as Prez backed around the emergency vehicles and spun down the dirt road. Del gritted his teeth. He would not complain of the divots in the road and the ruckus they caused in his head.

"So I'm not getting anything on Brina, yet," Sarge informed him. "But let me bring you up to date on everything else we've got."

"Go," Del urged, swallowing back his bile.

"My search into Reynold's records, a few days ago, showed him dealing with an import/export company running out of Dubai, with lots of big money going from there into an offshore account in Reynold's name. And remember I told you, I had just been starting to look into US AIM's inventory records for discrepancies when everything went white."

"Explain again what that means," Del queried.

"It means that every company record on-line, on the cloud, anywhere, was stricken from existence." He chuckled derisively. "And it was almost minute for minute, the exact timing as to when Reynold went up in flames with his office."

"So he destroyed everything. Or someone else did before Reynold died. Every loose end that could tie the two companies together is now gone. You just got lucky and found a connection before they had a chance to do their dirty work."

"Yup. And what I found was that Bri's father, Bennet Capadella, is the CEO of Wasem Trade Group. The very same company that paid Reynold untold millions."

"And Wasem Trade Group?" Del asked. "What have you found on them?"

"Nothing," huffed Sarge. "Whoever they've got working for them, they're as good as me."

It wasn't bragging. Del knew Sarge's capabilities. And if The Wasem Group had someone like Sarge hiding their information, they were taking no chances of anything being found.

Del's head hurt. "So how long before you can have dirt on them?" Just because the company's guys were good, didn't mean Sarge would give up.

"I'm not sure," Sarge groused. "Bri is our priority right now. Every few minutes I'll be trying her signal, but in-between I'll be fishing for something on Wasem or Bri's father."

"Good," Del commended, sinking back against the seat now that they'd left the pitted road and his head was no longer threatening to detonate. He closed his eyes, tired beyond anything he could ever remember. "Wake me up if anything comes in. I'm going to get a little shut-eye."

"Oh no you're not." Wiley poked him. "First, you have a possible concussion, so sleeping is out. Second, you're going to admit to us that Brina is more to you than just another job. We've been taking bets." Wiley smirked. "Although with you striking out on your first encounter, she might be thinking you're not a very good risk."

"I didn't strike out," Del growled.

"What?" Prez's eyes left the road for a minute and met his in the rearview mirror. "You told us you passed out. A big zero you called it."

"Well, apparently I didn't." Del didn't want to get into it, but his guys would be risking their lives to rescue Bri, so they needed to know all that was at stake. "She, uh, reminded me of a particular thing I do when I'm with a woman, so I knew we'd had sex." Del clamped his jaw shut. That piece of information wasn't going to be shared.

"Oh. You mean the three before me thing?" Prez countered.

Del's head snapped up. *Ouch.* "You know about that?" He looked at Wiley, then Sarge. They both had shit eating grins on their faces.

"Well, yeah," Prez gave a "phhttt" sound. "There was that time in Rio…"

"No. It was Cartagena," Wiley interrupted.

"Nope. I'm sure it was in Rio when he had the room next to mine."

"That might be where you heard it, but I got an earful when we shared a suite in Cartagena and our friend brought back company after a little too much to drink."

There was a distinct snort from Sarge. "Try sharing a tent next to his in the Selvas Basin when he's entertaining."

"Alright you guys. Enough." Del groaned. So he hadn't been as discreet as he'd believed. That life was behind him now. He may have sowed a lot of wild oats in the past, but since he'd met Bri, no other woman held his interest for a single minute.

He continued his affirmation of shame. "So Bri assured me that I provided all three preliminaries before we actually got down to the rest."

"Good job, man," Wiley punched him again. And dammit, the man was going to lose fingers if he didn't keep his hands to himself. Every time Wiles jostled him, Del swore he saw stars.

"Yeah, well. Now just back the fuck off." Del didn't want to talk about it. He knew where it would lead.

"Whoa," Wiley came back. "That means you got lucky while holed up in the cabin."

Bingo. Right where Del knew Wiley would go. Now he had to really 'fess up. "Not exactly," he admitted.

"What do you mean, not exactly?" Now it was Prez digging deep.

"I mean, we did some stuff, but not all the stuff," Del grumbled.

"She shut you down?" Wiles asked.

"No. I shut her down," Del divulged. Now they looked at him as if he had three heads.

"Forgive me if I'm not seeing the whole picture here," Sarge pondered from the front seat. "I thought you were attracted to her."

"Attracted, hell," said Wiley. "In the cabin he told the paramedic he needed to get 'his woman' back. Am I right?"

Del knew Wiley hadn't forgotten that one. Sneaky bastard. *Fine*. He'd give it to them straight.

"I pulled back from having sex because after she told me we'd been together before, she hit me with something else."

"She couldn't stand how small your…"

"Can it, Wiles." Del glared. "Brina is pregnant."

Chapter Nineteen

Brina had been awake for a while, but chose to make herself small and inconspicuous in the back of the van where she'd been dropped. Luckily for her, some kind of packing blankets had been piled on the floor. It kept her from getting banged around as the van sped up, slowed down, and took corners.

As far as she could tell there were two men up front. Both heavily accented when they— occasionally—spoke in English. Most of their conversation took place in a language that sounded distinctly middle-eastern, which had Bri worried. A lot of her father's business dealings took place in Dubai. If her foggy brain were to be trusted, these thugs had to belong to him.

For a time, while the sky grew brighter with the morning sun, Bri alternately wondered how long she'd been out, and worried that whatever they'd given her might have hurt her baby. But those speculations eventually got put on the back burner. She had other, more immediate concerns. Namely, her bladder. She needed to make a pit stop. Badly. She'd avoided talking to the two men for as long as possible, but now she could wait no longer.

"Excuse me," she called loudly, over the rattling of the van. The man on the passenger side canted his head around the seat to scrutinize her with dark eyes. She pushed to a sitting position.

"You," he grunted. "Don't speak." He turned back around as if by saying so, it would be the end of the discussion.

Not as far as Bri was concerned.

"Excuse me," she repeated. "I have to go to the bathroom."

He rotated once again, pinning her with his gaze as he regarded her blankly. *Dammit.* He didn't understand.

"I have to urinate." She knew she blushed up to the roots of her hair, but seriously? How long could anyone be expected to hold their pee? Not that she'd been aware that the two kidnappers had stopped to relieve themselves.

The man showed her a malevolent smile complete with one gold-filled front tooth. "Go ahead," he smirked. "Pee."

Bri wanted to scream. He was an ass, who looked like he'd come right out of central casting.

And no. *Uh, uh.* She wasn't going to let go in her pants, on the mats, or anywhere inside of the vehicle, and she let him know it.

"I'm clueless as to how long we're going to be in this van together," she stated, unequivocally, "but as the day warms up, you'll be pretty sorry if I take your suggestion. The smell of urine gets old, really fast."

Thankfully the guy understood, and his face wrinkled in disgust. He scanned ahead and pointed, saying something in his own language to the driver. The van slowed down, then pull over. *Thank God.*

Before she could move, the one who'd spoken got out, and wrenched open the side door of the rear compartment. Dull, morning light filtered in, and the smell of thick, exhaust-fumed, cool air hit her nostrils.

The guy signaled to her with...oh hell...his gun. Well, she should have expected that. Bri knew they hadn't taken her captive just for funsies.

Her legs were decidedly rubbery and unsure as she stepped to the ground. It took her a moment of hanging onto the van before she deemed herself steady enough to take a step. Her captor, however, lacked patience.

"Go. Now," he ordered, pointing to a spot on the side of the road where a bunch of short, scrub stood at the edge of a tree line. "There," he indicated with his weapon.

Great. If Bri didn't have to go so badly, she would have refused to do so in a place where her head and upper body would be visible to all who passed by—not that there were many at the break of dawn. But dignity took a back seat to need. Squaring her shoulders she walked on wobbly legs to the area indicated, insinuating herself into the densest part of the brush. Quickly she squatted, shoving her pants down and out of the way before relieving herself of hours worth of tension.

She let out a deep sigh. Now she could think again.

Pulling up her pants, she grimaced. *Gross.* There was nothing for it. No toilet paper was going to appear out of thin air, and she eyed the small leaves around her, dubiously. Nope. Not using them. She'd just have to deal with a wet crotch.

Putting as much stiffness as possible into her posture, Bri marched back to the van, head held high. If she caught so much as a snicker from the bastard who'd been watching her every move, she'd clock him, gun or no gun. Thankfully, he remained silent, shutting her back into her four-wheeled prison.

Hours passed. Bri dozed on and off. When she wasn't sleeping, she was thinking about Del. There was no reason to think he was anything but alive. Sure, there had been a lot of blood on the floor around him, but he'd been warm and breathing. That was something she'd seen for herself. And he was a bad-ass ex-military dude. He'd probably been in hundreds of worse situations before, and lived. She remembered the silvery scar running down the side of his temple. A keepsake of some super-secret job he'd undertaken? She'd have to ask next time she saw him.

Bri bit back a sob. *There* was a bitter question. Would she ever see Del again? Even if he survived his injuries, her *own* future was a complete unknown. No doubt these men had been sent by her father, and if the email she'd seen—was it really less than a week ago?—was any indication, he wanted her dead. So if that was the case, why was she being transported somewhere by van? Surely a killing in the woods of Maine counted as much as one done in New York City where her father lived most of the time. Still, being driven somewhere and kept alive was the only thing keeping her from losing all hope. Maybe, given enough time, she'd find a way to free herself.

Voices that had been speaking in normal tones from the front seats, suddenly rose into loud disagreement. Not one of epic proportions, but one that let Bri know the pair weren't seeing eye to eye on something. Her stomach lurched as the van suddenly swerved abruptly, and swept in what felt like a big arc. Had they taken an exit ramp? What did this mean where Bri was concerned, and did it bode well, or ill?

Sitting up now, and on alert, Bri was aware that the van took another few turns, and slowed to a crawl. Before she could say a word, the gun appeared between the seats, aimed right at her. Bri swallowed painfully in a very dry throat.

"You speak. You die. Understand?" The gruff gunman asked.

Bri nodded. She wouldn't even take the chance of saying 'yes'.

"Good." He changed his expression to one of mild disinterest as the driver pulled up to a fast-food window. *Ahh.* Food.

Bri caught a whiff of French fries as the driver lowered his window. Her stomach growled, loudly. She blinked at the gunman. *Good.* He hadn't heard it.

The driver, using a mild tone, ordered what seemed like a lot of food and drink, and Bri's spirits rose. Maybe they were including her in the bounty. And if they actually deemed it prudent to feed her, would that mean she'd be kept around for a while?

Bri focused on the food coming through the window, but even more-so on the few large, strawed cups, and several bottles of water. Surely at least some of that would be shared? Her mouth and lips were so dry, they resembled dust.

With the window rolled up, the van pulled away, and sped back toward what Bri figured was the highway's on ramp. Her nostrils flared at the smell that filled the van, and if she'd had any moisture left in her body, her mouth surely would have watered. She waited, not so patiently, and finally the passenger threw a few wrapped bundles her way, before he tossed back a couple bottles of water. Bri could have wept.

She quickly twisted the cap off one bottle, and guzzled half. So what if she'd have to pee again. It was the best water she'd ever tasted. Eventually, her captors who were guzzling extra-large soft drinks of their own would have to relieve themselves, too.

Sitting taller and reaching for what looked to be a burger and fries, Bri happened to catch a glimpse of the clock on the dash. It read 8:00AM. A funny time to eat fries, but that didn't bother her as she popped one in her mouth.

She continued to look ahead, and if she wasn't mistaken, the buildings—whose tops were visible from her low position—were ones on the outskirts of New York City. Adding to her certainty that they approached the city, was that the van slowed nearly to a stop. Traffic had come to a crawl. Nothing like rush hour going through the Big Apple.

None of that worried her now. She focused on the greasy meat, which a few days ago she might have scorned, and took a big bite. Any calories were good now. Right? And the fries? Never in her life had she turned down fast-food fries. Ever. The excess salt on the handful she'd just shoved past her lips, caused moisture to bead up in her mouth. Wonderful. For the first time in hours, she felt fully hydrated.

It looked like her captors were enjoying their feast as well. No arguing was taking place, and that was a good thing. It was a little disquieting to have them railing at each other so much of the time in a language Bri couldn't understand. Everything they barked out sounded to her like a threat.

More relaxed and feeling like herself for the first time since she'd woken up, Bri took stock of the interior of the van. The walls were stark and bare. With no padding or carpeting, the structure of the vehicle—welding and supports—was out in the open. The packing blankets, of which she'd made good use, lay in piles on the floor, but there was little else to see.

What caught Bri's interest, was that there were two points of egress. The side door that her abductor had used earlier when letting her out to use the bushes, and a set of double doors leading out the back.

Bri pondered the possibility of wrenching them open. If she could, how dangerous would it be falling out into nearly stopped, rush-hour traffic? And if she survived that, would her captors dare to shoot at her? Chase her? If they did, she'd probably be dead, but would they risk it since there would be no possible avenue of escape for them? They were just as stuck in highway gridlock as everyone else.

Dammit. It was worth a try.

Bri inched her way toward the back, slowly. It was a good thing the pair had purchased an endless supply of food, because they were paying her no attention. After what seemed like ages, she positioned herself within reach of the inside handle, and flexed her muscles, readying for escape.

It was now or never.

One, two, three. Bri grabbed for the lever and threw all of her weight into turning it downward. It didn't budge. She cried out and tried again. Nothing.

Laughter met her ears from the front of the van, and when she turned to look, two pairs of malevolent, amused eyes were on her. "You think we are stupid?" the driver laughed. "Not so much. You are the one is stupid."

Bri let go, rolled onto her back and groaned, weighing any other options. Surely there was something she could do to thwart these assholes? Bri thought hard. She could scream. She could beat on the doors of the van in hopes that someone in traffic would hear her, but chances were that the non-driving kidnapper would come back and shut her up before she could make enough ruckus to have someone pay attention. She'd risk a beating if it weren't for the little life growing inside her. As it was, she'd have to pick another plan, another time.

She crawled back to her nest of blankets near the front, refusing to look and see the gloating on her abductors faces. Instead, she gave herself a quick pep talk.

Things could be worse. Without the blankets, she would be rolling around on a hard floor, injuring herself and endangering her baby. And it wasn't winter. If it was, she would be freezing cold right now, in the back of an uninsulated van. Instead, with summer temperatures, and the pair up front using the air-conditioning full blast, enough cool air wafted to the back to make it bearable, if not comfortable.

Also on the plus side, she didn't have to pee since she'd been so long without water. *And* her tummy was full for the moment. So there. Positive boxes checked off.

Bri must have eventually dozed again, because when she awakened, traffic was moving along at a much faster clip. She checked the skyline, and saw nothing. Had they passed through the city? Strange. She'd figured New York City to be their destination. Weren't they bringing her to her father? If not, what was the point of this whole abduction, and where were they headed? She gave another look through the windshield. Nothing. But, tuning her ears in to what was happening outside of the van, Bri heard airplanes. Large ones, in a steady pattern. Newark? It was the only major airport she could think of outside of the city. It made sense, but perhaps it was about time she asked.

"Where are we?" she finally ventured, her voice raspy with disuse.

"Half way to destination," the passenger told her, and he received a punch along with an angry spate of words from the driver.

Bri winced, but didn't give up. "What's our destination?"

She got a glower this time, but using her upright position again, she managed to look at the clock. It was afternoon. She did some quick calculations.

They'd left Maine sometime after midnight, so if they'd been sticking to the coast—and Bri's nose, smelling briny air, said they were—an equal amount of time would bring them to where? Savannah, Georgia?

Wracking her brains, Bri tried to recall the port cities where her father's company did business. Was Savannah one of them? *Dammit.* She wished she'd paid more attention. She figured time would tell.

Of course, if they were headed to Savannah, that begged the question: what would happen when they got there?

Chapter Twenty

There'd been a lot of silence in the vehicle since Del had used the "p" word. He'd never taken his guys for wimps, but not one of them seemed to have the balls to call him on his actions, or...*hell*, how about just to congratulate him?

It had taken Del, himself, a while to warm up to the idea of a baby—but he was happy now, thinking about being a dad—which didn't mean he still wasn't scared shitless. A little back-slapping and moral support from his team sure would feel good at this juncture. Del sulked and nursed his bad head.

They hit the highway south toward Boston before Sarge—from the front seat—eventually spoke up. "So how far along is she?"

Del's shoulders dropped. He hadn't realized the tension he was holding until Sarge breached the silence. The answer rolled off Del's tongue easily. He remembered the exact date of their encounter; he'd played it over in his head so many damned times. "Three months and twelve days," he declared.

"Good," he nodded. "She's out of the first trimester when a lot of bad shit can happen. Your kid's in there like glue now, so as long as we can find her, Bri and the baby should be okay."

"And you know that, how?" Prez didn't take his eyes off the road, but if Del was seeing correctly in the rearview mirror, they'd certainly gotten wider. And why not? Del wanted to ask the same thing.

"Sisters," Sarge mumbled.

Prez's skeptical glance met Del's in the rearview mirror, but they both had the good graces not to question something that was clearly a lie. Or if not exactly a lie, certainly not the reason Sarge had his finger on the pulse of that information. It reminded Del sometimes, of the secrets they each held.

Quiet descended before Prez offered something up to get the heat off whatever it was Sarge didn't want to reveal. "Congrats, by the way. That is, if you're happy."

"Thanks for asking, asshole," Del teased, but instantly grinned, now that the ice was broken and they were talking about it. "I *am* happy, actually," he revealed, knowing in his heart that it was true. "I just have to fix a few things with Bri when we get her back...to make things completely okay. Although I think she's already forgiven me."

"Forgiven you for what?" Wiley asked, having held his piece up until then. Of all the guys, he looked the least amount of happy at Del's news.

Del ignored Wiley's sour puss, and answered the question. He'd look like a jerk, but he'd admit his mistake. "When she first hit me with the pregnancy thing, I kind of told her I didn't trust her enough to believe it was my baby."

Groans came from the front, but Wiles perked right up. "So maybe it isn't," he suggested with a certain degree of satisfaction. "It's not like you could do a paternity test or anything. Maybe she's lying."

Del fought back the sudden urge to punch Wiley right in the face. The only thing that stopped him was that his punching hand was pressed to the top of his head, feeling like it was holding his brains in. That, and the fact that he'd been guilty of pulling the same shit with Bri. Practically throwing it in her face that she wasn't telling him the truth. Del began counting to ten. Ah, hell. Five. This was his best buddy who probably was just looking to have Del's back in a worse case scenario.

"I trust her, Wiles," he finally spat out. "And what good would it do her to lie, anyway? In six months, she'll be able to prove it for sure, and she certainly doesn't need my money. Her dear old dad is worth a fortune."

"If you say so." Wiley clearly wasn't buying it.

Sarge broke in. "So how did you fix it with Bri?" he wanted to know. "Most women would have beaten your ass, and then threatened to sue the shit out of you."

Del removed the gauze on his head, cautiously, and when blood didn't drip down his face, he ditched it in the trash bag on the center console. It took him a while to think about what had happened, and he ended up shrugging after giving it some serious thought.

"I don't know." He held up his hands in a gesture of defeat. "She asked why I was so suspicious and the next thing I knew, I was giving her my life's story. At the end of it all, she got right up into my face and gave me some home truths." Del remembered how kind her eyes had been, even while laying him out about his distrust issues, and assuring him he didn't need to pin any of them on her. "And even though she didn't say much of anything new. It was the way she said it that had me. I just decided that I believe her."

Wiley crossed his arms over his chest, and sank back into the seat, sporting a huge pout again.

"So what is it you need to fix?" Prez sent back.

"We got the Reynold call from you, and started preparing for the worst, so I never got the *chance* to tell her that I believe her and that I'm happy about the whole thing."

191

"Well that sucks," Prez commiserated. "But don't worry, Del. We'll have her back, safe and sound before you know it. So feel free to start picking out baby names."

Silence descended again as they took the long route around Boston to avoid the morning rush hour. Luckily, circumventing the city saved them a lot of time, and the traffic on the outskirts of town was unusually light. Thank God something was going their way.

Del risked a glance over at Wiley, who was doing a good job staring out the window. Del didn't like the attitude that flowed off the guy like black waves. It was time for Wiles to reveal what had crawled up his ass.

"You want to say something to me, Wiley?" Del asked, in a voice he hoped didn't necessarily travel.

As if on cue, Prez cranked Led Zeppelin on the front speakers to let them have it out in private.

"Yeah. I do," Wiley didn't hesitate at the opening. "So once you get your girl back, and run off to make a new family, where does that leave us?" His face had soured. It was a look that Del hadn't seen too often on his normally goof-ball friend, and he didn't like it.

"What do you mean, where does it leave you?" Del probed back. "It leaves you exactly where you are right now. Working for me. Working with Prez and Sarge. Finding people. And what do you mean, running off to make a new family? Running to where?"

He hoped Wiley would take the gloves off and stop dancing around the ring, because the attitude he was displaying had started to bug the hell out of Del.

"Listen," Wiley huffed, still not coming completely clean. "Between the two of you, you have more money than God. You can be in the Caribbean, Switzerland, or the fucking Hamptons just by throwing down the platinum card. So why would you stick around and run a piddling search and rescue company out of Boston, when you can have the world at your fingertips?" The last statement finally spoke to the meat of Wiley's real problem. Abandonment.

Del ignored the pain in his head and reached over, grabbing Wiley by the front of his shirt. He twisted the material in his fist. "For the same reason I expect you'd do the same," Del growled. "We're a team, asshole." Del was just winding up. "We've been together a long time, and we're good at what we do. You think that something is going to get in the way of that? Break up what we have?" He shook Wiley a little bit. "Eventually, all of *you* will have new families, and I hope to hell you don't up and throw everything away that we've built together." Del took a few deep breaths and attempted to calm down. When he spoke again, it was with an edge of humor. "And that aside, just how long do you think I'd last sipping fruity drinks with paper umbrellas plunked in them, talking investments with a bunch of stuffed shirts? Huh?" Del really wanted the answer to that. If Wiley believed he was that kind of guy—could become that kind of guy—then he'd never known him at all.

Wiley actually got a whine in his voice. "Once guys have a wife and kid, friends go to a back burner," he complained. "I'm just not ready for it," he admitted.

"Wiles, believe me, no guy is ever ready for it. But it happens, so watch yourself. It could be you, next. And let me tell you something else," Del snarked. "You don't know Bri, but after spending time with her these last few days, I know she doesn't want a stuffed shirt for a husband. She likes what I do, and wouldn't *want* me to quit. And Wiles, I'm not sure why, but she likes your sorry ass," Del added.

Wiley had the good graces to look sheepish. "So you wouldn't take off and be the boss in name only?"

He still needed convincing, but Del could tell he was coming around, and Del would fight for their friendship, even if Wiles was being a jerk. "Of course not," Del huffed.

"And you think Bri could take it if you were in danger every day?" His buddy kept poking.

Del pondered that one. So far, this job was the most dangerous that they'd undertaken since leaving South America, but he had a feeling there would be more like this. Bri wasn't stupid. She had to know that, too.

"First of all, we haven't discussed it, but I'll tell you honestly right now. I love Brina." *Holy shit.* Where had that come from? *Damn,* he liked admitting it. And to actually say it out loud. Del felt lighter all of a sudden. "And danger or no danger, she won't change things up. I will say this only once, Wiles. Nothing, and no one, is going to keep me from doing this job." He let go of Wiley's shirt and smoothed out the wrinkles, sitting back and nursing his sore head again. "Do you hear me?" he asked, closing his eyes on the wave of pain.

"I do," Wiley finally gave in. Del could hear it in his sigh of relief.

"Good." This came from Sarge in the front seat. "Now will you two kiss and make up? I'm trying to work here, and Prez has my ears nearly bleeding, cranking the tunes to drown you out."

The sarcastic words broke the tension, and when Del opened his eyes, Wiley came at him with arms wide and lips puckered. Del pushed him away, laughing. "Come anywhere near me, and you'll lose your tongue," he warned. "I swear it."

"Spoilsport," Sarge interjected. "I was going to YouTube it and see…"

He broke off abruptly, a startled look coming over his face. Reaching swiftly to the volume knob on the radio, he turned it all the way down.

"What?" Del probed. The tension in the vehicle ramped up in an instant.

"I think we just got a hit on Bri's tracker," Sarge said, his hands flying over the keyboard.

"There!" he exclaimed, pointing at a spot on the map. "Got her. We were right. New York City. They had to have been stuck in traffic which allowed us to get close enough to pick her up. But Del," his face puckered, clearly baffled. "They're passing through the city. They're almost in Jersey, heading south. Where the hell are they going?"

"I don't know," Del ran a hand over his aching head in frustration. "Listen. Do a fast search on Wasem Trade Group and see where else they do business. There has to be a port city south of New York where they take shipments. We need to know where that is. I don't have to tell you that if we lose Bri's signal, the only thing we have to go on is a new point of destination."

"There are a ridiculous amount of possibilities," Prez groused, clearly thinking his way down the coast. "Newark, New Jersey, Norfolk, Virginia, Wilmington, North Carolina, Charleston, South Carolina, Miami, Florida. And that's only naming a few."

"Yeah, but it shouldn't take much to see where Wasem ships from. Most of what they do has to go through legal channels, so it will be public record." Del tapped his foot, saying it as much to make himself believe it, as for it to be true. He waited impatiently.

It didn't take Sarge long to come up a possible destination. "Savannah is the first one," he supplied. "Then Miami."

"Savannah it is, then." Del called it. They'd keep heading south. He couldn't say why, but the blip sound coming from Sarge's computer comforted him. It was as if he had a physical connection to Bri. He just hoped like hell it didn't up and disappear.

"How far ahead of us are they, Sarge?" Del needed to know.

"Just under a couple hundred miles, or two and a half hours at the speed we're travelling."

Del understood what Sarge was saying. They'd gotten lucky. Bri's abductors had to obey speed limits. If the bad guys got pulled over, their whole game could be blown to hell, whereas the worst Del and team could expect would be a ticket. Not only that, but by heading straight through the city at morning rush hour, the kidnappers had scrubbed a shitload off their lead. Del was now fairly certain they could catch up.

His optimism suddenly plummeted. They too would have to go through New York City, and dammit all to hell, by the time they got there the mid afternoon, rush hour exodus would be well underway.

It could cost them the time they'd gained, but at least they had a destination in mind.

Chapter Twenty-One

The next time Bri awoke, it was nearly dark. They'd had two road-side pit stops during the day, but Bri was hungry again. She didn't like not being in control of when she ate and when she relieved herself. Funny how she'd always taken such small things for granted.

She looked toward her captors. The passenger was dozing for the first time. That was good. At least his beady eyes weren't on her every few minutes. He really creeped her out. If it weren't for the driver who was clearly in charge, Bri was certain she would have been molested by now.

She lay back and stared around her rolling prison. Bare walls, bare except... For the first time, Bri noticed that the lack of interior insulation left a lot of the van's guts showing. And some of those guts could be useful. Bri narrowed her eyes. *Huh.* There were wires running from the front of the frame to the back. She traced one set from where it appeared next to the front seat, and followed it back to where it disappeared into the side of a tail-light assembly.

What she wouldn't do for a pair of wire-cutters. With darkness coming on, if the van was without tail-lights, any passing cop would stop them. Bri focused harder on where the wires entered the tail light. She couldn't be sure, but it looked like it might be a module that plugged in, rather than wires running directly into the housing. She needed to take a closer look.

With her ever-vigilant guard asleep, she wasted no time silently scooting to the back, and spent even less time on her inspection. She'd been correct. The wire simply plugged in. Giving herself no chance to have second thoughts, she reached up and yanked the wire. The plug easily popped out. Bri took a short, nervous breath, looked toward the front, then wiggled her way to light number two and disabled that one, as well.

Swiftly and quietly she made her way back to her nest and lay down again. Her heart thumped a million miles an hour. What had she just done? It was either a brilliant plan, or the stupidest thing she could do. Only time would tell.

When nerves had crept up on her during the day, she played a game with herself of WWDD. What would Del do? As darkness fell, she realized that she'd just scored big. If Del were here, he'd have to give her a bunch of points for her tail-light daring. That calmed her a little. Bri bit her lip. So what would Del do next, she pondered. How about demand something? That would be bold, in light of her stunt.

"I'm hungry," she spoke up in a loud voice. "And I'm almost out of water." She'd rationed the second bottle, not knowing how long it would have to last, but she only had a quarter of an inch of liquid left in the bottom. The two men up front seemed impervious to hunger or thirst.

The passenger woke up with a start and with reflexes that shocked her, had the gun pointing directly at her head within a second of her request.

"No talk," he yelled, but eventually pulled the gun back.

"But I need to eat," Bri cajoled, putting a little whimper into her words and lowering her eyes. She'd already found out that they were more likely to respond to her requests when she appeared meek and non-confrontational.

A spate of words flew back and forth between the driver and the passenger, before the gun-wielder turned back to her.

"We will stop, next food place," he grunted, and folding his arms across his chest, he sank into his seat and closed his eyes again.

Bri bit a fingernail nervously. Now all she had to do was wait.

Somehow, as boredom overshadowed nervousness, Bri fell asleep again. She didn't know how many miles they'd driven while she'd been out, but as the van slowed down and took a curve, she became instantly alert, pushing herself to a sitting position. Would someone now see the van's lack of tail lights?

There was a repeat of the other time they'd stopped for food. The wonderful smell wafting in as the window opened. The polite, even voice of the driver ordering food, and the gun trained on her between the seats so that she wouldn't give herself away.

As the food was thrown back, Bri almost forgot about the lights. She dug into the fish sandwich with gusto as they left the fast-food mecca and headed back to the highway. She'd been hungry for so long that despite her nervousness, she wasn't about to let it go to waste.

Stuffing a few French fries into her mouth, she'd just started to remove the bottle cap on a new water bottle when the whoop of a siren erupted behind the van. The fries got stuck in her throat and she coughed violently to discharge them.

"Quiet!" The passenger's voice hissed at her, and he leaned over the seat, waving the gun with one hand and pushing her down with the other. Once she was prone, he yanked one of the huge packing blankets from the pile behind his seat, and threw it over her. "You will stay there," he ordered. "If you move, or make noise, I will kill you and cop." He didn't wait for an answer. His weight shifted, once again to the front seat.

Bri wanted to cry. Tears of frustration and fear welled up in her eyes. She clearly hadn't thought her plan through. It was all for nothing. If she made any kind of a move, she had no doubt that her abductors would make good on their threat. But when they found out what she'd done, how would they react? Would they kill her and dump her body on the side of the road?

The van came to a stop, and Bri had everything she could do not to cough up the last of the fry that was stuck in her throat. It was stifling beneath the blanket, but she somehow managed to keep her breathing shallow and her body still, even when the back doors of the van were yanked open.

"It's rental." She recognized the voice of the driver. "I don't know why the lights would not work, officer." He was pretending to be humble and cooperative, which Bri knew would go a long way with officers who—because of a lot of bad press—were being extra careful these days with profiling.

"Well, here's your problem," the policeman's voice was easy and helpful. "The modules to your tail light assemblies aren't hooked up. It must have been an oversight at the rental agency. They must have had this one in for maintenance and forgot to hook them up."

Bri heard some fussing, and could picture the friendly cop plugging the wires back in. Frustration ate away at her. If she gave herself away, both she and the officer would be dead. And how could she let herself be responsible for his death? He sounded young. He probably had a wife and kids. Bri bit the inside of her cheek and kept silent.

When the doors finally closed, muffled voices moved away, and the driver got back in the van. She heard him turn the key and they were back underway. Maybe she'd just stay under the stuffy blanket and hide for the rest of the night. Bri wasn't anxious to see what kind of retribution her kidnappers had planned.

Not so lucky, the blanket was whipped off her head, and a fist came down to slam into the side of her face.

"Bitch," the passenger growled. "If it was up to me, I would kill you now." He punched her again, this time in the shoulder as Bri managed to curl up into a ball to hide her face and protect her baby. He rained a few more blows down on her before making a disgusted noise and turning back to the front.

Bri took a deep, tentative breath. No broken ribs. Still in her fetal position, she moved her jaw from side to side. As painful as it was, Bri didn't think it was broken either, only badly bruised. And as for her shoulders and back, where the rest of the punches had landed, she'd be sore and black and blue, but all the soft parts of her that really mattered were untouched. She could live with that.

Now. WWDD? Play dumb. Bri only gave herself a few seconds to think, before sitting up, moving out of punching range, and confronting her captors.

"What was that all about?" she wailed. "Why did you punch me?" She forced loud, accusatory sobs from her throat.

"You broke lights," the passenger snarled.

"What lights?" she bawled and played up her confusion. "I don't know anything about lights. The policeman said the rental company was at fault."

There was a quick discussion and some grunting from the driver.

"Maybe yes, maybe no," the passenger finally conceded. "But if lights mysteriously go bad again, I will tie you up. You understand?"

"I do," she sniveled. "And it won't be necessary."

"Make for sure," he responded curtly.

It was the best Bri could hope for. Certainly she hadn't been holding out for an apology. She settled back and groped around, looking for the rest of her fish sandwich. She found it smooshed underneath her hip. Her fries had fared little better, spilling out across the packing blankets. *Screw it.* She wasn't proud, and she was damned hungry. She piled the mangled food onto her lap, blew on it a few times to dislodge anything hairy, and started eating.

It took a while to finish. Her jaw reacted painfully to the chewing, but she certainly felt infinitely better when she'd finished. She held the cold water bottle to her cheek, and debated not drinking anymore since it made a nice compress, but thirst won out in the end.

Bri even managed another look at the clock up front. 1:23 AM, and oddly enough, while she'd been finishing her food, the van had gone off the highway again. Counting in her head, Bri realized that the timing was right for reaching Savannah. She'd at least had that correct. Gingerly, she sank back onto the mats, happy she remained alive, but wondering what the hell would happen next.

She didn't have long to wonder. Within minutes the vehicle came to a stop, and the side door slid open.

"Come," the cold voice she'd gotten used to, bade. "And no noise."

She scuttled across to the open door, and eased herself out. Her body, now that she attempted movement, was sore as hell. She took small, tentative steps, walking like a feeble old woman. Another beating would do her in, so she needed to comply with whatever these guys had in store.

They were in some kind of industrial park. Close to water, Bri's nose told her, but because of their position between two big, grey, metal buildings, she couldn't see it. The driver had a grip on her elbow, and was leading her to a people-sized door in one of the buildings. Bri didn't like it, but what choice did she have? If she fought them, they'd beat her to a pulp. Better to appear meek again, hoping they'd drop their guard and give her some kind of opening to escape.

Once inside the building, one of the men hit the lights. Huge sodium vapor's lit the interior with an eerie, bright orange glow. Bri blinked at the sudden corneal onslaught.

"Sit," said the one holding her, and pushed her into a chair, positioned across from another, with a laptop resting on a box between them. The rest of the room was filled with large crates. Each crate was marked with the understated logo of Wasem Trade Group. She'd seen it enough times in her life to recognize it immediately. So this was one of her father's warehouses. But what was up with the impromptu office set-up?

"We will make quick video call," the driver-guy stated, sitting in the second chair. He plugged headphones into a jack and turned the screen away from Bri, and pointed a remote camera right at her face.

Bri simply sat and blinked in the direction of the small, white camera. Who was on the other end, and why?

"Yes. As you see." The words coming from her captor's mouth seemed to be in answer to what someone was asking, via headphones. "She was uncooperative."

The person on the other end must have asked about her face. She probably looked hideous.

"Fine," the kidnapper said into the mic, then looked directly at her. "You are to speak," he ordered.

"What do you want me to say?" Bri sneered. "That you stole me away from my boyfriend in Boston, Del Songen, and stuck me in a van? That I—"

"That's enough," the one with the headphones ran a hand across his throat in a gesture that didn't make Bri feel all warm and fuzzy, and when the gun was put against the back of her head by creep number two, she shook in her seat. Could this be how it ended? Had they brought her here to shoot her and have it captured on video, live for whomever was on the other end of the transmission? She closed her eyes and prayed.

"No," the computer operator barked. "I have orders. She will be in container on next shipment out."

Bri's shoulders slumped in relief. It seemed there'd be no shooting in the head. At least that's what she believed his words meant. The gun lowered. That was a good thing. But wait. What was that about shipping her out? Shipping her where? The words sprang from her mouth before she could stop them.

"Where are you sending me?"

The blow from behind came unexpectedly, knocking her off the chair and to the ground. *Damn.* She needed to learn to keep her mouth shut. Her poor head. Luckily, the asshole had pulled his punch, but the back of her skull still hurt like a motherfucker. She'd have a doozy of a headache, later, to match all her other pains.

Bri was heartily sick of this shit. Sick of being a victim. She wanted nothing more than to get up and fight. She wanted to spit and swear, and gouge someone's eyes out, but she couldn't. Because this wasn't just her life on the line. There was another nestled deep within who needed protection. Bri bit her tongue and stayed down on the floor.

"It is not for me to say," the guy at the computer spoke to whomever listened on the other end. "Once I do my part, she is no longer concern for me. Talk to boss."

Bri saw him reach over and punch a button, terminating the connection before removing his headphones. He jerked his head in her direction. "Take her. We go now."

The one with the gun reached down and grabbed her by the arm, hauling her to her feet, while the other snagged the computer. Bri stumbled, but recovered quickly. She had no doubt that if she didn't find her feet, her aggressor would drag her the length of the warehouse.

She was surprised when she was taken back outside and tossed once more into the van. Having understood that she was to be "shipped out", Bri figured she'd be taken aboard an outbound freighter and locked in some store room or another. To say she was confused was an understatement.

When both men were back in the van and they were underway again, Bri moved out of striking distance and asked the question that was foremost on her mind.

"I thought I was to be on the next shipment out?" she asked.

She hadn't counted on the nasty laugh she got in return for her question. But she'd take it, because it looked like an answer was forthcoming.

"You will be. The next shipment does not leave from here."

Great. So even if the person on the other end of the video was a good guy, recognized the warehouse, and understood her plea to contact Del, she'd be long gone by the time help arrived. Why did her odds have to suck so badly?

Chapter Twenty-Two

He'd been pumped that they'd gotten lucky, but then things had gone to hell. Del shook his head in disgust.

He looked at his watch for the current time. Four in the morning. The minutes were ticking by, fast, and the ingested tracker would be out of Bri's system by three that afternoon, which gave them eleven hours to find her. He feared it wouldn't be long enough.

Their first break, after clearing rush hour in The Big Apple, had come when one of their military friends—working for the Georgia State Police—with whom Sarge had been in contact, had contacted them with a possible ID on their suspects. He'd had access to a report on a routine traffic stop for no tail lights on an unmarked, white van. The officer who made the stop, took note that the two gentlemen inside were of middle-eastern heritage, and had acted strangely. However, seeing nothing except the routine violation, he'd let them go.

Since the timing and positioning of the van fit perfectly, Del recognized, in his gut, that it was their target. They'd broken every speed limit after that, and eventually regained Bri's signal. Two and a half hours ago, her ping had become static in Savannah. The van had stopped.

Del and his friends had eventually rolled in, three hours behind their quarry, knowing—by that point—that Bri and the van had moved on, but needing to check out where they'd become stationary. It irked Del that Bri had gone out of range again, and that the thirty minutes it took to sweep the warehouse where Bri's marker had been, turned out to be fruitless. And what they'd come across, chilled him. One smashed microphone, a couple of overturned chairs, and a small bit of blood on the floor which he'd known instinctively was Bri's. It tore at his gut that she could be injured.

They'd had to make a quick decision. Get on the road again, hoping the van had traveled south to the next port of call which was Miami, or send out an APB on the vehicle across all the southern states, no doubt putting Bri's life at great risk by doing so.

No brainer. They'd taken to the road.

"At this speed," Sarge told him, as they barreled down the dark and empty highway, "we should pick up her signal again in just under an hour." His fingers flew on the keyboard and he brought up a visual of the Wasem docks in Miami. "Here's what we'll be dealing with when we get there."

The complex was vast, and the chances were good that the tracking part of the chemical compound would be within an hour of quitting Bri's body by the time they got there. Del wanted to punch something. They were cutting things too closely.

****

Too much time had passed and a tense silence blanketed the interior of the vehicle. Nobody wanted to say anything, but the fact that they hadn't gotten a hit on Bri's location worried the shit out of them.

"Run the numbers again, Sarge," Del barked into the quiet.

"Already done." Sarge shook his head. "There's no way, at this speed, we shouldn't have picked her up again. Unless they were driving at the same pace we are."

"Which they aren't, because they're afraid of being stopped." Del hissed in frustration. "They've been sticking to the speed limit like clockwork since we started out."

"So there's only one *real* answer then," Wiley spoke the obvious. "We've gone the wrong way."

"Yeah. Pretty clear in hindsight, but where else would they be headed?" Del's vexation heightened.

Adding to his aggravation, his phone vibrated in his pocket for the second time in two minutes. *Dammit.* One call from his office—forwarding to his cell—wouldn't be so unusual in the wee hours. Telemarketers worldwide made calls at all times, night and day. But two calls? Someone really wanted him. Del swore to himself. He didn't want to talk about another job right now. His priority was Bri. He ignored the pulsing phone as it buzzed a third time and wracked his brains.

Had the van turned around and gone back up the coast? Not possible. In that case they would have picked up Bri's signal passing them on the highway, and been alerted to her change of direction. So she had to be going south, or somewhere else?

Del's phone sounded off for a fourth attempt, and this time he yanked it from his pocket and looked at the number. Nothing registered on his caller-ID. Somebody better have a damned good reason for calling him.

"What." he barked, not even pretending to be polite. Maybe the person would hang up, encountering his unbridled hostility.

"Del Songen?" A computer generated voice asked.

"Who wants to know?" Del growled.

"Someone who's concerned about Brina Capadella," the voice came back.

Del sat up straight, every cell in his body on alert. He switched the phone to his dominant ear, and snapped his fingers to bring all eyes to him. "What do you know about Bri?" he barked, pegging the volume so his guys could hear everything being said.

"She's in trouble. You need to get to warehouse forty-two at the docks of the Wasem holding site in Savannah."

"What is this, some kind of a joke?" Del bellowed, but at the same time, he indicated to Sarge that the call needed to be traced. "We just left that warehouse, and there's no sign of her."

"You did? How did you... Never mind. I happen to know you're wrong," the voice insisted. "I saw her there."

"What?" Del's tone became shrill. "What do you mean, you saw her? You were there? When?"

"No, no. I wasn't there in person," the robotic speech was annoying. "I was contacted via a computer video feed."

That would account for the smashed microphone.

"Explain," Del ordered, getting a sign from Sarge that he needed to keep the call rolling in order for him to get a fix on it.

"They had her. Two men." Was there concern in the strange, disguised voice? "And they said that she was going out, in a container, on the next shipment."

"Why would they contact you to tell you this?" Del questioned.

"It's not pertinent," the voice responded impatiently. "You must listen. She's to be on the next container ship out of the facility."

"Next shipment to where?" Del's mind was churning. There was no way Bri was still at the Savannah shipyard, or even anywhere nearby. They absolutely would have gotten a fix on her—not that he could tell the caller that—so how could she be slated for the next shipment out if she was miles away?

"I'm not at liberty to say," was the response.

"Listen. If I don't get some answers from you, I can't possibly take you, or this call seriously." Del fished for answers.

"How serious are you?" the voice countered. "Do you value Bri's life?"

Del, loathe to show his hand, but unable to remain impassive, bit the words out. "Enough not to hang up on you."

"Then go back to that shipyard and find her. Please." This time he didn't imagine it. The intonation denoted fear.

"She's. Not. There." Del used his most commanding tone to get his point across to someone who could be emotionally unstable.

"But they said she'd be on the next shipment out. That she'd be inside a container," the voice wheedled. "She has to be there. And they hurt her."

"Hurt her, how?" Del experienced a twist to his mid-section again, hearing that someone had injured Bri.

"Her cheek and jaw were deeply bruised from what I could see, and when she asked where they were sending her, one of them hit her in the back of the head and she fell to the ground, hurting her again. You have to find her."

Del saw red. The caller was right. He needed to get his hands on the pair who had stolen Bri away, and he needed to make them pay. Big time. "Who are you and what do you know?" he howled, tired of the anonymity and the game playing. If this person truly looked for help in locating Brina, he was going to have to do better than that.

"I'm someone who cares greatly about Brina's fate. And if you want to help her escape the fate those men and their higher-ups have in store for her, then you have to go back to Savannah. Right now."

Del took a deep breath and tried to focus himself. "Fine. We're turning around." He gave Prez the signal, and got a thumb's up in reply. Maybe the person was right. Perhaps they'd overlooked something. Doubtful, but possible. Certainly heading farther south seemed to be doing them no good. "Now tell me what time the next shipment is supposed to leave."

"Midnight, tonight," the unknown caller answered.

Which would give the kidnappers plenty of time to have left, and then return, but something still didn't feel right. Why would they bother to send this guy a skype? And why would they send one that gave away their location? Del grimaced. His gut told him that Savannah was simply a decoy stop, and they should be looking somewhere else.

Del had a sudden epiphany. "Do you have access to all of Wasem's shipping schedules?" he grilled.

"Yes, but why? I've told you the next container ship out is at midnight." The voice answering sounded impatient, as if the individual wasn't used to being questioned.

"But is there one before midnight at another facility?" Del probed, his hunch growing stronger by the minute. "Any other facility?"

"Hold on for a minute."

Del heard the clicking of fingers on a keyboard.

"Damnit, yes," the reply came after only a moment of research. "There's one out of New Orleans at Nine o'clock tonight. You don't think…"

"I do," Del answered before the man could finish. It made perfect sense that heading down the coast, they'd lost Bri's signal if the van had gone inland.

"Prez," he barked. "Turn around and head for Jacksonville." They were only half an hour away from the

Florida city where it would be a straight shot to New Orleans.

"New Orleans is still a good eight hours from there," Wiley had his phone out, checking distances. Del did the math. If the traffic cooperated, they could be in Louisiana by two-thirty. That would give them a half hour leeway before Brina went off grid. God, he hated those odds.

"Tell me how I can get in touch, to let you know when we find her," Del queried. There was no "if", only "when".

"I'll get back to you," The voice stated, unequivocally. "And have your friend with the computer give it a rest trying to find me. I have firewalls up he'll never get past. But I'm rethinking my position, and I suggest you check your office files every few hours. If you get Brina out of danger, I may have some very interesting information for you." The line went dead.

"What do you think about that?" Del asked his men.

"I think that person knows what he or she is doing," Sarge smirked. "I traced the call to the east coast, but then it bounced around to show its point of origin anywhere from Nova Scotia to Key West. I'd say they've got one of our auto-scramblers."

"Damn. I hate it when technology becomes mainstream," Del groused.

Nine hours later, Del knew that a super-phone was not his biggest problem. They'd met an enormous accident, which caused a traffic tie-up coming into Mobile, Alabama. They'd regained Bri's signal, then lost it again. And even now that they'd cleared Mobile, they remained in construction gridlock outside of Gulfport. Three PM had come and gone long ago. They'd be lucky if they made New Orleans by seven. And they'd be going into the Wasem shipping docks, blind. Bri's signal was completely spent.

Chapter Twenty-Three

Bri heard the activity around her, but couldn't see it. One of those sunscreen things had been stretched across the front window of the van, and for hours she'd been chained to a strut inside, sweltering in the mid-day heat. She'd also been told that her captors would forgo a gag, but if she made any noise, many people would die because of her. Bri didn't want to test that theory, so remained quiet.

The only thing that had gone her way was that they had left water bottles, and although warm, they'd kept her hydrated.

Once again, with nothing to do, she'd dozed on and off, dreaming of Del. She wondered where he was, and if he'd recovered fully from his injuries. She speculated, too, that if he had, would he and his team be trying to find her? The precautions he'd taken with his magic bug-juice, and the dark clothing—that although covered her completely, also wicked the heat and moisture from her body—would say he hadn't planned to lose her.

That brought her some comfort. And when she'd pondered shedding layers, she knew she'd be better off keeping them on. For a few reasons. First, once darkness fell, if she had an opportunity to escape, Del had told her that keeping covered, her body's heat signature would not be found. Second, the creepy guy who had been the passenger for the entire trip, had, in their last few hours together, eyed her in a far too lascivious way. She got the feeling that any provocation—such as baring some skin—would scream "whore" to him.

Bri grimaced and tugged at her wrist again. Her hand being slightly elevated, it had long ago turned numb, and the discomfort kept her from falling into a real sleep. Bri sighed. Whatever they had planned, she hoped it would be soon. Waiting had never been her forte. Time never passed fast enough when she was filled with anticipation, good or bad.

Turning her mind to the computer chat in the warehouse, she pondered again who had been on the other end of the transmission. How had they reacted when she'd been knocked to the ground, and could the unknown observer possibly have been her father? If not, who else could even be remotely concerned with her whereabouts? What had her abductor said to him? *Oh yeah.* That she'd been uncooperative. Well, duh. Who went with armed strangers without a struggle?

But the next thing from the kidnapper's mouth made her rethink it being her father on line. "I have my orders," he'd said. "She will be on the next shipment out." And, "it's not for me to say. Talk to the boss."

Bri had always assumed that the boss was her father. She had various relatives working for Wasem, but she hadn't paid strict attention to the hierarchy. And really. Who could possibly even remember she existed? Images of distant cousins and uncles wafted through her mind, but were quickly dismissed. She hadn't seen any of them since her mother died.

The only other person in the world who cared for her—besides a handful of friends—was her aunt Celia. Could it be possible that her father had orchestrated a computer call to her, perhaps feeling some remorse, and wanting to reassure his sister that Brina was still alive? *Damn.* Brina didn't have a clue.

Vaguely she noticed as time passed that the van was becoming more comfortable, and that the ambient light sneaking around the corners of the sunscreen had diminished. Evening was surely creeping in. Noise outside had dropped to a minimum, which probably meant that all of the day-workers had gone home. If a move was to be made by her abductors, Bri assumed it would be coming soon. She hoped it included food. The water had gone a long way towards assuaging her thirst, but it hit her now that she hadn't eaten since she'd picked fries off the floor after her aborted escape attempt. They'd stopped a couple of times after that, en-route, to let her relieve herself, but no food had come her way. And she was hungry.

When the back, double doors finally opened, the sun, low and hidden behind large buildings made it so she didn't have to blink at the sudden intrusion of the outside world. The breeze that immediately wrapped around her might as well have been heaven, and the fresh air entering her lungs was almost as good as food. Almost.

She put aside pride and caution. "I'm hungry," she said

The gun-wielder indicated with a pointed barrel that she should get out.

Bri rattled her hand-cuffs. "Chained, here." She pursed her lips into a "really?" frown.

He grunted, and handed off his gun to his partner, moving forward to let her loose. His knee came uncomfortably close to her thigh as he worked, and his elbow managed to arc a path into her left breast, twice. She flinched away, but couldn't get far enough because of the restraint.

"Stop moving for me to unlock," came the unhelpful answer. He knew what he was doing. His leer told Bri the story. She gritted her teeth and endured his slimy touch, but if he thought he'd get away with more, she would scream the bloody area down. Threats or no threats. Her narrowed eyes in his direction daring him to try.

Even if he'd been about to attempt anything, his buddy wasn't having any of it. The guy standing at the door griped tersely in his foreign language, clearly telling the un-locker to get on with it. If Bri wasn't so nervous about what was next on the agenda, she would have almost felt relief. And speaking of that, along with her hunger had arisen the need to use the facilities again.

"Hungry and in need of *urination*," she announced the word, emphasizing every distinct syllable. She'd long ago passed the point of being ladylike.

"It will all be taken care of," the head honcho told her.

With her wrist released, she rubbed and shook feeling back into her fingers, scooting toward the back doors of the van, but not before Mr. Leer-face shoved her in that direction.

"I'm going," she hissed. *And I'm so done with your bullshit.*

Her legs, initially, refused to work, and she literally growled at the man who'd followed her out of the van when he propelled her forward again. "Unless you want to peel me off the ground, you'll wait a minute until I'm able to walk."

With a grunted word from the boss, her tormentor took possession of his firearm again, but backed off. *Huh.* Maybe she should have attempted to be more forceful all along. *No*, she grimaced as her hand crept, inadvertently to the side of her face where dried blood now crusted. Tried that. Wore the result.

Bri took a few tentative steps forward. "I'm good now." She aimed her words at the more reasonable of the two men—or the more disinterested anyway—attempting to ignore the one who once again waved his weapon about.

She took the opportunity, as she was prodded along, to look around. The scene was nothing unusual to her. She'd been to Wasem's various shipyards many times when she was young, before her mother died. Her father had been loathe to invite her once he'd taken over the reigns.

Ahead of them loomed a couple of ships, but one in particular caught her eye. It was loaded with containers, and its running lights were on. There wasn't a large crew scrambling around above-decks, but Bri recalled that these huge cargo ships needed very little in the way of man-power to make sure they made it across the ocean. A crew of fifteen on a panama—the size ship predominantly owned by Wasem—would be the norm. Most of the workers they needed to get the ship loaded would have been on the docks, and long gone by now.

Her eyes travelled upward to the three deck cranes. From what she'd learned over her internships at the companies where she'd been placed by her father, Wasem had these geared ships, which was unusual. Most companies preferred to use shoreside cranes. She remembered her father explaining that a lot of times their ships docked in smaller ports that didn't have adequate equipment, so they preferred to have their own, aboard.

Strange though, one of those cranes was still lit and unlashed. Bri could only assume it was nearing time for the vessel to weigh anchor, and wondered why the gantry crane hadn't been put to bed. She watched it move handily along its track and took stock of its trajectory.

She didn't have to wait long to find out where it headed. There was still one open cargo container on the siding. And she was being led right to it. *Oh, hell no!* It didn't take brains to figure things out. *She* was the cargo going into that one.

Her feet stumbled over each other, her chest seized, and she tried to suck in air, all the while, being yanked by the arm toward her prison.

"No!" she screamed. "I..." her mouth was suddenly stuffed with a foul tasting rag, and because her arms were held on either side by her vile escorts, she couldn't remove it. Her eyes darted around wildly. There had to be someone here who would stop this.

They marched her forward, relentlessly, and the more she struggled, the tighter their vice-like grips became. There was still plenty of light to look into the twenty foot container where she was being led. Bri saw cases of water stacked side by side against the back, right wall. A pallet of sorts that looked to be a low cot with blankets thrown on top sat against the left. A couple of closed buckets stood in the front right, and a half dozen or so medium sized, unopened cardboard boxes lay opposite. She couldn't read the words on them, but assumed since they were giving her other amenities, they had to contain food.

She got one final lurch from her companions, as she was dragged into the box and dropped to the floor. She pulled at the rag which had caused bile to back up in her throat, but by the time she had it out to scream, the metal doors had slammed shut behind her and Bri was thrust into total darkness.

Fighting back tears, she took a few cleansing breaths, relieved—at least—that the container didn't smell. *Damn.* She knew what was next, and she needed to be prepared. Attempting to remain calm, she visualized what she had seen before things had gone black. Slowly she came to her feet, and spreading her hands to the front, shuffled her way toward the cot. It seemed to take a long time to reach it, and before she did, the unmistakable—and very loud thunk—of the spreader came to rest on top of the container.

Bri didn't have much time to secure herself, but she refused to panic. Dropping to her knees in case of any sudden movement, she continued her trajectory, groping forward as she listened to the spreader being secured to the four corner castings of the container. It would only be seconds now.

Her hand hit the cot, and the pile of blankets. She pulled on it, and thank God it had been secured to the wall. Bri moved the rough covers aside and quickly climbed up and into the cradle of the canvas, then gripped the metal sidebars tightly as her container began to move.

Bri tried not to panic, alone, swaying in the dark. She pictured her metal enclosure making its way skyward. She'd had a look at the ship for which her prison was destined, and knew she'd go high up, on top of one of the piles. With the locking system in place, she assured herself that there was no fear of being dropped, and once the container had been placed, no chance for it to move around. But having been on ships before, Bri realized that if there were any rough seas, the pitch and roll of the ship would be most apparent from her high perch, and that disasters still occasionally happened. But she couldn't think about that right now.

She hadn't even had time to worry about where she was being taken. She could only assume it would be to the parent company offices, or thereabouts, in Dubai. Whoever wanted her, they'd gone to a lot of trouble, so at least they didn't plan on killing her.

The shifting of the box, without anything to visually anchor her to reality, made Bri nauseous. But she refused to give in to it. Clearly one of the buckets in the corner, meant to be her bathroom would suffice for puke, but she wasn't going to risk trying to get there until the container became static.

In through the nose, out through the mouth. The mantra had served her well during her first trimester, and would have to suffice now. Surely the crane trip would be over soon, and at least she'd made it to a secure spot before she'd been in danger of rolling around on the hard floor.

A harsh drop, and a grating noise told her that she'd landed. The top bracket released with a scrape, and the ones that secured her to the container beneath, engaged. She was safe. For the moment.

Before the ship got underway, Bri needed to explore her confines. She once again conjured a mental image from the quick peek she'd had at the interior, and with the aid of a few streaks of light entering through bad welds in the metal—now that her eyes had adjusted—she got to her feet. Most containers were forty feet long, but this one was clearly twenty. All containers were a standard eight feet wide, so at least she knew what she was dealing with.

Gingerly, Bri placed one foot in front of the other, and bending at the waist with hands extended, came to the shadowy pile of water. She didn't need to drink yet, but using it as a point of reference and keeping her hand on the wall, she cautiously slid toward the front corner of her prison. Her toe purposely bumped one white bucket, and by the way it didn't move, she immediately knew it contained something. She knelt to explore.

Huh. There were two of them, with covers. She pried one cover off, and the smell of the blue liquid that fills porta-potties, assailed her nose. *Whoa.* She'd pegged it right the first time. Bathroom facilities. She supposed it could have been worse. Gaining confidence, she reached for the mysterious pile in back of the buckets and found several rolls of paper towels. A little rough, but they would suffice.

After taking care of her full bladder and replacing the cover on the bucket, she used her hand on the wall again and made her way to the cardboard boxes. These babies would take some effort.

There were no knives to help her split seams, so Bri patiently went to work at the tape on the first box she picked. It took her several minutes, but she managed to get the thing open. Not that it helped her a lot. Inside, there were packets. She counted. Twelve. Each one appeared to be a mixture of aluminum and plastic, with writing on them that Bri could not make out. Exterior light was fading, so her room became darker by the minute. She picked one up.

If she had to guess, she'd say the thing in her hand felt the way tuna fish got packaged at the grocery store in those squishy packets. But in a much larger quantity, and this one had lumps.

Bri turned it round and round until she encountered what had to be a tear-strip opening. She would get heartily sick of tuna fish if that's what these were.

When she tore the top off the pouch, a series of smaller things fell into her lap. She recognized the utensils immediately, and what had to be a small packet of salt. Several other items accompanied it, and she explored each one, slowly, starting with the smallest.

Score! The first was a chocolate bar, and Bri didn't hesitate to pop it into her mouth. Saliva pooled at the unexpected boon. As she chewed, opened and explored the other packages—some with trail mix, another with a bit of meat in gravy that she suspected was chicken, and a pouch of rice—Bri's brain clicked onto what these had to be. MRE's. Meals-Ready-To-Eat. She settled down, as happy as possible under the circumstances and counted her blessings.

One: She had plenty of food and water

Two: She no longer had her evil captors pointing guns in her face and hitting her.

And three: She felt closer to Del as she chewed, knowing he'd probably spent a lot of time eating these very same things while deployed in the jungle of South America.

Chapter Twenty-Four

True to what Del had speculated during the last frustrating hundred or so miles of their trip, it was after eight o'clock when they arrived at the shipyard. What didn't take them long, once they were there, was to locate the ship that was scheduled to depart. The enormous vessel was loaded, with running lights up and operating.

"Looks like it's on schedule to leave at nine o'clock," Wiley nodded in the ship's direction from their position, hidden around the side of a warehouse. It looked that way to Del, too.

"I agree, but we need to find our suspect's van first and make sure Bri isn't in it. I'd hate to head out to sea if she was still on land." He quickly perused the area, and pointed to a nearby warehouse. "That's Wasem's logo," he told the guys. "How many buildings can there possibly be? We'll split into pairs and check them out."

Del and Prez went left, Sarge and Wiley right. It wasn't difficult to get into the structures. Standard locks were on the personnel entrances, and were easily picked. Del and Prez were at their second building when the text came through.

Van in warehouse 17.

They took off, running, and by the time they arrived, Wiley and Sarge had made a complete inspection.

"What did you find?" Del looked into the back of the vehicle and saw a pile of packing blankets and some empty bottles.

"Nothing much left behind," Sarge said. "You won't be happy about this, but they clearly kept her confined to the back and secured with cuffs to a strut."

Del punched at the metal so hard he left a dent.

"The good news is, by the looks of the trash, they kept her in food and water."

It was something, but Del couldn't imagine the hell Bri had been in, spending nearly thirty five hours in the van. He cut off his emotions at the knees. If they were going to find her now and get her free, he needed to be all business.

"Back to our vehicle," Del barked. "We'll get what we need and board the ship."

They hurried back and loaded their backpacks with necessaries; their guns and their goggles. Wiley held the grappling hook. They'd find the most likely place to throw and attach it to the gunnels where they wouldn't be spotted. That was the good thing about a container vessel. The vantage point of anyone inside the superstructure was severely impeded to the sides and rear due to the containers. They were also lucky because this ship was fully cargoed, which meant there wasn't a lot of freeboard, and the gunnels weren't too high off the dock.

They found a likely spot near the port stern, attached the hook with one throw, and climbed the line, one after the other. Piece of cake. It had been no more than fifteen feet from dock to deck.

Once on board, Sarge headed forward to a secure location to see about jamming navigational controls. To be on the safe side, Prez slinked his way to the engine room below to create a small distraction; an explosion or a fire. Whichever struck his fancy, Del was good with it. It was always interesting to see what Prez concocted. With both of his guys doing their jobs, the egress of the ship would be impeded on two counts. It would be a very short sea voyage, if they got underway at all.

Del looked at the towering columns of containers and squared his shoulders. While Prez and Sarge were working their magic, he and Wiley would be scaling the hundreds of metal boxes, looking for Bri.

Unfortunately, she'd been at the shipyard since early afternoon if Del's calculations were correct, which means she could be in any container, not just the ones near the top. That would suck but it wouldn't keep them from their objective. What might impede them was whether or not Bri remembered the compound she'd ingested, and had removed her black, protective clothing. Since there was always at least one end or one side of each box visible—they were packed that way on purpose—with their special goggles, they'd be able to see Del's bug-juice glowing from within her container, through cracks in the welding.

But if Bri hadn't stripped down, or had been sedated or restrained before she could do so, the search—having to inspect inside every box—would take an interminable amount of time. In that case, her retrieval would have to take a back seat to overcoming the crew. Yelling and opening all the crates was not something they could do with Wasem employees, and Bri's kidnappers walking around. If the van was any indication, the assholes who'd stolen her were taking the sea voyage, too.

Del hoped it wouldn't come down to combat first. His optimal plan was to secure Bri ahead of everything, make sure she was away from anyone who could grab her, and then neutralize the opposition.

Goggles in place, Del and Wiley worked each row, starting at the middle with one going starboard and the other port, until all containers had been scrutinized. The boxes were stacked as many as eight deep in most places, and as frustrated as Del was, they moved slowly and methodically to make sure they wouldn't miss her.

By the time they were at the third row, Del was beginning to wonder what had happened to his two men. He'd felt the vibration of the ship's anchor being pulled, and knew by the slight rocking and the thrum of the engines beneath his feet, that the ship was underway. Where was the...

Ahh. A lovely little explosion from below decks, and at the very same moment, all the lights onboard blinked out. The ship went dark in the water.

Del heard yelling, but got back to business. Time enough to subdue the crew if they got in the way. He had a woman to find.

****

Bri had filled her belly then settled down on her cot, feeling the ship come to life. The pulsation of the engines wasn't unpleasant. On the contrary, it was a fairly comforting hum. Still it brought slow, quiet tears dripping down the sides of her face to puddle in her ears. She couldn't even be bothered to wipe them away. The sound certainly signaled a finality to any escape on US soil.

The ship was truly leaving port, and now that they were underway, the chance of a rescue—which she'd held in the back of her brain as a real possibility—bottomed out to nothing. For the first time since she'd been kidnapped, she allowed herself a moment to wallow in self-pity.

What had she done to ask for this? Why was she even involved in a situation this strange? If she ever managed to get out of this predicament, Bri would rethink her life in a million different ways; the biggest being a complete termination of any contact with her father. The second would be to tell Del her true feelings. She actually fantasized about how that would go, and looked forward to it.

She'd inform him that since the first time she'd met him she'd known he was special, and his feelings about her pregnancy notwithstanding, spending time with him in the cabin had cemented her feelings. He was a big dope, but she loved him. *Yup.* She actually loved him, trust issues and all. And before she let him speak, she'd poke him in the chest and tell him if he wasn't man enough to handle her, fine. But in her daydreams, he did nothing of the sort. He actually captured her hand and dragged her close for one of his soul-searing kisses, and then—

A completely alien sound ripped through the ships droning, and had her abandoning her fantasies to sit upright. Had that been an explosion? The sound of the engines died. Something had happened to the ship. Her heart beat faster. Surely that was good news. Although the men who'd stolen her probably had enemies who would commit sabotage, wasn't it more likely that Del and his guys had caught up to her? Bri wanted to cheer, and yell. As a matter of fact, why not? If someone was looking for her, they needed to know where she was!

Bri opened her mouth and then closed it again just as fast. Wait. If Del was here, she wouldn't have to yell. She knew what he'd be searching for. Her hands stripped off her clothes as fast as she could tear at them. If she was correct, Del would have his goggles on, and he'd be sweeping containers for her rainbow glow. She glanced down at her almost nakedness. Left in her days old bra and panties, she was suddenly conscious of their deplorable condition. *Oh hell, no.* If her knight in shining armor was on his way, she was greeting him clean and naked, not swampy.

The offending scraps came off, and Bri staggered to the water bottles. There were certainly enough that if she used a couple for cleanliness, a trans-Atlantic supply would still be available in case she was hallucinating a rescue. And—she grabbed two bottles and tripped toward the food boxes—some sour-ass, dried strawberries had made her mouth pucker so she hadn't eaten them. But if she mixed them up, along with a couple of salt packets and water, couldn't she make a yummy scrub? *Hell, yeah.*

She poured fresh water and salt into the strawberry pouch, folded the top over and shook it. Into her hands went the gooey mixture, but damn, it smelled really good. She scrubbed her face—which stung, her armpits, and all the other bits that needed attention. She even dumped a bottle over her head, scrubbing away and removing the tangles in her hair with her fingers. She avoided taking the majority of sweat from her skin, afraid she'd wash away too much of Del's compound, but when she finished and rinsed down with the bottle of fresh water? She felt a million times better. She'd be ready for her rescue, dammit. And glamorous. Just like a waiting damsel in distress from the movies.

She moved back to her cot, drew a clean blanket loosely around her shoulders and sat down. Perusing her naked body, she giggled. What if the whole glowing bug-guts thing had been something Del had made up to mitigate her fears. Well then, the joke would be on her. He'd eventually find her, sans clothes, and have a good laugh for himself. She'd be too busy telling him how much she loved him to even care. It was her first order of business, in case they didn't get off this damn ship.

Bri stopped spinning wistful tales in her head, and got serious, chewing her lip. Another possibility was that the cessation of the ship and the noise she'd heard were nothing out of the ordinary. In reality, it was just as likely as being rescued. If that were the case, and nothing happened, she'd eventually put her dirty clothes back on to resume resigned-prisoner status. But certainly nothing ventured, nothing gained.

She strained her ears in the darkness to listen for anything that might alert her to either possibility; rescue or resumption of the ship's propulsion. At one point she imagined there were men yelling, but that was from far away. It could be they were trying to fix an engine problem.

In time, Bri began to drift off. But a new noise startled her awake. A distinct grating of metal on metal, and it was right outside her container. Dare she make noise? If it *was* a rescue, would she raise attention that would alert her kidnappers? Maybe a whisper?

She moved to the doors, treading carefully in the dark, and with her hearing attuned to what might be going on, she swore she heard the steady tread of feet, moving up from below and closing in on her position.

"Del?" she dared murmur, and at a long pause where no pandemonium broke loose, she repeated his name a little louder. "Del?"

"Bri." A masculine voice breathed out, nearly in her ear. The sound of Del's quiet rasp right outside her prison sounded like heaven. And if she hadn't loved Del before, his rescuing presence would have tipped the scales in his direction.

"I'm here," she scratched on the doors, willing them to open.

"I know," Del answered with a relieved amusement in his voice, "And you're lit up like a firefly."

"Ha, ha," she laughed, alleviating the near hysteria that threatened. "You ain't seen nothin' yet." Bri dropped her blanket to the floor.

Chapter Twenty-Five

"Let's get these doors open and get her the hell out of here," Del ordered. He needn't have spoken. While he reached for the lever and pulled up on it, Wiles already had his fingers curled around the edge of the metal, pulling one side apart.

Holy shit! Del nearly swallowed his tongue when the door swung outward. The saving grace being that Wiles was behind the metal. He quickly drove a hand toward his partner's face, keeping him in a blind spot. "Don't you dare move," he barked.

Wiley started sputtering so hard with suppressed laughter, Del thought he might choke. "Naked, huh?" he managed to wrench out.

"You know it." Del moved forward with the speed of a cheetah, dropping his backpack at the door.

"God, am I glad to see you," he breathed out as he gathered Bri's body up against his.

"The sentiment is mutual," she returned into the front of his flack-jacket. "And you feel so good. Can I stay just like this for the rest of my life, please?"

Del grunted in response, his cock springing to life in an instant. He pushed his goggles to the top of his head and ran his hands up and down Bri's warm, soft back, making sure she was all there. And how in hell could she manage to smell like fucking strawberries after being enclosed in a van for days? Only Bri. It was good, but he missed the lemon smell he associated with her. They'd get back to that.

"Ahh, shit sweetheart. I'd like nothing better. Are you all right?" he questioned, raining kisses on her cheeks and eyelids. For some reason she kept him away from her mouth.

"Some bumps and bruises," she told him, then let off her held breath over his shoulder "And really, really bad morning mouth even though it's nighttime." A hiccup-y giggle emerged between them.

"I don't give a damn," he said, claiming her sweet lips, gently. She ran her fingers tenderly over his head as Del forced himself to lighten his own touch. Instantly he felt like an asshole, not remembering that Bri had been roughed up. Here he was, gripping her so tightly she had to be hurting, but not a complaint came from her mouth. Only concern for him.

"You were unconscious and bleeding when they took me." Her fingers found the gouge in his head where he'd been whacked, and Del winced, but he didn't care. He'd take pain any day if it meant Bri's hands on him.

"A bullet grazed me—" he told her.

"But he's got such a hard head, it didn't do anything but make him grumpier," Wiley groused. "Now if the two of you are through with your reunion, can we get the hell out of here before someone notices us?"

Del reluctantly took his hands off Bri and went for the blanket on the cot. He quickly wrapped her in it. When he looked up, Wiley was at the door. "You didn't see anything, Wiles, right?" He clenched his jaw.

"Leprechauns and rainbows. Magically delicious," he hedged, before a sharp report sounded from somewhere below. "Uh, oh." Wiley fell to his face.

"Shit!" Del pushed Bri to the back of the container. "Get under the rack and stay there." His voice gave no room for argument.

"But—"

"Do it!" Del dropped and moved forward on his belly, reaching out to touch Wiley.

"I'm okay," his friend answered him, but clearly in pain. "Lucky the guy's a lousy shot. Hit me in the back of the thigh," he hissed. "Couldn't help but go down like a sack of potatoes. Sorry for scaring you."

"Hell, Wiley," Del blew out a sigh of relief, rolling to his side and getting a firm grip on his Beretta, sliding it from its holster. "I'm just glad you're not dead. Shot in the ass is something we can give you shit about for a long time." Del teased, then changed his tone. "Now go stay with Bri. I'll take care of this."

He got a caustic laugh in return. "Always wanting to hog the glory," Wiley smirked. "Screw that. Just give me a second to do a ninety, and I'll make sure *your* ass stays in one piece."

Wiley drew his preferred Colt from the small of his back, and executed a slow spin.

Watching, Del almost missed the slight movement behind him, but being strung tight at the moment, he didn't. He turned his head to peer back over his shoulder, exasperation in his tone. "Dammit, Bri. You need to move deeper, and now."

She reached down with a tentative hand and laid it on his shoulder. "I just have to tell you one thing, first," she hesitated, clutching the blanket around her naked body with her other. "I promised myself I would, and you may not want to hear it, but just in case we don't get out of this... I love you, Del." She finished strongly, the word love echoing around the metal chamber.

"Well, shit," Wiley interjected in an ironic tone. "Isn't that sweet, and doesn't that just make two of you."

"What?" Bri stared blankly at Del. Clearly she'd expected him to speak, not Wiles. Now he felt like all kinds of a jerk.

He raised his eyes skyward, avoiding her stare. "Umm. I might have told the guys that I have feelings for you," Del bit out. *Dammit.* How stupid did that sound? But give him a break. There were better times to have this discussion.

Bri gave him a brilliant smile that was unmistakable even in the darkness. She tilted her head and turned on her heel to skip away. *What? Skip?*

"That'll do for now," she called back to him, and Del blinked twice as she shimmied beneath the cot.

A stupid grin came to his face. Not only did she love him, apparently they would be having a conversation later. *If* he could take care of the guys shooting at them. Del growled. There was no way they would get the better of him twice, and cheat him out of declaring his love.

"I'm going to have a look, Wiles. I'll draw some fire and see how many we're up against," Del said, lowering his goggles. "Cover me."

Wiley had moved into position. He set up some smokescreen fire, and Del stuck his head out. It looked like one heat signature below, and another moving to the side of the containers. Del quickly drew his head back in. "We have two tangos in sight. One is firing from the base of the containers across from us to the left, and the other is on the move to the right. That second one will be scaling our pile, attempting to come at us high."

"We'll have to keep our ears open," Wiley grunted, and Del didn't like the sound of his voice.

"Hey," he poked. "What's going on Wiles? Tell me?" When all he got was a huff in return, Del refused to relent. "I want to be sure that you have my back, and won't go Tango Uniform on me."

"From an ass shot?" Wiles returned, but still not sounding entirely like himself. "Not happening. But I might feel a little light in the head. Must be losing a bunch of blood."

"Then go have Bri wrap it," Del barked. "And that's an order. It's not going to do me any good having to work around your passed out carcass."

"Copy that." Wiley huffed. And Del knew how bad his friend really had been hurt as he moved slowly away, pushing backward towards Bri's position. But he still gave a final warning. "Listen buddy, stay frosty with that tango on the move."

"Not planning to screw the pooch here, Wiles," Del assured him, trying to keep things light. He knew Wiley was going down for the count since he'd taken the retreat option. "Calling for back-up now." He clicked his mic to get Prez and Sarge's attention. "Two armed tangos on our twenty," he snapped. "Wiles out of commission. Could use some help."

Sarge's voice came back. "Copy. Oscar-Mike, Del. What's your twenty?"

"Fourth row from the stern, middle, top." Good. There was one friendly on the move, but where the hell was Prez? Del clicked his comm-unit again. "Prez?" Still no answer. He made a fast, executive decision. "Sarge. I've got things covered here for a few minutes, but Prez seems to have gone Elvis. Priority change. Find him."

"Copy that," Sarge acknowledged, signing off.

"I'm still good if you need me," Wiley sounded as if he'd stopped mid-crawl toward the cot, and Del wasn't having any of it.

"Get your bloody ass bound up, then talk to me." A shot came in over his head, pinging off the metal doorframe.

"And stop distracting me," he mocked. "Thank god these guys can't shoot worth dick." He gave it one additional second. "But you know what? I'm through with their crap." He reached toward his backpack and withdrew his M4A1. He'd be using trigger group "F". Fully automatic. "They wanna play?" Del snarled, "I'm ready to rock'n'roll."

Part of his mind detached, and he became one with the shooter on the ground. Although he vaguely registered the sound of Bri taking care of Wiley's wound, his brain predominantly centered on his enemy's shots, and kept track. Once he had the predictable cadence embedded in his muscle memory, he let his trigger finger take over. The next time the guy took a shot, Del would be a split second ahead of him, and open fire.

But nothing happened. Del cautiously peered out. He couldn't see anything. He regulated his breathing and waited for the next move.

Minutes went by, and all was quiet. Del had the feeling that Wiley had passed out, but he didn't want to raise his voice and ask. He'd rather the pair's exact position in the back stay anonymous. It was damned hot in the container, but even though he was sweating bullets, in a game of waiting, Del always excelled. He hunkered down, keeping his body taut and at the ready.

When all hell broke loose, it came in a big way. Gunfire erupted from below to spray the bottom front of the container in a steady, non-automatic, barrage. While Del tipped the barrel of his gun over the edge and answered fire, a noise from the right—on the outside of the one still-closed door—startled him.

He whipped onto his back toward the left just in time to see a rifle pointed directly at him, and his weapon was not angled correctly to counter.

Out of the shadows next to him, a flash of movement took place, so fast it almost didn't register. Bri swung the blanket from around her shoulders like a bullfighter, snagged the rifle that was pointed at him, and pulled it upward while at the same time covering the assailant's head. It was all the distraction Del needed. He shouldered his carbine and let loose.

Bri's fingers let the blanket go, and the wrapped bundle, man and gun, plunged fifty feet to the deck. Del used his momentum, rose to his knees and strafed the area below, hearing a grunt and the drop of a body that meant the second target had been neutralized.

Only then did he let the reality of what had happened wash over him. Bri had made her way around the right perimeter of the container, hidden behind the closed door, and put herself in the way of danger to save his ass. His head nearly exploded. He was going to paddle her backside until she couldn't sit down.

"What the hell do you think you were doing?" he hollered, letting every bit of his anger show. "You could have been killed."

"And so could you," she told him, her eyes gone wide. It registered, with his goggles still engaged, that she remained stark naked. He turned to find Wiley, and when he saw that his friend was back to the land of the living, his anger found a new outlet.

"Dammit, Wiles. Turn your eyes away or I'll shoot you myself."

That got a weak laugh. "And here I figured you'd be glad that I'm distracted from my pain." But Wiley obliged, shutting his lids and his mouth at the same time. *Smart man.* Del was in no mood.

"Clothes on, Bri," Del snarled at her. "And get to the back again. We don't know who else we might be up against.

Just then, his mic clicked to life.

"Prez here, Del. Shots registered. Are you okay?" It sounded like he was running.

"All good here," Del assured him. "Two tangos down. Proceed with caution until you're sure they've been wasted. Sarge with you?"

"Yeah. He found me in the bowels of the engine room. I wasn't getting a signal there. I stayed to make sure the crew could put the fire out."

"Good thinking," Del assured him, and for the first time in hours he breathed easy. "And what have you found out about the crew?" He knew one or the other of his guys would have been on that.

"No bad-guys to report. Just a regular crew trying to earn a living. The only wild-cards, from what we've been able to find, are the two you've taken care of. The regulars had no clue they had human cargo aboard."

"Copy that." Del let out a long, relieved breath. "Time for some clean-up." Del turned and shook his head. Bri was covering up with her black clothing, albeit commando, after she'd taken a brief peak over the edge and confirmed it looked like he'd killed the two men who had kidnapped her.

"Assholes," Del ground out. "Got what they deserved," he muttered. "I'll put in a call to the FBI."

Chapter Twenty-Six

Hours later, the ship had been led back to port by a tug, and everyone; the crew, Del and his men, as well as Bri had been thoroughly questioned by the federal agents. After what seemed an interminable amount of time, they were finally cleared to leave.

Bri felt pretty good, all things considered. Del had made an enormous fuss over getting her medical attention and food before any of them would agree to an interrogation. She'd had actual green stuff—an enormous Caesar salad.

Unbelievably, she'd needed butterfly tape on her cheek. She hadn't realized her injury was that bad. She'd also been given antibiotics, since the cut had seeped and oozed for so much time without treatment.

Eventually she became couched in the back of Del's SUV, and at the moment was snuggled up tight against the man himself, feeling like she'd never let him go. She *had* noticed, despite her tired stupor, that they were going west, instead of east.

"Aren't we going home?" she queried.

"You didn't think we were going to drive all the way back, did you?" Del countered, his commanding eyebrow rising as he dropped a kiss onto the top of her head. "Not a chance. I don't want to spend another minute in this vehicle with these smelly oafs. I've chartered a jet. We'll be back in Boston in under four hours." He smiled down at her.

Bri had picked up the prevalent and overwhelming guy smell in the SUV, but she wasn't going to complain. It masked her own, she imagined, not-so-pleasant odor.

"And what will happen to your vehicle?" she questioned.

"Torched," Wiley's irreverent answer came from the third seat, where he reclined on his side after having a bullet removed from his ass.

"I'm leaving the keys, hoping it will get stolen," Prez added.

"Actually," Del interjected with a roll of his eyes. "I'm having it fumigated, then shipped home."

Bri didn't think *that* was a joke.

"Hey guys?" Sarge interrupted from his position in the passenger seat up front. "I just got hit with a huge, anonymous file." He shook his head in disbelief. "It's encrypted, but nothing that won't take more than a few minutes to decode. Any idea if we're expecting anything?"

Del gently moved Bri aside to sit up and look over Sarge's shoulder. "Not that I'm aware of," he said. "Open it up."

"Could be a hack," Sarge warned. "Although all of our good stuff is safe and secure in alternate cyber space."

"Then what are you waiting for?" Del queried.

"What if it's…you know," Sarge answered, indicating Bri with a tilt of his head.

"If it's about what just happened, or the FUBAR situation with my father, I'd rather know now." Bri pursed her lips and received a small grin from Del at her use of military slang. "After all that's gone on, I doubt the shock will kill me."

"Okay. Working on it." Sarge's fingers flashed like lightening over the keyboard. Bri was now sitting up too, extremely curious. Del had told her about the help they'd had from someone "anonymous", and she knew they were thinking the same thing. This latest file had to have come from the same source.

When Sarge's screen finally filled with legible text, he came out with a soft and long whistle, accompanied by a "holy shit".

"Take a look at this." Sarge turned the first page so she and Del could see, a deliberately conscious effort by the computer genius to keep her in the loop, which she greatly appreciated.

"Names, dates, manifests." Del's eyes scanned the page as did Bri's. The only difference was, she recognized a lot of the individuals mentioned.

Number one on the list was her godfather. A scary, ancient man whom she hoped never to see again. She'd been brought by her mother, to visit him abroad several times when she'd been small, and he'd been her idea of the bogey-man.

Several other names popped out. A few cousins, an uncle, some of the "guests" whom her father had brought along as business associates on the trips she and her aunt had made to meet him for vacations.

"I know so many of them," Bri breathed. "What does this mean?" She brought her eyes to focus on the text beside the names, and realized that someone—the person sending them the files—had kept years of documentation on the comings and goings of Wasem Trade Group. And all of it had to do with munitions, explosives, military issue arms. There was so much, it almost looked fake. *Almost.* But considering the volume of legal shipping Wasem was involved with, the amount of trade here could easily have been disguised.

"Do you know what we have?" Del asked her.

She nodded slowly, having had time to digest the contents.

"Enough to bring Wasem Trade and all its principals down," she told him, sorrow and regret filling her heart. "So you'd better notify the FBI before we take off," Bri told him. "They have a lot of work ahead of them."

****

Bri slept off and on during the flight home. When she did force her eyes open, she noticed that everyone else was following suit. It had been a hell of a few days, and according to the FBI—when Del had talked to them at length—the next few wouldn't be much easier.

When their expert had received the files, the request had come back that Del and crew be recruited to join a team to Dubai to "clean things up". When Del had asked why them, the answer had come back that since he and his men were already involved, and since the government didn't want an international incident arising from the take-down, the fewer factions involved, the better.

Bri understood, but she didn't like it. Remembering some of the evil faces she'd encountered over the years, she knew the job wouldn't be an easy in and out. She also knew that the net they cast would include her father. How would Del feel about her once he'd met the man who'd sired her, the one who'd had her fooled all these years into thinking he was simply an uptight businessman with too much on his plate to spend time with his only daughter. She'd been a chump, and had mixed feelings about seeing him again, herself.

One thing was certain, there was no way she would let Del go without making sure he knew the depth of her feelings. Wiley had mentioned that Del loved her, but she hadn't heard it from the stubborn father of her child. He would have one night on American soil before heading overseas, and Bri would do everything possible to get a declaration past his lips before he left.

The plane touched down in Boston, and the sleepy bodies woke up in various states of grumpiness. Del had ordered a car to be available, and he proclaimed his intentions to drive so none of his team had to face the Boston traffic. That looked like a good call...for the Boston traffic.

Each of the guys, in turn, were dropped off at various addresses. Wiley at a brownstone in Brookline, Prez at the T station for the red line headed southbound, and finally Sarge in front of a high-rise on the harbor. Bri wondered when Del would ask about her destination, but he remained silent, so she took her cue from him, and waited it out. It wasn't long before they were headed out of the heart of the city, and she realized he must be bringing her to his home.

When they pulled up in front of a rambling, one story ranch overlooking Wollaston Beach, Bri blinked twice. This wasn't the address she had imagined, although why she'd conjured anything about where Del lived, she couldn't remember. Maybe it was the way he talked about his upbringing, that he'd loved his old neighborhood, but also hated the rich suburbs. Perhaps this did make sense. A happy medium.

The home was well cared for and had a timeless feel, as if it hadn't changed since the fifties, or the seventies. It hadn't been modified on the exterior, and the charm of it remained true to the beachy neighborhood.

"I like it," she told him, happy not to have been brought to her sterile hotel-apartment overlooking a street and a parking garage. Since moving out of her father's estate, she'd been determined to do things on her own, so money didn't exactly flow freely, and US AIM hadn't offered upscale accommodations. She'd never invested in a place of her own. Living out of a suitcase suited her, and when she missed luxury, she had always had the option of going back to the estate for a visit.

Of course, that didn't mean Bri didn't have a lot of money socked away in the bank, deposited by her father over the years, but it had remained mostly untouched, just as she wanted.

"I'm glad," Del replied, turning in his seat to regard her fully for the first time in several hours. His eyes glinted like obsidian glass. "You know it's been hard keeping my hands away from you where the guys could witness it," he told her, "but once I get you inside, all bets are off."

"And what would those bets be," Bri gave what she hoped was a sexy smile, and ran a finger down his chest.

"First off, a shower...together," he informed in a voice that brooked no argument. "And then perhaps a well-deserved spanking for scaring the shit out of me back in that container."

Bri's girly parts clenched. Could Del be serious? She'd never imagined that the idea of a spanking would turn her on, but the picture of Del's huge, capable hands on her bare skin? Well. She'd reserve judgement.

"And then what?" she asked breathlessly, unable to make her voice come out with its normal authority.

"And then, girl who's GGLL, we'll see how many ways I can make you orgasm."

Bri's nostrils flared and her nipples hardened. *It was about damned time.*

Chapter Twenty-Seven

Del unlocked the door and pushed it open. With what could only be considered a war-cry, he scooped Bri up and stalked with her in his arms, across a brightly colored living room. She twisted her head to get a better look, but whoops! Tactical error. Del used the opportunity to fasten his mouth to her neck. Not that she minded.

Had she just purred? God, she was pathetic, and she also needed to stop the overwhelming physical, Del-tsunami if they were going to have a coherent conversation.

He kicked open the bathroom door, and Bri blinked. No massive tub for Del, but a shower the size of her entire kitchen took up most of the space. She snorted laughter. "What do you do in there, run laps?"

"You're close," Del chuckled, dropping her feet to the floor and tugging at the hem of her shirt. She slapped his hands away.

"Explain." She took two big steps away from him, turned her back, and seductively worked the material he'd fondled, slowly up her back.

"Uh. Explain what?"

Bri smirked to herself. Nothing like a good strip-tease to knock all the smarts out of a man's brain. "What it is you do in the shower?" she reminded him.

"If you'd stop talking and move along on removing that shirt, I'll show you what I'm *going* to do in the shower."

She turned, clutching the material so it just covered her breasts. "Not before we talk, Del."

He groaned. "Ah, Bri. Are you sure that's what you want to do?"

"I want to do everything you want, and more," she promised. "But first I need to know how you feel about me, and not just hear it second-hand from Wiley."

Del's teeth showed white in his swarthy face as he gave her the most delectable grin. He pulled his own t-shirt off in one tug over his head, and lowered his hands to the front of his black camo's. She couldn't help her tongue coming out to rest on her top lip. His chest was ripped, and the fine, silky line of hair that led southward from his belly button? Lick-able.

"You already know I love you." His eyes twinkled as he reached into the clear glass shower. Manipulating one dial, he turned on at least a half dozen heads. "No guy in his right mind admits that to his buddies unless he's long gone. But instead of starting out with me stating it, how about I begin by telling you all the ways I'm *going* to love you," Del's voice rumbled deep in his throat.

Oh, Lord. Bri swallowed. How could Del possibly know that talk could seduce her faster than all the foreplay in the world? And she only knew that from the erotic books she'd picked up over the years, because certainly her few, disappointing lovers went right for the textbook hot-buttons on her body, and skipped the fun innuendo. It was like she'd been waiting for the right lover all of her life, and Bri knew, down deep, that Del wouldn't disappoint.

She dropped her shirt to the floor, and Del's hungry gaze swept over her breasts, causing a flush to spread across her chest.

"First," he said, popping the button on his pants with deliberate movements. "You're going to follow my orders to the T. And after we clean you up, if you're good, I'm going to reward you by sucking on those raspberry nipples until they're so hard under my tongue that you'll ache with need."

Bri was aching already, and brought her hands up under her breasts to offer them up to Del, nipples stiff and erect. But damn him, he ignored the invitation. His fingers, instead, worked the zipper of his pants down, ever so slowly.

"And then when you're screaming my name, I'll gather your fine ass in both my hands, and lift you up to straddle me, right on my cock where you'll feel how much I want you, and how lucky we're both going to get."

Bri gave up on her breasts and removed her pants faster than he could speak so he wouldn't tell her no. She wanted to be ready.

She saw his eyes darken and heard his sharp intake of breath. *Oh, yeah.* She preened, and couldn't help but posture just a little, her shoulders thrown back. He wasn't as in control as he pretended.

"Get in the shower, Bri." It was an order given in his best, superior officer bark.

With a delightful frisson of anticipation, Bri complied.

"I want you soaped up," he continued, as warm water hit her hyper-sensitized skin. "So that when you run your hands over your body, they glide slowly to all the right places."

As far as she was concerned at this point, there wasn't a wrong place. If she touched the tip of her elbow, she'd probably go off like a thousand sky-rockets. But she took a deep gulp of air and strove for calmness. Two should be able to play at Del's game.

Bri picked up the bar of soap from one of the many holders, and gave it a good rub between her hands. If applied correctly, she'd have her man abandoning his misplaced restraint within minutes.

Starting with her neck, she rolled her head to one side and spread the lather from her ear to her shoulder. She lifted her arm and continued from her armpit to her hip, making sure to linger on the side of her breast. Bri repeated the process on the other side.

Keeping her eyes languorously half closed, she witnessed Del shedding his pants and briefs in double-time. His impressive package—and oh boy, she loved what he had packing—made a statement that he would not be long denied.

But keeping to her agenda, and what he'd believed was his, Bri turned her back to Del. Bending at the waist, she gave him a clear view of her backside. She smoothed the soap around her ankle, up her calf to her thigh, and spreading her legs ever so slightly, worked the soap into her blond curls. He couldn't actually see, but he knew what she was doing.

Without turning, she used the bubbles on both hands to round the mounds of her ass and wash the valley between. Now she most definitely heard a moan.

Ah! When had he entered the shower? Bri smiled. She had him.

Moving her body slightly, and looking over her shoulder, she met his eyes with hers. He'd grabbed his own bar of soap and was quickly washing all of the parts where she wanted to have her hands.

"Couldn't you save that job for me?" she purred coyly, but the catch in her voice gave away the lust that whipped through her body

"Nope. There are other things I want you to do," he countered. "Rinse off."

Bri shivered and obeyed, making sure to raise her hands into the spray of the water to bring her breasts high and taut. She wondered what he had in mind.

"Now turn to the wall and place your hands on it, leaving your arms up straight," he ordered. "Then give me a thirty degree bend and spread your legs."

Bri wasn't terribly good at math, but she got the picture. And she couldn't have kept her legs together if she tried. The slick heat of her pussy demanded Del's touch. She did as he required, quivering with anticipation.

"Good girl," he crooned, right beside her ear, and the vibration on her neck had her near fainting. His hands smoothed across her back and inched slowly around her sides. And just as she was about to scream with frustration, he cupped her breasts, bringing his thumb and forefinger together on each sensitive nub. A moan escaped from her mouth.

"Feels good, doesn't it," he said, running the hard, slickness of his cock against her ass at the same time his hands played. "Wait 'til I have them in my mouth." His body moved away from hers and Bri almost screamed, until she saw his intent. He insinuated his body between her and the wall, ducking to the right height to make good on his promise.

At the first flick of his tongue, Bri's legs gave out, and if it wasn't for his hard, muscled arm quickly surrounding her waist, she would have fallen to the shower floor.

"Hang in there, baby," he growled against her breast. "We're just getting things started."

Bri would have laughed if she had any moisture left in her mouth, but it had all traveled south. He might just be getting started, but she was pretty damned near finished. When his free hand dipped down into her slick, wet pussy at the same time his mouth closed around her nipple, she detonated. Her hands left the shower wall of their own volition, one to press his head closer, and one to make sure his digits stayed right where they were. She screamed his name and pulsated around his fingers, cascading breathlessly downward from what had to have been the fastest orgasm she'd ever experienced.

"Well doesn't that just make me a lightweight," she joked, when finally able to speak.

"Hell, no," Del's face when he moved it to look up into hers, held a masculine pride that couldn't be disguised. "That was beautiful."

Bri was too relaxed to dispute his point, but still contrary enough to tease. "From my reading, I understand pregnancy enhances one's speed and ability to finish."

He laughed against her chest, then lowered to her tummy. "You hear that, baby? She's blaming you." He teased her right back. "I guess I'll have to wait a few months to prove your theory wrong."

Bri had a feeling Del was right. She doubted if a few hormones could account for the strength of her attraction to him. Hell. She'd wanted him from the first minute she'd laid eyes on him, and even after just having the orgasm of her life, Bri wanted him again. Right now. She edged closer.

"Give a man some breathing room, Bri," he chuckled. "I just need a quick taste of..." Instead of finishing his sentence, Del dipped down and brought his tongue to the spot his fingers had just abandoned, gathering up her creaminess while making noises of satisfaction.

And just like that, Bri climbed toward the peak again. Del must have noticed, because he looked up with a lazy smile.

"Oh, no you don't," he stated, giving her a smart little smack on the ass that had Bri ramped almost to the top again, immediately. "This time I get to join you."

She gave him her best, lascivious look. "What happened to three before me?"

He came up between her and the wall, turning them both around until her back was pressed to the cold tiles. "Every good covert operator has a plan B," he informed her. "You'll like mine. I promise." Then just like he'd teased, he cupped her ass in both hands and lifted so Bri's only move was to wrap her legs around his waist.

"That's it," he urged as her cleft splayed open and she ran her wet heat up and down his hard shaft. "Right there." Now his breath was coming in panting gulps. Bri was thrilled she wasn't the only one spiraling out of control.

"I can't wait, Bri," he warned, and he looked to be half out of his mind. "But...damn..."

Why had he paused? She couldn't understand his hesitation. They were right there, ready to go.

"Condom," he snarled, his lids nearly closed and his jaw clenched.

"Condom?" Bri didn't mean to, but she broke into a cascade of wild giggles.

Del came out of his trance, scowling. "What?"

"Uh, we already passed go and collected two hundred dollars on that score, Del," she chortled. "Pregnant. Remember?"

His eyes screwed up and his mouth dropped open. "Shit. Programming," he said sheepishly. "Sorry."

Bri rubbed up and down his length again. "I'm not," she said. "I wasn't about to interrupt the flow, but I'm getting pretty prune-y. Do you think we could move this to a dryer spot?"

"My pleasure," Del beamed, but instead of letting her go, he maintained their entangled position and carried her to the glass door. She turned off the heads and obligingly pulled the portal open. Not because she wanted to be helpful, but because she was enjoying his hands right where they were.

"Good teamwork," he declared, giving her full globes a squeeze. How quickly they'd gone from torrid to playful. Bri had a feeling Del would never let her get complacent when it came to sex-play.

They spent the next few minutes—after Del convinced Bri that she needed to be on her feet—drying each other off; finding secret places that tickled or enticed. Bri had never had so much fun with a man before, and this humorous side of Del was as appealing as all the other facets she'd seen. She had to fight back happy tears at what a wonderful father he would make. Kind of like her own dad, before things had changed.

"What's got you so serious all of a sudden," he said, wiping a spot on her nipple with more diligence than necessary. Not that she was complaining.

"Thinking about our child…and my dad," she admitted.

He looked her square in the face. "I'll never be like him, Bri. I promise you. My love is permanent. I will never leave you or our child alone. I know how much it hurts, remember?"

And Bri did remember. His father and mother had gone off to South America and left him with his grandfather. Their situations were so similar. Maybe that's why they understood each other so well.

"And I'll never leave you," Bri tapped him on his chest and kissed his chin. "But I wouldn't mind testing out the goods one more time before I commit," she teased. "I had my first sample so long ago, I might be remembering things wrong."

Once again she found herself in his arms. "I'll give you plenty to remember," Del handled her like she weighed nothing, jogging out a second bathroom door, straight into his bedroom to lower them both to his bed. Bri landed on top.

"How's this for a start," he said, lifting her to a hands and knees position above him before sending his digits down between them to guide his rock-hard shaft up and down her wet pussy.

"Wonderful," she moaned, swinging her curls into a curtain around them. "But I have a better idea." Bri shuffled downward and easily persuaded his fingers aside, her mouth hovering over him in seconds.

"I'm not so sure that's a good plan, Bri," Del gritted out.

"And why not," she asked, licking the tip of his weeping cock and blowing out a soft stream of air.

"Because I might be done before we've gotten to the good part."

"I'm patient." Bri brought her mouth down in a long, slow swoop before bringing it up again and popping him free. "And someone convinced me that fast isn't the end of the world. That there's plenty more *after* that."

Del lay back against the blankets, clearly giving up. "Okay," his laugh was pinched. "But be gentle."

****

In the end, he couldn't stand it. Her mouth felt so damned good, but his need to be in her, joined to her, took precedence. With a growl, he pulled her up and flipped them over.

"Hey!" Bri's hair was mussed, and her lips were swollen and cherry red. God didn't that turn him on, knowing that she looked that way from sucking his dick. He bent and captured her mouth before she protested more.

His knee parted her legs, and it didn't take long for Bri to get on board with the change of position. She dropped her hands to knead his ass, drawing her nails up and down his sensitized skin. He pulled back from their kiss.

"I want to watch your face this time," he smoldered. "I got cheated before because somebody got me drunk, so this time I'm not missing a thing."

Bri whimpered her agreement, and tried to pull him in, but he held back. He would do this slowly, no matter how badly he wanted to be buried inside of her hot snatch. Del looked at her face, then looked down where the tip of his cock nudged at her opening. He slid in an inch, and observed as her mouth drop open in a pant. He glanced down and fed in another few inches, gritting his teeth against the velvet pull of her pussy.

Her cry snapped his eyes back to hers.

"Bri? Did I hurt you?" he asked, horrified. Del had no idea if pregnancy made things uncomfortable.

"The only hurt I have is the ache to have you completely inside me," Bri bit out. "Please," she begged. "Right now."

Del abandoned his hard fought restraint and with a groan, plunged into her welcoming heat. Planted to the root, surrounded by pulsating pleasure, he was just able to pause and ask. "Okay?"

Bri must have been in the same boat, vocally, because she looked at him with wild eyes and simply nodded. They began to move together.

Del had never before lived in every inch of his skin, while being buried in a woman. For him, it had always been a quick in and out. But with Bri? Every breath on his face stirred his ardor, every drag of her nails and every tug on his scrotum had him harder than before. His shaft had become sensitized almost to the point of pain. It was excruciating, it was glorious. *Damn.* He needed to finish. But Bri had to go first.

"Come for me," he ordered. Refusing to take no for an answer, he lowered a hand to the small bud nestled within her curls. "I'm going to pinch your clit until you scream," he threatened. And just as he'd planned, the verbal picture he put in her head, along with a reduced version of the actual act, had her careening over the edge, instantly. Bri did scream, and that signaled his turn to let go.

Del pulled back and drove into Bri's welcoming pussy, holding her ass up to go as deeply as he could. A half dozen strokes, and then with a mind-boggling clench at the base of his spine, he exploded into her, coming apart into a million little pieces.

His lungs seized and he held still, embedded deeply for the longest time, until finally his breath returned with a gasp. *Damn.* He'd never felt anything as intense in his entire life, and he refused to let the feeling go by pulling out. He was loathe to separate from Bri; to give up this feeling, this connection that warmed him from the inside, out. He buried his face in her hair and reveled in her scent. *Lemons.* His cock twitched and Bri giggled, finally breaking the spell.

Del lowered himself and rolled to the side, making sure they stayed entwined.

"Wow." He finally conjured the energy to give her that one word.

Bri beamed at him and licked one salty trail of sweat from his chest. "Uh, huh."

Chapter Twenty-Eight

"We've been over this a hundred times," Del told her, his eyebrow running rampant with frustration. "You need to stay here until I get home." He'd already slung his back-pack over his shoulder, and he looked bad-ass standing in the kitchen doorway, dressed all in black and ready to go do covert-type things, the likes of which made Bri shiver.

"Yeah. I get it. The house has this state of the art security system, blah, blah, blah." Bri rolled her eyes. He'd given her an interminably long lesson in its use, but that's not what Bri was concerned about right now. "I want to know how long you'll be gone?" she asked determinedly. She knew that Del's various jobs would keep him away from her for long stretches of time. She was okay with that. But this particular venture had to do with *her*. She had the right to know about this one.

"I've already told you as much as I can," Del groused. "Fourteen hour flight, however long it takes us to mop things up at Wasem headquarters, and the same amount of time back give or take a few hours."

Bri looked at the clock on Del's bright yellow kitchen wall. 9AM. They'd slept and worshiped each others bodies from late afternoon yesterday until getting up for breakfast this morning, mooning at each other over bacon and eggs. Now it was just past rush hour, and Del was headed to Logan.

"So by this time, two days from now, I should expect you back?" She crossed her arms over her chest. That would give him flight time plus twenty hours to clean house in Dubai. It simply bugged Bri that he expected her to stay indoors—not even venture out for a walk—until he got home. She needed to pin him down on timing for her own sanity.

"I think it's safe to say I'll be back by then," Del finally allowed.

"Good," she nodded. Going up on tiptoes she kissed the end of his nose, the only spot she considered she might have missed in their exploration of each other. "Now promise me you'll be careful." Her voice choked up. She had no illusions about the work he did. She'd seen first hand the danger that could come his way. But this was part of Del, the man she'd fallen in love with. There was no way she'd ever ask him to stop, no matter her anxiety.

"Don't worry," he told her. "The guys won't let anything happen to me, because if they do, they'll have to face you," he teased.

She swatted him on his fine behind. "And for that, they should be shaking in their boots," she answered. "Now go, before I get all weepy and maudlin."

"Yes, Ma'am," Del gave her a million watt smile, a scorching kiss, and walked out the door.

Bri watched him drive away, a fake grin pasted to her face as she waved, but she hadn't been kidding about the weepy and maudlin thing. She maintained her dignity until his car disappeared, but as soon as he was out of sight, she sank to the kitchen floor, tears flooding her eyes. If it wasn't for her, Del would never have gotten involved in this mission. If anything happened to him, she didn't know if she could live with that knowledge, and without him.

****

Exactly two days later, Bri hadn't heard from Del. Not that she'd expected to before now. He'd told her they'd maintain silence until they landed safely back at Logan, but as far as she was concerned, his time was up and the phone wasn't ringing. Bri stared hard at the door, willing Del to walk in. She just wanted this to be over.

In between their physical love-marathon, they'd talked about their pasts and where their futures would go, together. And as much as Bri looked forward to being a mom, they'd agreed she'd have difficulty being a full time, stay-at-home parent. She'd admitted to having more of her mother in her than she realized. The difference between them? Whatever Bri ended up doing, she wanted to pursue her career with Del's support, and a huge involvement in her child—or children's—lives.

Bri needed to find something that would give them, as a couple, the flexibility to swap off childcare-time, and Del was enthusiastically onboard. He'd talked about putting a nursery in his office, complete with nanny, one who could then easily travel to Bri's workplace, if that's how it played out.

Bri had plenty of great references. Even if the companies with whom her father had placed her were in bed with Wasem, it didn't necessarily mean they had illegal dealings. On the contrary, she'd done most of her work in what had seemed like legitimate Import/Export companies. That's not what had her worried. She simply recalled the amount of time needed on the jobs she'd had, and there wasn't enough left over to be spending time with a family.

Ideally, she'd start her own consulting firm, but after the shake-up at Wasem, she wondered if she'd have any money left in the bank. She'd never touched it, but it had been put there over the years by her father. Whether it was dirty or clean would be the government's call.

Of course, Del had assured her he could more than adequately finance any venture she wanted to attempt. It was just that she'd always been independent.

Bri stopped struggling with something that had consumed her during Del's absence. Of one thing she'd become sure. If she and Del were going to be a team, they'd both have to learn to trust.

A smile lit her face. Which was why, when he hadn't met his good intentions of being home, he'd have to trust that she could take care of herself.

Number one on her agenda? She needed to talk to Aunt Celia. Del had told her that the cascade of events leading the foreign kidnappers to the cabin had most likely begun with her call to her aunt, but Bri couldn't imagine gentle Auntie Cee having anything to do with kidnapping, murder and arms dealing. But just in case, she wouldn't call her aunt this time. She'd make an unannounced visit.

The family home was located on the outskirts of New York City in Great Neck. Bri looked at the clock. It would take 4 hours without traffic, which would bring her to a late lunchtime. Perhaps she could convince her aunt to go out for a few cocktails, which would loosen the older woman up.

Without giving in to wimping out , Bri threw a couple of Del's t-shirts—which she'd been living in since she had none of her clothes—the laundered pair of black pants and a few of his cotton boxers into a paper bag. She wore one pair of his boxers now. With the waistband turned over several times, they covered more than her normal shorts. A toothbrush and comb she'd resurrected from underneath his bathroom sink concluded her packing, and before she could talk herself out of it, she'd called a cab which would take her to the car rental place down the street. Her own car still languished in Maine. She and Del would have to take a trip to retrieve it, and at the same time thank Maygan and her cousins for all their help. They had been truly amazing, and so relieved to learn that Bri was safe.

She scribbled a fast note for Del before a car horn outside alerted her to her ride.

An hour and a half later Bri was on the road, happily blasting tunes on the radio and relishing her freedom. She hadn't realized how much she'd missed being in charge of her own time and agenda until it had been snatched away. This was a good first trip, to clear any lingering trepidations she might have about travel. Yes, Del would be furious when he got back and found her note, but he'd understand. Independence was very important to her.

****

Del wasn't feeling good about this. They'd spent too many hours rounding up the principals of Wasem Trading Group, many of whom had proved to be dangerous. Those cousins of Bri's, and her damned godfather were a bunch of high-class thugs. It had taken an arsenal and some delicate negotiation, but they'd finally managed to wrangle everyone on their list. Well, all but two.

When things were cleaned up and done, a pair of individuals remained unaccounted for. Bennet Capadella, and their unknown informant. Not a trace could be found of either. Del wanted so badly to confront both parties, for two very different reasons. He wanted to thank the mole who had leaked the pertinent information that had saved Bri's life, and he wanted to put his fist in the face of her father, a man for whom he had zero respect. Failing to apprehend those two key people, partly accounted for Del's bad mood. The rest of it was compliments of the freaking FBI.

He growled at the agent in charge. Even now that they were on the plane headed back, he was told that radio silence had to be maintained until their last loose ends had been tied up. And that if he went against those orders, they'd throw him so deeply away, that no one would ever find him. He believed it. Which meant he couldn't talk to Bri. Which meant he wouldn't be able to touch base with her until well after the time limit she'd specified.

Damn it all to hell, she figured she'd pulled one over on him. But Del already knew Brina too well. When she'd extracted the promise for a definite ETA, Del had known that it would be the time she considered herself free. Free to leave his protected home. And could he blame her? Additional hours—on top of what she'd already suffered—before she could get on with life would have seemed interminable to him. He could only hope that shopping for food and clothing were the primary things on her to-do list. His gut said differently. Couldn't the damned plane fly any faster?

He must have dozed off, for the next time he looked out the window, instead of seeing ocean he saw buildings. *What?* Del bolted upright. That wasn't the Pru. He kicked Wiley—asleep next to him—in the foot.

"Huh?" His friend scrambled to an upright position, grabbing for a gun at his back that wasn't there. He shook his head to clear it. "Asshole," he griped, but then noticed Del's agitation. "Do we have a problem?"

"We sure as hell do." He eyed the complacent FBI agent in charge, malevolently, while at the same time jostling Sarge and Prez—sitting in a pair of seats facing him—to wake them up. "Why aren't we landing in Boston?" he called across the small jet. Immediately he wanted to knock the smug look off the agent's face as the ass turned to regard him.

"We've had a change in plans," came the conceited reply. "New intel says that Capadella is at his house on Long Island."

Fucking hell. Del had conflicted feelings about this. Finding the elusive CEO was a priority, but leaving Bri to her own devices sent a cold finger of apprehension down his spine.

Chapter Twenty-Nine

How could she have been so stupid? Bri stood in the enormous foyer of her childhood home and stared at her aunt and father. The former looked defeated. The latter held a gun. Bri's ire grew. *Really?* Fucking, really? She suddenly became more angry than scared. It was way past time that she received some answers.

"Just who are you threatening with that thing, *Daddy*?" Did the sarcastic emphasis she'd put on her greeting make her father wince? Bri must have imagined it, but just the same, he lowered the gun.

"Close the door and set the alarm behind you," he said, a blank mask dropping over his face. "Then join me and your aunt in the kitchen."

Bri didn't like being bossed around, but reluctantly complied, engaging the security system. She dragged her feet when it came time to head toward the back of the house. The kitchen was a place of good memories and she didn't want to sully it. She'd always had her best childhood chats there, with her father, perched on tall stools at the counter, usually over a slapped together peanut butter sandwich. Her mouth actually watered. *Damn Pavlov.*

Daddy and Auntie Cee preceded her, and she knew she should use the opportunity to dial 911. He had a gun, after all, but she *needed* to hear what he had to say. This was a man whom she'd loved and trusted for the first half of her life. He owed her this. And despite the bravado with the firearm, she just couldn't believe that he'd shoot either her or her aunt.

Deliberately making her way to the long, designer-distressed, pine kitchen table, she sat down slowly and crossed her ankles.

"Illegal arms dealing? Truly, father?" she queried bitterly. "It couldn't have been something more forgivable like hiding offshore accounts or…" She struggled for something ludicrous. "…jewel smuggling?"

Her aunt came to her side and put a hand on Bri's arm. "It's not quite as black and white as you believe, Bri. Just give him a chance to explain. Hear him out, sweetheart, please," she begged, retreating to stand nervously by the counter. Bri huffed, but gave a tilt of her head that told them she'd listen.

Her father sat down heavily, opposite her at the table, resting the gun on the scarred surface in front of him. "I never wanted you to find out," he shook his head, regretfully. "I never wanted you involved."

"So I understood from the e-mail you sent Reynold," Bri scoffed. "You took care of him, didn't you? So now what? You give me a speech and a few minutes to be convinced of why you have to kill me, too?" She couldn't help her eyes filling with tears at this ultimate betrayal.

"No! No." Her father looked to rise from the table, but one watery glare from her had him sitting back down. Strange how she still had some emotional control over him, even as he became set to end her life.

He reached out a hand toward her, as if imploring. "You don't understand," his voice broke. "For years I've kept the true nature of the family business from you, staying between you and your mother's people. My only goal, ever, since your mother's death was to keep you safe."

Bri stared into her father's stricken face. She wanted to believe him, but he'd dug a deep hole between them, and would take a lot filling before she trusted him that they stood on level ground.

"Tell it from the beginning," she choked out, sitting back to cross her arms over her chest. "I'll reserve judgement."

He took a deep breath, and started. "Your mother's family, specifically your godfather who is her great uncle, has owned and operated Wasem since she was small. They've been dealing arms illegally overseas for years, but back before you were born, they decided they wanted to expand; to take money from those whom they considered foreign infidels."

When Bri narrowed her eyes, he held up a hand. "Their words, not mine," he sighed and continued. "But let me get back to our personal problems, first."

Bri gave a slight inclination of her head. This ought to be good.

"When I first met your mother, it really was love at first sight." His face took on a far-away cast. "We were both in our senior year at Harvard, and had signed up for the same foreign politics class. I was surprised we hadn't run into each other on campus before, but didn't find out until later that she'd done her previous years abroad. She was the most beautiful woman I'd ever seen." He gave a self-deprecating chuckle. "And I was shocked when she seemed to take an interest in me."

Bri didn't interrupt to tell him he'd always been handsome in her eyes.

"We had a whirlwind romance, or so I thought," he shook his head. "If I hadn't been blinded by my feelings for her, I might have been more cautious." He took time here to look at Aunt Cee.

264

"We tried to tell you," she lamented quietly. "Mother and Father were so upset that you wanted to marry so fast, and we weren't shy in letting you know how against it we were."

"Which only made me more determined," her father acknowledged. "Instead of taking the position that Father had been holding for me in *his* company, I married within months of graduating school, and joined her family business. With my American citizenship and credentials, Wasem was able to open an office over here within the year, with me as titular head. But we all knew differently." His face showed pain.

"I was nothing but a puppet. Your mother had all the real power. I was still in the dark as to the real agenda of the business, and couldn't understand why my newly acquired business expertise wasn't being tapped.

"Eventually with the aggression from her family undermining any interest I initially had in Wasem, I began to work less and less, staying home more. With you." Now his expression softened. "And I have to say, those were truly the best years of my life."

Bri tried to understand where this was going, and shook her head slowly. Confused now if the man she was hearing about was truly her father.

"By the time you were two, your mother was showing her true colors. She'd never really wanted me. The whole 'being sent to Harvard' thing was only so she could find a husband with the right connections. She become cold and distant to me, and in a foolish move I found out about much later, she laid plans to take over Wasem."

"Which got her killed," Bri supplied. The pieces were fitting together.

"Exactly," her father concurred. "But with her death, there came a dangerous gap in Wasem's hierarchy. They had no one to man the helm and maintain their status in the United States…except me." His face became blank. "When the family approached and threatened that if I refused to bow to their wishes, they would take you away to groom you for the position, what choice did I have? There was no way I'd let them put the US side of their business in a trust using your name, an innocent twelve year old. They would have taken your American identity and exploited you for the rest of your life." He turned imploring eyes to hers. "Can you see that I had to do what they asked of me? They would have turned you into pure evil if they'd been allowed to get their hands on you, and I couldn't let that happen."

"So you took over the company and distanced yourself from me," Bri whispered, finally seeing the whole picture. "You decided to cut me out to save me, but do you know how much that hurt?"

"I do," her father replied, a tear leaking from the corner of his eye, lingering in the deep lines etched there. "Because my heart was breaking right along with yours."

She swallowed the enormous lump in her throat. "So what happened when I finished school? You insisted I work at the companies where you set up jobs. It seemed like you were making sure I had experience in the industry. That you were grooming me to join Wasem." Bri remained confused.

"At your godfather's behest," her father's lips drew together in a hard line. "I was ordered to have you learn the ropes, and I agreed, but only if we apprenticed you to companies other than ours. *Uninvolved* companies. I convinced him it would help us in the end if you learned all angles and legal aspects of the business before you joined us. And if, eventually, you forged connections for us with these upstanding concerns, so much the better."

"So even though you kept me safe, I was to eventually join Wasem?" Bri was grateful her father had delayed her involvement, but why bother if she was still to become part of the corrupt family business.

"No." He sat taller in his chair. "I never would have let that happen. What your godfather and the rest didn't know, was that I used my time to amass a huge data-base, outlining Wasem's illegal activities, and implicating those involved." Now he actually laughed. "My major in college was actually not political science, you know. It was computer programming." He smiled, but sadly.

"Oh my God." Bri sat up straighter. "You were the one…"

"Yes. I was the one who led that team of young men to you in New Orleans."

Bri drew her brows together. "I still don't get it. Not entirely. You were apprenticing me to companies who had no involvement in Wasem's illegal activities, but then you sent me to US AIM. To Reynold. Why?"

A huge sigh escaped from her father. "Your godfather had begun to get anxious. I'm not getting any younger, so he foresaw a day when I might not be around anymore, and demanded we start making you a part of the dirty companies with whom we did business. He wanted you to marry Reynold so that he had one more puppet on board."

"But the email?" Bri's voice had gotten smaller. "You said that if Reynold let me in on any of US AIM's arms dealing, you would have me killed."

"No. Not me. Your uncle. If you recall, my warning stated that if you found out what was going on, you were both as good as dead. Which was true. I knew the minute you got wind of the true nature of the family business, you'd run. And that it wouldn't take your godfather long to find out and come after you, which is exactly what happened. Reynold panicked when you left, and made some blunders trying to cover up his involvement. It triggered a cascade of red flags with the higher-ups at Wasem. They had him eliminated, and then they went looking for you."

"So why didn't you reveal everything you had for evidence against them, then?" she puzzled.

"Because once you disappeared, I needed leverage so they wouldn't harm you. They weren't stupid. They knew I'd been documenting their movements for years, and all along they planned to use you to keep me in line. But you ducked out of their well-formed agenda.

"Therefore they needed to apprehend you, make sure I saw that you remained alive, and assure me you were being brought to them in Dubai. Of course, once you were there, they would use you as leverage for me to hand over everything. I'm sure I would have been killed, and you would have been married off to one of the cousins who would then become head of American operations."

"And I would have rotted in a guarded cell somewhere, putting my signature on things they needed, but never seeing the light of day again," Bri quaked. Bri understood. If not for Del and his men, this whole thing would have had a sinister outcome. She owed him everything.

"But how did they find me in Maine?" she continued, already sure she knew the answer.

"The phones here are tapped," he confirmed. "They always have been, but I never told you or your aunt. How could I without raising questions? It was a huge mistake, because the minute you called Celia, they had your location."

Bri processed that. "And it was you who watched me on the computer feed from the warehouse?" she swallowed.

"Yes. They wanted me to see that they had you. They knew I'd be desperate to do anything to keep you safe. It was another way to try and keep me in line and save their asses here."

"But you dared to go against them," she marveled.

"You, my dear, are the one who gave me that opportunity," he smiled into her eyes. "I might never have given up the information to the FBI, knowing that Wasem held your life in their hands, but once you gave me the name of Mr. Songen, I did a quick search for him and learned a lot about that young man. I took a chance, and trusted him with your life. I contacted him, giving him not only the means to find you, but the means to shut down the illegal arms dealing at Wasem."

Bri put her hands up and held the sides of her head. It was so much to take in. But one thing became crystal clear. Her father was not a bad-guy, and everything he'd done had been to protect her.

Slowly she rose from her chair, and took the steps separating her from her father. She didn't have to go far, because he stood up and met her half way, wrapping her in his strong, loving arms. Bri couldn't hold back the sobs that wracked her body. After so many bleak, lonely years, it felt damned good to be back where she belonged.

They held each other for a very long time, and after a draining cry, Bri eventually became aware of her aunt's soft sniffles behind them. She pulled back far enough to wipe her eyes. "Did you know about any of this, Aunt Cee?" she choked.

"No," her aunt blubbered. "Bennet had only finished filling me in on parts of it right before you showed up."

Bri was loathe to let go of her father, but the scene she'd walked in on suddenly came back to her. She gently pushed away. "So Daddy," and this time she meant it with love, "what's with the gun?" she probed.

"I'm certain that the FBI will be here, soon," he responded sadly, going to pick the weapon up off the table. "Once they find I'm not in Dubai or New York City, there's really only one other place to check. Which is why I want you to take your aunt and disappear right now."

"So what?" Bri started out in a tentative tease. "You plan on having a shoot out with them?" And she didn't even want to contemplate the possibility that Del and his guys would be part of the FBI task force sent to retrieve her father.

She noticed a look passing between her still despondent aunt and her dad. "What?" she demanded. "What am I missing?" When her aunt's gaze dropped to the gun clutched in her father's hand, Bri had a horrified dawning. "Oh my God. You're going to let them kill you," she said on barely a wisp of air.

"It's the only honorable thing," her father answered quietly.

"No! That's not true. You've done everything under duress…to keep me safe! I won't let you do it. I—"

Just like in a bad movie, she was cut off by the sound of the perimeter alarm. She turned frantic eyes to her father. "Put the gun down. We'll explain everything. It'll be all right." Her heart hammered in her chest. "Please Daddy, don't do this."

He backed away, toward the French doors that separated the kitchen from the pool area. "I love you, Bri," he said with sad eyes, and walked out into the balmy, afternoon.

She took one step forward, but the kitchen was suddenly full of bodies and Bri was tackled from behind and thrown to the ground, cushioned by strong arms. Yelling and gunfire erupted from the back yard. She screamed and tried to get up, but whoever it was held her firmly to the floor. Bri wailed in frustration, kicking to be let free. But the body holding her in place, gave no quarter. She sobbed.

Frantic seconds passed until like a thick blanket, an eerie silence descended. Bri lowered her forehead to the tiles. It was over and the quiet didn't bode well. She didn't want to know. The fight drained out of her with the finality of those shots.

"Are you okay?" Wiley's voice sounded in her ear. His weight shifted and she could almost breathe again. She'd had an idea that it might be one of Del's men who had kept her immobile, trying to be gentle no matter her struggles.

"Daddy," she wept. "Del!" Had either one of them been hurt?

Wiley leaped to his feet and offered her a hand up. "Sounds like things have wrapped up. Let's go find them."

With his support, Bri made the short journey out of the back doors, but when she glanced to the pool and saw blood spreading through the water, she instantly flashed back to the night her mother died. It was too much. Her eyes rolled back in her head, and she slumped into darkness.

****

Del hauled his pissed off ass out of the pool and glared at the FBI gunman he'd ordered to stand down. Prez was helping a shaken Bennet Capadella from the water on the opposite side from where they stood, positioning himself so that no other unauthorized shots would be fired.

"What the hell was that?" Del looked down at the torn and bloody mess that was his dripping ribcage, then back at the agent, and his anger grew, exponentially. "I told you I had him, and you took your shot, anyway?" His voice rose in volume and must have held an edge of danger, because the agent backed away.

"He still had his gun," the man defended in a whiny tone that ramped Del up even more.

"Pointed in every direction but ours," he roared. "Have you heard the term suicide by cop?" he growled. "If you'd taken a second to scope out the situation, you would have seen that's what this was about." Del didn't know why Bennet Capadella had wanted to die, but the man wouldn't get his wish, today. Del had already made up his mind, driving here, that Bri would have answers from her father, and that meant taking him in alive.

"I'm calling a medic." Wiley's voice chimed out from somewhere to his left, and he almost told him to can it until he realized that Wiles wasn't talking about him or Capadella. Instead, he hung over the prone body of Brina.

"What the hell?" Del sprinted to her side and dropped to his knees. "Is she hurt? Shot?" Del's heart leaped into his throat.

"Calm down, Del." Wiley laid a hand on his arm. "She saw the blood in the pool and freaked. She passed out, but it might be a good idea to have her checked. She's been through a lot the last week. Not to mention…" he quirked a head toward Del, where blood dripped freely from his side. "That's no glorious ass wound, but it still might need some attention."

Del tried to come up with something witty to say, but his brain had slowed to a crawl with the realization that his girl was down.

"Del?" Bri's weak voice dragged his eyes downward, and damn, this he could do. Del took over from Wiley, gathering her up, and holding her close to his good side.

"I'm here," he told her. "Everything's fine."

"Blood," she whimpered. "Where's Daddy."

"Prez has got your father," Del informed her gently. "He's fine, too."

She struggled to sit up. "But the blood…"

"Mine, I'm afraid," he told her, shrugging, and she shakily pushed his hands away to draw her head around his body. Bri gasped when she saw the bloody path the bullet had taken.

"Don't worry. It's just another flesh wound," he assured her, and she must have believed him because she wrapped her arms tightly around his neck instead of pushing him prone for first aid as would have been her first priority if things looked bad.

"I don't know how you did it," she sniffed beneath his ear, her voice full of tears. "But thank you for saving my father."

"You were inside," Del teased, trying to lighten the situation. "How would you know if I saved him?"

"Because that's who you are, Del Songen," she said with conviction. "And you wouldn't have done anything less."

Bri pulled her face away from his neck and turned earnest green eyes to his. "I love you," she pronounced.

"I love you, too," he returned, "And now might not be the time to tell you this, but I'm never letting you go. Ever again."

Bri smiled brilliantly up at him. "And I don't want you to," she acknowledged heartily. She reached up and tugged the hair above his left eye. "Especially now that your eyebrow's been tamed."

"I don't know if I'd say tamed," he drawled.

"Yeah, more like whipped," Wiley mocked.

But Del wasn't listening, he lowered his head to Bri's and they sealed their future with a kiss.

Epilogue

Del sat in his office, happy with the way things had turned out. Especially the part where he got the girl. Wasn't that how all good gum-shoes finished things up? Except this certainly wasn't the end. Since their involvement with the high-profile Wasem case, the phones had been busier than ever. His company was taking off, and a very pregnant Bri had been doing them the favor of answering phones and taking care of office work.

His new wife was satisfied with the outcome for her father. Since the elder Capadella had turned in the evidence he'd amassed on the family business, he'd received only a two year prison sentence for his cooperation. It could have been much worse, but he really had been just a pawn in the greater scheme of things.

As for her godfather and cousins? They'd been tried under the laws of international terrorism, and would never again see the light of day, outside of federal penitentiary walls.

Del gave a sigh that things were back to normal, and with a newfound calm, picked up the intercom that buzzed.

"Del?" Bri's voice sounded shaky. "I think I'm having contractions."

Holy hell. Here we go again.

GET PREZ NOW!

https://www.amazon.com/S-S-Prez-Book-Two-ebook/dp/B06W9H4HYX

OTHER BOOKS BY LJ VICKERY

MORE SOS:
Prez
Wiley
Sarge

IMMORTALS SERIES
Immortals Rising
Immortal Bewitched
Going Deep
Frozen Stiff
Royally Screwed
Blown Away
Tied in Knots
Erecting Barriers
Summer's Heat
Justice has Claws
Tendril Hearts
Something Old
Illogical
Immortals Redeemed

GEMMA-HYDROX SERIES:
Paranormal Dating Agency
Federal Paranormal Unit

NIGHTMARE MEN
Hutch

LJ Vickery